TELL ME HER NAME

KATE WILEY

Storm
PUBLISHING

This is a work of fiction. Names, characters, businesses, places, events and incidents are either the products of the author's imagination or used in a fictitious manner. Any resemblance to actual persons, living or dead, or actual events is purely coincidental.

Copyright © Ashley MacLennan, 2026

The moral right of the author has been asserted.

All rights reserved. No part of this book may be reproduced or used in any manner without the prior written permission of the copyright owner. This prohibition includes, but is not limited to, any reproduction or use for the purpose of training artificial intelligence technologies or systems.

To request permissions, contact the publisher at rights@stormpublishing.co

Ebook ISBN: 978-1-83700-159-0
Paperback ISBN: 978-1-83700-161-3

Cover design: Blacksheep
Cover images: Shutterstock, Depositphotos

Published by Storm Publishing.
For further information, visit:
www.stormpublishing.co

ALSO BY KATE WILEY

Detective Margot Phalen Series

The Killer's Daughter

Her Father's Secret

The Killer Instinct

In the Blood

Out of the Woods

Margot Phalen FBI series

The Wolf at the Door

As Sierra Dean

The Secret McQueen Series

Something Secret This Way Comes

A Bloody Good Secret

Deep Dark Secret

Keeping Secret

Grave Secret

Secret Unleashed

Cold Hard Secret

A Secret to Die For

Secret Lives

A Wicked Secret

Deadly Little Secret

One Last Secret

The Genie McQueen Series
Bayou Blues
Black Magic Bayou
Black-Hearted Devil
Blood in the Bayou

The Rain Chaser Series
Thunder Road
Driving Rain
Highway to Hail

The Boys of Summer Series
Pitch Perfect
Perfect Catch
High Heat

As Gretchen Rue

The Witches' Brew Mysteries
Steeped to Death
Death by a Thousand Sips
The Grim Steeper

The Lucky Pie Mysteries
A Pie to Die For

For everyone who loved these books enough to ask for more, thank you isn't enough. You are the wind in my sails.

ONE

Margot Phalen refused to think about serial killers until at least her second cup of coffee of the day.

As life rules went, it was one that served her pretty well.

She'd had her first cup before sunrise, something she could never have imagined possible in her old life. But in her old life there hadn't been chickens demanding breakfast, and a house full of rescue animals requiring food and medication at specific times.

Margot smiled to herself as she triple-checked the bolt on the feed shed outside, slipping the key into the pocket of her oversized cardigan as she went. The chickens clucked happily to themselves, pecking the ground for wayward insects as they wandered their pen. A coterie of aging dogs trailed behind her as she left the shed, another part of her new life she could never have envisioned before.

The sun was up now, turning the late-fall morning a lovely buttery yellow hue, warming her face as she walked back to the house. She loved this time of day, when it felt like she was the only person in the world awake to appreciate these little slices of beauty.

After making herself a second cup of coffee and feeding the cats, she headed to the porch swing, ignoring the creak in the floorboards that told her more work and more money would soon be leached into the old farmhouse. She tucked her feet up under her and cradled her hot mug in her hands.

There was a time when Margot couldn't have done this. Any of it.

She couldn't sit outside, couldn't live in a house where some of the windows didn't even lock right, couldn't live with—

"Move over."

Wes Fox, his own steaming mug in hand, bumped his hip against hers as he sat down, forcing her to share her precious bench space.

He was lucky she loved him.

She was lucky he'd decided he was so in love with her he had been prepared to change his entire life. It must be love for a man to be willing to quit the police department and move to Elk Creek, California, because his girlfriend of less than a year decided to buy a one hundred and thirty-acre ranch in the middle of nowhere.

It was *definitely* love that made him stay the next six years.

"Good morning to you, too," she snarked, settling her feet into his lap. He squeezed her toes with a practiced familiarity.

"No pleasantries before caffeine, you know the rules." He tipped his head back, his eyes closed, turning his face towards the barely risen sun with a faint smile. His thumb kneaded the arch of her foot through her thick socks. Her hideous Ugg boots were sitting on the porch beside the swing, saving him from having to mock her about them this early in the day. They were comfortable, and Margot didn't care how she looked when she was on the ranch.

She and Wes had never gotten married. In Margot's experience a marriage was just a place where people lied to each other and trust vanished over time. Marriage was people being tethered together by a piece of paper and societal pressure.

She wanted Wes to know he could leave if he ever got sick of her.

She knew *she* wasn't going anywhere.

Every year Margot expected Wes to decide he'd had enough of living on the ranch, enough of being away from San Francisco, enough of *her*, but it turned out the fool had it really bad, and, even through her sourdough and puzzles phase, he still loved her.

He still loved her even when she filled their dining room table with the grisliest photos of serial killer victims imaginable and sought his opinion on motives over homemade pot roast.

If Margot had said when she'd been thirteen what her dream life looked like, it wouldn't have resembled this one at all.

But there was a lot thirteen-year-old Margot hadn't known.

She hadn't imagined herself rescuing senior dogs because one had accidentally come home with her during a homicide investigation.

She couldn't have imagined that six cats would rule over the house and property, tripping her up wherever she went, from feeding the chickens in the morning to cutting wood for the stove.

And she certainly couldn't have imagined Wes.

Margot shifted her position, pulling her feet from his lap so she could turn and rest her head on his shoulder. She breathed in his scent. He smelled extra-clean, like Irish Springs soap and the fancy shampoo he insisted on ordering online because he was sure it would keep him from going bald. She wasn't sure if he was paranoid or if it was working, because his hair looked wonderful.

"When do you go back?" he asked her, a catch in his voice, as he knew the answer. Sometimes he did that, as if he hoped that if he played dumb her response might suddenly change.

She wished it could. While she loved her job, over the past six years she had come to begrudge it some days. Especially the days she had to leave *this* behind.

But when she left, she had something thrilling to sink her teeth into: solving murders for the FBI. While she enjoyed the slow pace of life here, her day job was never boring.

"I'll be loading up once I've had this." She lifted her coffee. "I'll be there about five days, Andrew figures."

Wes nodded.

Elk Creek was a million miles from anywhere. The closest town, Willows, was a good fifteen-minute drive away, and getting back to San Francisco took two and a half hours. It shouldn't have worked for her job, but, as it turned out, over six years and one work-from-home pandemic, Margot had proven to the FBI that she was perfectly capable of being useful to them from home.

There was only one thing she *couldn't* do from the comfort and convenience of the ranch, and that was the face-to-face part of the job.

The part she didn't think about until after her second coffee.

"And what are you going to do without me?" she teased, to avoid her mind wandering into work territory.

"Pine. Maybe unlock the attic and air out my first wife for a bit."

"A *Jane Eyre* joke? What *have* you picked up at that school?"

Wes could have stayed in law enforcement. He was wildly overqualified to be part of the Glenn County Sheriff Department—he *was* a volunteer deputy, he couldn't resist—but he and Margot had both been burned by their experience with the SFPD, and when they'd moved to Elk Creek, he had committed to it being a fully fresh start.

That manifested in him becoming the PE teacher at the local high school in Willows.

Just as Margot had assumed he would grow weary of her and her various mental and emotional flaws, she'd assumed the teaching gig would be short-lived before he found something else.

But it turned out she'd been wrong about that, too. Wes loved teaching. He loved the kids, and the place he had found for himself in their new small-town life. He could fit in anywhere, she should have known that. Her therapist, Dr. Singh, kept telling her that if she only expected bad things to happen, she wasn't giving herself permission to see the good.

She had to work on that.

It was hard, though, to see the good in things when your entire childhood had been a lie. It was hard to trust that the good thing *was* good when your own father had turned out to be a serial killer.

Ah, there it was. She'd broken her own rule.

She let out a disgruntled sigh, cursing her brain, and pressed a kiss to Wes's cheek. "Alas, duty calls."

He stayed out on the swing while she headed back into the house, all the well-fed cats now vanished to their various hiding places to nap away the day. All except for Lucy, the ruler of the roost, a chubby calico who followed Margot upstairs to the bedroom.

Five days on the road required some very specific packing, but it was something Margot was so accustomed to at this point she didn't bother to put her bag together until right before she left. She didn't like to stare at a packed suitcase in their room, even if it was hers. It made her uneasy.

Into a carry-on, she threw a garment bag with two dry-cleaned blazers and one pair of dress pants. She rarely needed to go *full* Special Agent on the job but, if something came up where she would need to face the press, she couldn't wear jeans.

She also packed her typical prison getup. Khaki pants, a neutral polo shirt. Nothing that could be mistaken for a prison uniform or gang colors, no denim, all the rules she had learned from visiting her father in San Quentin before he died.

Before you killed him, a voice in her head said.

She ignored it and put her gym clothes in the suitcase just in case the hotel they were staying at had some kind of setup. The odds of that were about fifty-fifty.

Wes came into the bedroom, set his coffee on the dresser and grazed her waist with his hand as he passed her to go into their bathroom.

It sent a little thrill through her, even now. It had taken her some time to move past the idea that they *couldn't* touch. She'd held him at arm's length for so long because they'd been partners—and because she'd been afraid—that sometimes she felt that same forbidden elation being near him, despite the fact they were basically an old married couple at this point.

When he returned, he had her travel toiletries bag in his hand. She didn't need to check it. Wes was so much better at knowing what she'd need than she was, he had probably even packed whatever makeup she might require, something she didn't bother to think of most days. On the ranch, sunscreen and SPF lip balm were about as close as she got to a beauty routine.

She put the kit in her bag and changed from her pajamas into her usual work uniform of jeans, a cotton V-neck, and ankle boots. She pulled her red hair back into a long ponytail, then took her gun out of the locked nightstand drawer, securing it in the holster under her jacket.

Wes had leaned against the door frame in the bedroom and was watching her dress as if the reverse striptease was as appealing as taking it all off. Her cheeks warmed.

"Stop *staring* at me," she chided.

"No, I don't think I will." He picked up his coffee and took a sip. "I want to get a really good mental image for while you're gone."

She made a face at him. "I'll be back in five days."

"A lifetime." He held his hand to his heart.

"You know the schedule for everyone's meds?" she asked as she set her suitcase on the floor.

"The laminated schedule that is on both the fridge downstairs and the one in the feed shed outside? The one you've been doing the same way every day for the past two years?" he teased. "No, please tell me again."

"Feed the cats their wet food by seven, please, otherwise Mustard gets mad and pees on the guest room bed, and I won't be doing the laundry if that happens."

"Margot, I've got it. You're just stalling now." He rested a hand on his hip and smirked.

Busted.

But who could blame her? Everything she loved in the world was right here.

When she left their driveway, she entered reality again.

And this week, reality was serving her a real monster, a vicious murderer who had targeted children, earning him the eerie moniker of the Sleeping Beauty Killer.

She kissed Wes goodbye, lingering for a moment, enjoying the taste of coffee on his lips, the warmth of his body, all while she knew time was ticking and her drive wasn't getting any shorter.

"Don't get in any trouble while I'm gone," she teased, her usual goodbye.

"Hey, I make no promises."

TWO

Margot hated the pang of driving away from her home, but the truth was, as soon as she got to the FBI headquarters in San Francisco, she felt a little thrill of excitement, because she knew she was about to get into a puzzle. And Margot was good at solving puzzles.

Killers like this left an air of something unfinished behind them, and Margot had a hankering to figure out what that was.

Stiff from the long drive and feeling a little homesick already, she sent Wes a quick text to let him know she was safely back by the Bay. It was a small gesture, but one that still amazed her sometimes. Someone out there cared about her enough to want to know she was okay. There was someone she cared about enough to want to tell.

She was glad to be in the building before the rest of the team. She made a detour before anyone had time to stop her, heading to her small office to deposit her suitcase and quickly check her emails. As soon as everyone else started to arrive, she probably wouldn't get another moment to herself until she reached her hotel room at the end of the day.

For someone who spent most of her time in the quiet of the ranch, office weeks were difficult to adjust to.

She was proud of the work that she and the team had accomplished, though.

Over the five and a half years the cold case unit had been operating, they had managed to solve over sixty unsolved homicides or missing persons cases, just by talking to killers who were already behind bars.

It was astonishing, really, how much you could learn about a person if you were willing to ask the right questions and listen to what they had to say. And that was the thing about serial killers—most of them *loved* to talk.

Margot's job was to listen.

She'd proved her mettle by interrogating her own father, using the information he was willing to share to help close almost a dozen additional cases.

She had also put him in the grave for good, but that wasn't a service the FBI typically offered for the people they were interviewing, despite most of them already being on death row.

Margot quickly checked her notes on their current file: Richard DeGraff. Before their team meeting she wanted one last look at the case so it didn't look like she wasn't ready.

She'd been a homicide detective for over a decade before joining the FBI, so speaking to killers was well within her wheelhouse. Since she'd moved to this team, that job had in a sense gotten easier. These killers were already behind bars; it wasn't up to her to make sure they secured an arrest. These men—and the rare woman—were already convicted and they weren't going anywhere. Margot just had to find a way to get them to unlock the secrets they were hiding.

Easy might not be the right word for it.

Simpler perhaps.

Margot stepped out of her office and scanned the work floor to see who else was already in.

Their office reminded Margot, honestly, of her and Wes's space back at the SFPD: sterile and a little the worse for wear. It was nothing like the fancy space the FBI had provided for

Andrew's last task force, when they had been working to find Ed Finch's missing victims. While some of the other members of the team complained about the change in their digs, Margot actually found that it made her feel more at home. She kind of missed the scruffy old couch and the creaky chairs of her old workplace.

She didn't see anyone lingering, so she headed to the small kitchenette to get another coffee, something she'd likely regret later, but which seemed like a perfect idea now. When she had only been a visitor to this world, she'd marveled at the stories staff mugs could tell about the people who worked on a team. The #1 *Dad* mug, or the red and white Stanford logo. Over the years she had come to know who belonged to each of them, and it made those mugs feel like emblems of her fellow team members.

Her own mug was a Willows High School PE mug—gold and cornflower blue—that she had stolen from Wes's office years earlier. They no longer sat across a desk from each other solving cases, so having the mug made it feel like a small part of him was here with her whenever she came into the city.

Alana Yarrow, one of the other team leads, came into the kitchen, her signature cloud of Baccarat Rouge perfume lingering around her and her pristine red lipstick in place. Alana, now in her forties like Margot, somehow wore her age with a polish and grace that Margot didn't dare try to duplicate. Alana had started to go gray a few years earlier and simply stopped bleaching her hair blonde, so now her pristine chin-length bob was a natural silver hue that somehow looked *more* youthful and chic than the blonde had.

Disgusting.

"Morning, Margot," she said with a smile, filling up her own cup, the Stanford mug. Margot had learned that Alana had gone there on a joint scholarship for academics and volleyball. She'd been so good she qualified for the Olympic team when she was twenty, but then a knee injury had ended her athletic career.

These were the little things Margot rarely tried to learn about people she'd worked with in the past. The small talk and backstories.

Back then, she had kept almost everyone in her life at arm's length, terrified that when they learned who she really was they would only have the capacity to hurt her more. She was slowly learning most people weren't bad. It was a hard thing to believe, when her day-to-day work, not to mention her home life, had been steeped in death, but she believed it now. Most people were good people.

And when she had learned to start letting them in, she found that, rather than getting hurt, she got to experience what it was like to have friends.

Even now it was still something she was getting used to.

"You ready for the trip?" Alana asked, spooning sugar into her mug.

Margot looked at her own watery brew. She missed Wes bringing her coffee every day when they were partners. It turned out she didn't make it as well herself.

"Yeah, I did another deep read on him." Margot shuddered involuntarily. "I also reviewed notes from the last few people who spoke to him, which was helpful."

A few more staffers were arriving now, the sound around the office buzzy with small talk.

Margot and Alana walked together towards the conference room, where Andrew Rhodes and Greg Howell were already sitting. Greg was in presentation mode, and was practically on the edge of his seat waiting to get started. Once Margot and Alana took their seats, Sydney Onyema hustled in, carrying a stack of files and looking as if she hadn't gotten any sleep in the last three days.

Her black hair was in long braids, and as usual she wore no makeup whatsoever. But who could blame her with such a flawless complexion?

Sydney had been their best researcher on the old team, and, although she had taken a break to move to a different field office for a few years, she had recently requested to rejoin the unit. This would be her first time joining them on site for an interview since her return.

Of the ten people working the cold case unit, most of them never left San Francisco. Andrew, who ran the unit, tried to keep the on-site teams small intentionally. But Sydney had been proving herself invaluable over the past several months, and she'd been expressing a lot of interest in field work. It was time for her to get her shot.

Sydney let out a little huff as she slumped into a chair, keeping the files in a haphazard pile in front of her.

"Sorry I'm late," she whispered to Margot.

Margot looked at the clock, which said it was five minutes to nine. Sydney was just the kind of person who believed ten minutes early was on time, and on time was late.

"You're good, don't worry," Margot said, with a smile.

No one else in the room was at all bothered by her arrival time, but Sydney had an uneasy look on her face like she was just waiting for someone to get mad at her. Margot knew how badly the younger agent wanted this field opportunity to be a success. She just hoped Sydney wasn't being too hard on herself.

Alana checked her lipstick in the reflection of her iPad screen. Most of the team were old school, with paper files, but Alana kept everything digital. It was a side effect of her computer science background.

Andrew got up to close the conference room door. He was in his early sixties, but looked great for his age. The mandatory retirement age at the FBI was fifty-seven, but Andrew had somehow been overlooked, and he wasn't about to remind anyone it was his time to go.

He wore a tidy beard that matched his salt-and-pepper hair, and tortoiseshell glasses. He always reminded Margot of a liberal arts college professor that all the freshman girls harbored a secret crush on. He had been the FBI agent responsible for capturing her father decades earlier, something that had formed an unlikely bond between them.

When everyone was settled, Andrew nodded to Greg. Greg was the dictionary definition of *gangly*, all limbs and elbows. He was pale because he never went outside unless they were on a case, and Margot wasn't certain he ever left the office most days. He had wavy red hair and a smattering of freckles on his face, and a penchant for being overly enthusiastic about some of the more macabre elements of the cases they worked on. Back in the day, it had earned him the nickname *Gory*, but over the past six years people had just accepted his foibles and finally stopped teasing him about them.

Margot was glad that he wasn't the outsider of the crew he had once been. She'd always had a soft spot for Greg. He reminded her of her brother, David.

She worried a little less about Greg than she did about David, but Greg also wasn't as much of a hot mess as her brother.

Greg typically led their meetings, but the true mastermind who made everything flow was an agent named Harper Talbot who could churn out gorgeous, professional PowerPoint decks in the time it took some people to pour a cup of coffee. Margot had admired her work immensely before ever knowing her name.

Harper had no interest in being a field agent, which was good, because her work with tech was where they needed her the most. Harper was also the one they could count on to scour any suspect's social media presence and find out things about them no one else knew. Comments they made on TikTok years earlier? She'd find them. A short-lived YouTube account that hadn't been updated in fifteen years? Harper could get there.

Margot was eternally grateful that in her teenage years in the early to mid-nineties, she had avoided social media entirely. She couldn't imagine what embarrassing things armchair sleuths might have dug up on her if they'd had old Myspace and Tumblr accounts to rifle through. Those hadn't cropped up until she was in college and already too wary of protecting her identity to dip her toe into the online world.

But if they'd existed Harper would have found them.

Margot scanned the window of the conference room until she spotted Harper at a desk in the open-plan space outside, her black hair in a pixie cut, cat-eye glasses with rhinestones glinting in the fluorescent lights. Harper caught Margot looking and waved, flashing a toothy grin. She dressed like an emo kid from the aughts, but had the sweet energy of an adoptable puppy.

Margot waved back before turning her attention where it belonged.

Greg launched the PowerPoint and a face they had all become very familiar with over the past several weeks filled the screen.

Richard "Ricky" Floyd DeGraff, the so-called Sleeping Beauty Killer. Margot didn't love to use the names that the media came up with for these guys, but for everyone like Ted Bundy who the public knew by name, there was a Green River Killer or a BTK, guys who became synonymous with a moniker and who most people couldn't actually name.

Gary Ridgeway and Dennis Rader.

Margot could name them.

Ricky DeGraff had been arrested in the early aughts, following several high-profile child murders. The stuff of nightmares. His victims had been aged from six to sixteen, but most of them were at the younger end of the spectrum.

All ten of his known victims had been beauty pageant contestants.

Now it was up to Margot and the team to see if Ricky had more victims he hadn't owned up to yet. He had, during the mid-aughts, been a chatty guy, agreeing to press interviews, talking to some of the best profilers in the Bureau, but he had always been cagey when asked if the ten girls they knew about were the only kills he was responsible for. There was also something about his victim profile that bothered Margot, though she couldn't put her finger on what it was yet.

He'd faded out of the public eye, but the rejuvenation of the true crime genre in podcasts and documentaries meant there was renewed interest in his case and, as always, that brought new pressure to ensure that all his victims were getting the justice they deserved.

DeGraff couldn't get any more imprisoned. He was on death row—not that Montana State Prison had executed anyone in almost twenty years—and would never see the light of day again. But just because a man was behind bars didn't mean that justice was done. Margot had learned all too well before joining the FBI that there was still plenty of damage a killer could do from a prison cell.

What Andrew had put together with this unit was an opportunity to unearth the crimes that serial killers *weren't* known for. The ones they had, to all intents and purposes, gotten away with. Margot had been able to find several new victims that her own father had been responsible for, ones he had been willing to admit to her, and that was how—without wanting to—she had learned to get what she needed from convicted killers.

Margot had finished with her father, thinking her days of sitting in prisons were done, only to turn it into her main job. It was funny the way the world worked.

Greg cleared his throat to get everyone's attention. He was typically one of the most awkward among them, but when it came to giving a rundown of a case file, he settled into a zone like nobody's business.

"Richard 'Ricky' DeGraff, colloquially known as the Sleeping Beauty Killer. DeGraff was a beauty shot photographer on the child pageant circuit. He would take headshots and other professional photos of girls at events, which gave him an established credibility in that world. People trusted him, and he was provided with home addresses and other information relating to the girls. He used this information to mark certain victims for death, and because he knew the timelines for all the events, he knew when the girls were likely to be home and not. He specifically targeted the daughters of single parents—he would often offer these mothers discounts to earn their trust further—and then he would kidnap and murder the girls in the lulls between pageants. He was able to get away with this for years, because he worked the circuit over eight states, and because the girls weren't attacked at pageants, that connection was only peripheral and not noticed initially because of the departmental issues."

Greg navigated to another slide, where there were photos of ten smiling girls. The most commonly known images of them were photos that DeGraff himself had taken. The FBI team had opted not to use those photos, choosing instead to use candid pictures provided by the victims' families.

The girls were mostly very young. Six, eight, nine. The outlier was the first victim, Laycee DeLine. Laycee had been sixteen when she died, and the theory they had developed was that she had been a bit more challenging than DeGraff wanted. Too big, too strong, too hard to subdue. So he had switched his MO.

"While we believe there was a sexual element to DeGraff's motivations, none of his victims showed any signs of sexual assault. It is highly unusual, but sometimes with sexual sadists they derive their satisfaction from the act of killing or inflicting pain rather than actual sexual penetration."

Everyone in the room knew this, but the presentation needed to be thorough. They were going through multiple cases at a time, and details mattered. Margot leaned forward, keenly waiting for Greg to get into the meat of the case.

Greg glanced out at the room and said, "Okay, now let's talk about the other victims."

THREE

Greg looked at all of them to ensure everyone was focused on him. This part was important, because they needed to know as much about these girls as possible. It could be the smallest bit of information that might trigger DeGraff to loosen his lips and let him know that he *was* responsible for their deaths.

While Margot had spent hours—*days*, even—looking at every aspect of this case, she appreciated the way Greg presented everything like it was new information. Hearing him give a high-level overview could often rattle something loose for her when she had been stuck in all the finer details of a case. She was hoping somewhere in his brief he would say something or show something that would reveal the hidden key to this case that had been evading her, the thing that kept her coming back to the same notes over and over.

It also helped remind her why they were here. It wasn't about the killers, despite the one-on-one work she did with them. This was all about the victims.

The team had done a thorough search of missing persons cases as well as cold case homicides for victims who were anywhere from two to twenty. It was a broad net, but by connecting those deaths to the pageant world—even if the victim had only been in a single pageant—they had narrowed their scope down to six girls they believed could have been among DeGraff's unknown victims. If they could get him talking about one of these, the hope was that this might get him to talk about all the others.

Once a killer got talking, they tended to love the sound of their own voices. They liked attention, they liked to be important to someone, and Margot knew how to make them feel that way. Threats and badgering didn't work. Not the way they would in an interrogation room.

That was something she had needed to learn the hard way as she changed career. She was *great* at interrogation, but the rules were different once it was a man behind bars doing the talking. That change had been difficult but enticing, a new learning curve that had been similar to picking up a second language. She'd spent six years honing her fluency in breaking down incarcerated killers, but it never ceased to be exciting when she finally made them crack and admit to crimes they'd kept hidden for years.

These men had nothing to lose but time. It was the one thing they had in abundance, even though being on death row should mean there was a ticking clock over their heads.

Margot had to learn how to make talking to her feel worth it to them, and that changed from killer to killer.

Now that Greg was sure they were all paying attention to him, he proceeded, clicking the remote in his hand to advance the PowerPoint deck. A photo of a round-cheeked young girl with dark hair and unevenly cut bangs appeared. "We have Reese Whittaker, age seven. She went missing in Red Field, Arizona in 2009. She only participated in a single pageant in 2008, and while there is not a specific record of DeGraff having been a vendor at that event —it was a locally organized event, not affiliated with any groups, and they don't have the most rigid records of who did and didn't attend—he might have been there. We have good reason to believe he made several trips to Arizona that year, as it was part of his normal pageant route. Whittaker is technically still a missing person. She disappeared from Flower Grove Trailer Park on a

Sunday afternoon while her mother was at work at a nearby diner. When a neighbor went to check in on Reese—who had been playing in the yard between the houses—they found she was missing. No body was ever located, and about five years later her mother declared her legally dead. There were several suspects, including two ex-boyfriends of the mother, but nothing ever stuck with them."

Sydney scribbled something down, looking through a file in front of her. "Remind me again why the girl's father was never considered a suspect there?"

Margot hid her smile by lifting her coffee mug to her mouth. She was so accustomed to Greg's various tics and oddities, she knew Sydney's interjection was going to bother him.

Greg's mouth twitched. He liked to field questions at the end, which everyone else in the room was used to, but this was Sydney's first time in the inner circle. She was an inquisitive person, and knew a lot about the cases, but with all the research they had done sometimes smaller things could slip through the holes in their memories.

Greg got his equilibrium back and answered. "Reese's father had moved to Florida and wasn't in contact with either her or her mother. The possibility was explored, but he had a rock-solid alibi for the day of her disappearance and there was no reason to believe he had a connection to her kidnapping."

Sydney made another note and then closed the file. "Okay, great."

It was a sensible question. In most scenarios of child abduction, the perpetrator was someone connected to the family, either a parent, family member, or close friend. Stranger abductions—despite the eighties obsession with "stranger danger"—were actually very uncommon. It was the reason the original investigators had spent so much time focused on the men who had come in and out of the mother's life.

But now they were exploring the possibility that her fate had fallen into the hands of a stranger after all.

Margot briefly imagined it. A child playing in her yard, happy and oblivious until a man came to stand over her. He would be friendly and kind, and any warnings her parents might have given her about talking to people she didn't know would fly out the window. He'd offer her an easy lie. Her mom had sent him. The girl would go, and she would never be seen again.

She thought of her own father, pulling the family car over on a deserted highway for a teenager with her thumb out. She imagined all the ways these men could make a girl feel safe until it was too late for her to get away.

Margot fidgeted with her coffee mug and refocused on Greg, trying to chase those images from her mind.

Greg continued through their list. "Rini Fawcett, age two. We think she would be a real outlier for DeGraff if she is one of his victims. She was very young according to his typical tastes, but we know he shifted his victim profile in the past and we also know he *was* present at one of Rini's toddler pageants. She'd also be an unusual choice in that she had a two-parent household, and her mother was a stay-at-home mom, so not a lot of opportunity. But she did go missing from her home, the same as his other victims. She was playing in a pool in the yard, her mother went inside to answer a ringing phone, and when she looked back outside Rini was gone."

Margot stared at the photo of Rini, with her sunburned cheeks, still cherubic with baby fat, and her light blonde curls. Even after all her years of crime scene photos and horrific case files, she still couldn't understand how a person could look at a face like that and wish the little girl harm. Besides that, she wasn't convinced Rini was a good selection for the shortlist. There were too many things that didn't align with DeGraff's standard victim profile and MO. But he had been present at one of her pageants, so they couldn't ignore that connection. Rini was also another victim whose body had never been found.

"We have Tawny Uecker, age ten, from Palm Springs, disappeared in 2010, which would be very close to the time he was caught, and we theorize that there might be more victims in this time frame as he got a bit more frenzied towards the end of his run. Uecker's body *was* discovered, but unlike DeGraff's standard profile she was assaulted and then manually strangled, whereas DeGraff tended to use pantyhose. While there are differences, the similarities are enough to keep her on the list, especially if he was becoming sloppier at the end. All of these victims have things that made them unlikely to be connected to him initially, but we're obviously revisiting a lot of these options."

He continued through the rest of the list, refreshing them on details they already knew. By the time he completed his presentation, Margot felt as if she had just speed-run the entire DeGraff case.

She was grateful for the overview. It would help keep her from getting stuck on one topic when she met DeGraff. She was looking forward to the interview now, in a strange way. Seeing all those girls' faces had reminded her of the reason they were doing this, and that was to make sure at least one of the names on their list finally had a resolution to her case, a sense of closure and justice that Margot could offer if only she asked the right questions.

It was now Andrew's turn to address them, and Greg took his seat beside Sydney. Margot noticed that his body language was rather stiff around the new arrival, and she wondered if there was a little bit of jealousy that there was a new person on the team and he was no longer special as a younger participant. Greg was typically very happy-go-lucky no matter how dark the discussion. She might need to give him a gentle nudge to be nicer to their new member.

Margot knew all about prickliness. Before this job she had never been accused of being a team player. Her partnership with Wes when they'd been on the SFPD together had helped teach her it *was* possible to work alongside someone. Until then she had spent much of her life putting as much distance as possible between herself and others, because close connections were too much of a risk. But what she had learned since—an education hard-earned—was that life could often be a heck of a lot easier if she allowed people in.

She didn't think Greg needed that same kind of lesson. He probably wasn't even aware of what he was doing. But sometimes it didn't hurt for people to have a reminder of the value of a team. Margot had come a long way if she was going to be the person to explain that to someone else.

Andrew was speaking and Margot realized she hadn't been paying attention; her mind had been off wandering until she heard her name.

"—that's where Margot is going to come in. While we will all be on site at the prison, Margot and I will be the primary ones in the room with DeGraff. We have to limit the in-person contact with him, but the room will be set up with a camera and Alana, Sydney, and Greg will be in a nearby visitation room watching the interview. If you see something you don't think we do, make a note of it. We have five days of visitation approved, so we can revisit the things you notice on subsequent days. No matter what it is, if it stands out to you, make a note of it. Nothing is inconsequential."

He walked them through the rest of the process of the day. Reminders were issued about what they could wear—and a not-so-subtle reminder was pointed in Alana's general direction about makeup and perfume—so that they would all show up in their matching khaki pants like they were running interference for the Best Buy Geek Squad.

Margot was an old hand at all of this, as were most of the team except for Sydney, so much of this was likely for her benefit. But it could often be six months in between prison visits, and it never hurt to be refreshed. Margot's suitcase was already expertly packed. She had a laminated checklist at home.

Knowing she was ready, she drummed her fingers on the table, a heady sense of anticipation buzzing in her.

"All right, are there any questions?" Andrew scanned the group seated around the table. Margot glanced at Sydney to see if she would ask anything else, but everyone was silent; there were just a few quiet nods. Andrew looked at his watch. "All right, the plane is wheels up in two hours, so if you need to go home and get your gear now is the time to do it. And if you came prepared, you can spend the next little bit refreshing yourself for the week ahead. We'll be in Montana in time for dinner, then we'll head to the prison first thing in the morning. We've been given two hours a day to meet with DeGraff, so we want to use that time wisely. Everyone feel prepared?"

Margot never *really* felt prepared for these visits, no matter how much reading or review they did. Knowing the case was one thing, but sitting across from a killer was always another situation altogether, one that no level of preparation could really get a person ready for. Still, every time she took that seat, it was like being in a plane as it took off. Thrilling, but with the edge of danger never far from her mind.

"All right, everyone. Now let's get going." He clapped his hands together and the meeting was over.

FOUR

Margot didn't think of herself as a private-plane person.

She hadn't grown up with money, even before her father had been arrested for murder, and after the fact they'd had even less. She'd been underpaid as a cop, as they all were, and only frugality and good investment had allowed her to have enough to buy the property she had up north.

That, and an unexpectedly robust inheritance from her father.

Ed Finch, it seemed, had generous benefactors, people who believed in his innocence and regularly sent him money or made donations towards future legal defenses. When Ed had died, he had been a millionaire, albeit a minor one.

She didn't *want* the money, but she found that when the time came, she didn't refuse it. Call it justification but she told herself that, after all the years of her life she had missed because of the fear he had sown in her mind, he owed her.

She put most of it aside into a savings fund for her nephew, Cruz. Giving it to her brother hadn't been an option, because of his complicated history of substance abuse issues. She felt bad that their father hadn't chosen to leave him anything, and admitting that she didn't trust him with the money was hard. But even though she had only met Cruz a handful of times, she did want to do whatever she could to make sure his life was easier than theirs had ever been.

But *money* was not something Margot felt comfortable with, and displays of wealth made her uneasy, even if this plane wasn't as lavishly outfitted as many private planes likely were. There was no one serving them drinks on the flight, and, while the seats were made of soft leather and the whole interior smelled faintly of a new car, the bells and whistles were minimal.

Margot was also a little afraid of flying.

Not that she would ever tell anyone here.

She had confessed it to Wes once and then on her next trip he had asked her if she needed to take an emotional support chicken with her, and, while it had been hilarious, she didn't need anyone else adding good-natured ribbing to her experience.

So, she made sure she was the first one there when the flights were scheduled, so she could find a familiar seat by the door—heights weren't what bothered her about flying, it was the sense of being trapped somewhere with no way to step outside, so she liked to be able to exit as soon as they landed—and practiced some exercises her therapist had given her to cope with situations that triggered her panic response.

It had worked well enough over the past five years that she was fairly certain no one had realized she was uncomfortable.

Or if they knew, they were kind enough not to say anything.

She buckled herself into her seat and got out her laptop. Flipping through Ricky DeGraff's file grounded her in the moment and the task at hand. Before she knew it the stairs attached to the exterior of the plane were rattling and Andrew appeared, ducking his head as he came aboard and grinning at her.

"Always have to show me up and get here first, don't you? You know we could have left the office together."

Margot smiled. "Then I'd need to go to the office to pick up my car when we got back. You know how I operate."

She would immediately head north the moment they landed back here in six or seven days' time. Her in-person commitments were done at that point, at least until the next case. She knew she was lucky, and she was grateful that Andrew gave her special privileges to perform her job. It went a long way to show how valuable both he and the Bureau found her work to be.

His support had allowed her to live a life for the past five years that worked for her. She could help solve some truly hideous crimes, and speak with some of the most vile monsters in the country, but at the end of it she could go home and sleep next to Wes, with a half-dozen rescue dogs snoozing on the floor, a cat on her head, and a window open letting the breeze in.

To sleep securely, that was worth its weight in gold.

"I'm glad you're here," Andrew said with a smile.

He said it to her every time they went on one of these trips.

Andrew, who understood her demons better than anyone else. Who had been there for the worst day of her life.

Both of them.

She was fairly certain he had set her up in this unique role as a way of apologizing to her. When he had dragged her in to help solve her father's cold cases, he had seen how it tore her apart. It had almost ruined her relationship with him. He knew he'd pushed her to the very brink.

By giving her what she needed now, he was saying he was sorry without saying he was sorry.

By continuing to stay on his team, she accepted his apology.

The rest of the team arrived together and settled into whatever places suited them. Margot, it seemed, was the only one who needed to have the same seat every time. She liked things she could control, and on trips like this those things were few and far between.

On the three-hour flight from San Francisco to Montana, Margot focused on her laptop, deep in the detail of the case, occasionally glancing out the window to ensure that the world was still there and everything else was a faint white buzz in the background.

Once the wheels touched down, a little *bump* on the ground jostling her seat, Margot let out a little sigh of relief, her fists unclenching, jaw loosening.

They were staying at a motor lodge outside of town, the fanciest place available in the area. After checking in, Margot dumped her bag in her room and called Wes.

"Did you crash twice?" he asked, rather than saying hello. It was a little endearment he had stolen from an old stand-up special.

"Only once, I'm afraid," she countered. "You'll have to wait for the return trip to see if you can collect that sweet, sweet insurance money."

"Well, shucks, there go my yachting plans. Very inconsiderate of you." She could hear the familiar sound of children shouting at each other in the background when he paused.

"Are you at practice?" she asked. It was unusual for him to still be at the school at this time.

"Girls' softball. Mimi had a last-minute appointment." He dropped his voice slightly when he spoke again, obviously wanting to make sure none of the kids overheard him. "She's doing another round of IVF, and I guess she's in a fertile window, couldn't be missed."

"I'm pretty sure I could go the rest of my life without hearing you say the words *fertile window* again, thanks. But that's sweet of you. Do you know anything about girls' softball?"

"Sure, it's like baseball but with more overt sexism."

Margot snorted. "You'll do great."

"You okay?" he asked. His tone wasn't heavy; he was just checking in, not actually concerned. It had been a long time since she'd heard genuine worry from Wes, and she liked knowing he didn't think she was as fragile now as she once had been.

Kid gloves no longer necessary.

"Yeah, I'm fine."

"This guy is a pretty fucked-up asshole."

In the background she heard a girl squeal, "Mr. Fox! Five bucks in the swear jar!"

Margot chuckled. "Watch your language, Mr. Fox. Impressionable youths."

"I thought you were talking to your *wife*," another girl said.

"I am talking to my wife," he replied, and Margot couldn't help but feel a thrill at the word *wife*. They weren't married, they'd never be married, but just knowing he claimed her like that even when she wasn't around made her feel an intense amount of love for him.

"You shouldn't swear at your wife," the first girl said.

"My wife is an FBI agent, she'll survive." This caused a chorus of excited noises to go through the girls, and they began talking over themselves. Someone was asking if she knew "Mindhunter," and, while the themes of that show weren't all that far removed from her current work, she wasn't sure Robert Ressler would be thrilled about being reduced to being called "Mindhunter" in place of his real name.

She *had* met John Douglas once, but she wasn't sure the girls would have a cultural connection to him.

"I'm going to let you go before you lose them completely." Margot laughed. "I'll call you tomorrow when day one wraps, okay?"

"Okay. Love you, glad you didn't die."

"Love you, too, don't let those girls eat you alive."

He snorted and hung up the phone. Margot felt lighter. She always felt better after she talked to Wes. There was a reason he was her person—he made her life better and easier just by being in it. It gave her the boost she needed to continue with this week and her job.

She needed a reminder that love existed, because tomorrow she would sit face-to-face with a human incarnation of evil on earth.

And even though she loved what she did and felt a sense of pride in what she and the team accomplished, it could be hard to keep hope alive in those circumstances.

FIVE

Prisons all had a similar smell.

Piss. Disinfectant. Desperation.

It was a smell she'd never experienced anywhere else. The closest she'd ever found was a hospital, but hospitals had that lingering hope to them. There was no hope to be found in a prison. Everyone here had long since given up.

Margot and Andrew were led by a guard in a khaki uniform to a small meeting room, a place designated for one-on-one meetings with prisoners and lawyers or small family gatherings. The rest of their team was already situated in a room down the hall, having set up the recording equipment ahead of Margot and Andrew's arrival.

Margot preferred not to see too many people before she sat down across from a killer for the first time. She found it made her think too much about the input of her team, what they were thinking, what had been discussed in previous meetings. She needed a clear head going in, because it wouldn't be until she spoke to Ricky DeGraff that she would know precisely how to work him.

Every killer was different, no matter how much they all had in common.

The guard waited until Margot and Andrew were seated

before he knocked on the glass of the far wall. Two more guards appeared on the other side, a man in an orange jumpsuit wedged between them. Margot watched intently as the guards guided him in, leading him to the table like he was a lost dog and then fastening his chains to the floor and the table so he wouldn't be able to move more than a few inches while they spoke.

In the past, in other interviews, Margot had sometimes asked for the handcuffs to be removed. She found that this often established a friendlier relationship between her and the killer. But that would have to wait. She needed to make DeGraff feel like he'd earned it. If she let him have little freedoms right away, he wouldn't respect the power she had in this scenario. She would seem too easy, too pliable.

Margot needed him to realize he had to please her to get what he wanted.

That was why they sometimes needed more than one day—to work up to it.

Once their charge was seated, the guards stepped out of the room, leaving Margot and Andrew alone with DeGraff.

Ricky DeGraff wasn't much to look at. He was skinny. Not lean, skinny. Bordering on gaunt. His elbows were knobbly, cheekbones taut, and, when he smiled, Margot saw that his teeth were yellow and one of his incisors was missing. But his eyes were bright, sharp.

In the pictures she'd seen of him from the time of his arrest, he'd been a little fuller in the face, and his teeth had been straight and clean. She supposed that after a while there wasn't much point in keeping up appearances. His hair was lank, a little greasy, and old acne scars marred his forehead and cheeks.

He looked like a man who hadn't seen a lot of sun in a very, very long time.

He also smelled faintly of stale sweat and body odor, which Margot was familiar with in places like these, where some men simply abandoned the typical attempts at hygiene and became more feral versions of themselves.

Here, it was easy to imagine Ricky doing the things he'd done, because the exterior had come to mirror the man he was inside. But when he'd been out in the world, he had done the thing most men like him did so well: learn to blend in. It was similar to the way that predators in the animal kingdom had evolved to disappear into their surroundings.

Serial killers did the same thing by affecting the words and actions of normal people. They learned by watching, and their mimicry skills were scarily good.

Ricky smiled at Margot, and it was the smile of a crocodile, toothy and dangerous.

"Feel like I'm famous, got the FBI in talking to me. The boys at dinner are going to ask if I'm getting a Netflix special. A book." He eyed Andrew specifically here, and Margot knew he was referencing the book that Andrew had written about the crimes and death of Ed Finch.

Margot had written the foreword of the new edition.

It was the closest she would ever come to writing something about her father, and it had felt necessary, because she was part of the lore now. She had closed Ed's cases. And she had killed him.

"No book deals just yet, Mr. DeGraff," Andrew said, his voice soft and slow, inviting, to a point where it didn't even sound like the Andrew she knew.

Margot added, "Mr. DeGraff, my name is Special Agent Margot Phalen, and this is Special Agent in Charge Andrew Rhodes."

Ricky let out a whistle. "Special Agent in *Charge*. Ooh la la, so fancy. You a fancy man, Rhodesy?"

Andrew didn't make a habit of correcting anyone who gave him nicknames, which seemed to happen with some frequency. Andy. Randy Andy. Rhodesy wasn't even original to Ricky.

"Can't say that I'm very fancy, no."

"Good, keep yourself humble. It's good for the soul."

Margot would keep that one in her pocket. If you were willing to listen, people would give you so many little treats you could use against them later on. She tried very hard to turn this technique off the moment she left an interrogation table, because she'd found it could come back to bite her in the ass in her personal life.

She didn't *always* need to weaponize the knowledge she got from others.

"Do you mind if we call you Richard, Mr. DeGraff?" she asked.

He stiffened, smile vanishing briefly as he sat back in his chair and scratched his bare arms. He sniffled. "Ricky's fine."

Richard had been his father's name, too.

Many killers had complicated histories with their mothers, but everything she had read about Ricky DeGraff suggested that he—like Margot—had pretty damaging daddy issues.

Margot would ask him about that, in time, but these interrogations were kind of like dating. You don't ask a prospective partner their dirtiest secrets or kinkiest fantasies on a first date. That was a surefire way to spook someone. No, the key was to earn their trust first, or at least find a baseline level of comfort in the conversation.

Even serial killers needed a little foreplay. *Then* you could ask them about the worst traumas of their life.

"Ricky, we might be here a little while," Margot said. "Can we get you something to drink? A coffee, a pop?"

"I'd take a soda. Ginger ale." He didn't include a barb with this, and, while he didn't say *thank you*, she noted the way his posture shifted slightly, becoming less stiff. They were already making headway.

Margot nodded to one of the guards who was standing out in the hallway watching them. This had all been discussed in advance; she wasn't treading on any toes by asking them to do it. The guard returned a few minutes later with a cold can of ginger ale. Margot noted that the tab on top had been removed. She was surprised the drink hadn't been poured into a paper cup, but she wasn't really worried that he would try anything.

Ricky's prisoner file was that of a man who kept very much to himself and caused no trouble. As a murderer of children, he was at high risk from other inmates, so he spent most of his time in his cell in an area with other death row inmates. At the moment, there were a grand total of eight of them, and they didn't exactly socialize as a group.

But Ricky's report said he was polite, obedient, and worked hard to complete a remote college degree while he was locked up. He was a voracious reader, and the notes indicated that he seemed to favor non-fiction DIY titles, like amateur soap-making and beekeeping, rather than fiction.

Margot would ask him about that, too, if it came up.

But first, as she watched him take a sip from his can, the soft, fizzy sound of the bubbles filling the quiet of the room, she leaned forward and said, "I want you to tell me about the very first girl you killed."

SIX
ARIZONA

2001

He couldn't get the hair right, and it was making him angry.

He thought he'd known what to expect, how to make this all work, but now that there was a body in front of him, her features placid, her skin cool, Ricky found that the way he had anticipated this going was not quite the way it was playing out in real life.

It was like taking a picture. You could give all the right directions, tell someone how to pose, but often there was no way to get around an awkward smile or a face that just didn't want to look good on camera.

Some people were not meant to be pretty, and the camera could tell.

He had planned this whole thing out, but the girl—Laycee, one of those names with a unique spelling that let him know she was fresh out of the trailer park—hadn't made things easy for him.

He was a *man*. He was supposed to be able to take what he wanted, do what he wanted. She was a girl. Skinny, small. Too short, even, for a real modeling career. She should have been easy to subdue. But the throb in his ribs and the bruises on his legs and arms were a testament to the fight she'd had in her.

None of this had been what he had wanted.

He wanted a doll.

He had seen Laycee over the years, and he liked the way she never really lost the roundness in her face. She also kept out of the sun, unlike some of the other girls who sported dark spray tans, or spent their time baking in sunlight to give themselves an almost orange glow. Laycee was fair, her skin unblemished, like porcelain. She had long eyelashes, and her dark hair offset her light complexion.

Every time he saw her, he imagined her propped up on a Victorian bed, her limbs still, eyes unmoving yet somehow seeing everything.

Like the dolls his mother had kept in pristine condition.

The ones his father said he couldn't play with, unless he was queer.

At the time, Ricky hadn't really known what *queer* meant, but he'd had an innate understanding from his father's tone and expression that it wasn't something he wanted to be.

The dolls sat behind glass cabinet doors, and Ricky would wait until his parents were out to take one down. He would brush their soft hair, adjust their delicate dresses to sit just so, and drink in how beautiful they were.

He suspected his mother knew, the way mothers do. That something was just a little different, a little out of place when she passed the cabinets. But she never said anything to him. He would catch her looking at him sometimes, a little differently, wary and somewhat perplexed, but never angry.

She never said anything to his father.

Somehow Ricky understood why. Because if there was anything wrong with him, anything *queer*, it would be her fault, not his father's. And she didn't want to deal with that particular explosion.

She and Ricky had learned to sidestep the landmines his father had littered all over their home. It was a tense way to live, always holding your breath, but after a while it just became the way of things.

It didn't always work, and sometimes there were fits of rage.

Sometimes there were fists.

Eighteen years living in that house was enough.

Ricky left for college—he'd saved every penny, studied hard enough to get a partial scholarship—and he didn't look back. He felt sorry for his mother, leaving her like that, but he believed his absence would make life easier for her.

In a way, she made it easier on herself by dying only two years later.

It gave Ricky an excuse to leave that part of his life behind him. But after the funeral, a stodgy-looking lawyer with a bad comb-over sent him a box, and in it, alongside some old photo albums and bits of memorabilia, was a note from his father.

She would have wanted you to have this.

And under the other items, a doll.

The one he had loved the most, with her dark hair, her smooth porcelain skin.

Ricky put her in his closet, careful to avoid the mockery of anyone who might see it. But whenever he got dressed for the day, there she was, her all-seeing eyes looking right into him.

Wanting a friend.

And he promised her every day he would bring her one.

Laycee was supposed to be that friend, but now he was sure she wasn't good enough to present to his doll. She'd been pretty enough, certainly, but that was all fucked up now. There were bruises around her neck; those he could easily cover with makeup, but the hair was all wrong.

She'd thrashed around so much when he choked her, flailing like she'd been possessed by a demon. Aside from making him angry, it had also completely ruined that beautiful, shiny, dark hair of hers. Now it was tangled and, as he tried to ease a comb through it, the hair split and frayed, looking frizzy and unkempt.

No, she wouldn't be right. She was too big, anyway, too grown. She didn't look like someone who still played with dolls, even if she resembled one. He would need to change his approach, find someone smaller, easier to subdue. Someone where there was less risk of ruining her picture-perfect appearance.

He finished posing Laycee the best he could, though the results were unsatisfactory, and took a photo. She might not be the right one, but she was his first attempt, and he knew from his work as a photographer that it was important to chart your progress, so you could see how far you'd come.

He would just need to try again.

SEVEN

Margot used to have trouble sleeping after visiting with men like Ricky.

But over time, the mind can come to accept just about anything.

So, when her phone rang at eleven o'clock, she was already asleep in her lumpy motel bed, with Ricky DeGraff's file on her chest and a half-finished carton of surprisingly decent kung pao chicken on the nightstand.

She fumbled for the phone, and considered letting it go to voicemail. A sharp pang came as she briefly wondered if it was her father. A thought she would probably never be able to shake.

Ed was dead and gone, of course. But that didn't change the fact that she still felt his presence clinging to her like an unwelcome second shadow.

Margot pushed down the anxiety, not wanting to let that kind of fear rule her anymore. She'd worked too hard for the life she had now to fall back into those old habits, that nagging fear. But there would never be a time, she knew, that Ed wasn't at the back of her mind.

She answered the phone. "Hello?"

"I've never been so glad you were a light sleeper," Wes's

familiar voice said. It was impossible not to hear the tension in his voice. Something was very wrong.

Margot sat upright in bed and the files she'd been reading when she fell asleep dropped to the floor, grisly crime scene photos decorating the ugly hotel carpet. "What's wrong?" she asked.

Wes cleared his throat before speaking again. "I don't want you to panic."

"That's probably not the best way to start this conversation, then," she pointed out.

"It's probably nothing, but..." He paused again, trying to find the right words. "I just got a call from the parents of one of the girls on the softball team, Whitney. They said she never made it home again after practice."

Now Margot felt clear-headed and awake, any remaining dregs of sleep shaken off with his words.

"Have they called all her friends? The other girls on the team?" She was immediately in problem-solving mode. She could tell from his tone that this news was weighing heavily on him, and Margot was not the type to placate and coddle when a problem arose. She had always been the kind of person who immediately offered solutions.

"They've called everyone. Local hospitals. The sheriff. But the thing is, Margot, I *know* she got home safe. I dropped her off myself."

Margot held her breath for a moment. Surely it wasn't standard procedure for the coach to be giving teenaged girls rides home. That could lead to problems down the road, and she was sure the school wouldn't allow it.

He must have sensed her hesitation, because he continued. "Her car wouldn't start, and it was pouring. She was supposed to give rides to a couple other girls on the team, so I took them all home. I couldn't just leave them stranded."

She could hear a slight defensiveness to his tone, and she suspected that was because someone else had already questioned him about this. Perhaps the angry father of a missing girl. "I know,

Wes. You were just doing what you thought was right." She struggled to find the right thing to say, wishing she could be there with him. Words were never her strong suit. She had a difficult time expressing herself and her feelings to him, even after all this time together.

If she could be with him, she could hold him, let him know that he wasn't alone in this.

"Do you want me to come home?" she asked softly.

He let out a sharp laugh. "As much as I would love that, no, you have important work to do out there. But thank you, just having you offer is a nice feeling."

Margot bit her lip. She wasn't even sure she could make good on that offer if he had said yes. They were in the middle of an investigation, and leaving when they had such a short window with DeGraff seemed impossible.

"Do you know what's happening next?" Margot's mind was running through what she would be doing if she were in charge of the case.

"No, I'm just waiting for an update."

"She'll turn out to be at a friend's place," Margot said, knowing that *was* the most likely scenario. Even though, in the back of her mind, a little voice said, *Don't be so sure*. "She'll show up in the morning with some story about a dead phone and falling asleep on a couch and she'll be grounded for a month, but it'll all be fine."

"You're probably right," Wes said. "Teenagers, right?"

"Not famous for being the most responsible people on the planet."

"I'm sorry I woke you," he said.

She shook her head, even though he couldn't see her. "Wes. You wake me up any time, any day. You are the most important thing on this planet to me."

"Except Lucy," he said jokingly, a little lightness returning to his voice. "Don't think I don't know she's your favorite."

"Don't say it out loud, it will go to her head."

"Oh, she already knows."

Margot closed her eyes for a moment, pressing her fingers into her temple to ease the headache starting up. "Are you going to be okay?" she asked, feeling as if her words simply weren't enough. She wondered if there was anyone local she could call who might be able to help, but knew almost immediately that doing that would just be seen as an intrusion by the local cops.

"I will be," he said. "Just hearing your voice really helped."

"Let me know if there are any updates, okay?"

"I will. I'm sure it will all be fine in the morning. Just a misunderstanding, like you said."

After they hung up Margot stared at the ceiling for a long time.

She hoped he believed it, that things would all turn out just fine.

Because she couldn't quite manage to believe it herself.

EIGHT

The next day didn't allow Margot much time to dwell, though Wes's situation was on her mind from the second she woke. She checked her phone and there were no texts from him to let her know that the girl, Whitney, had been recovered. She sent him a message asking if he was okay and whether there was any news, then tried to focus on the day ahead.

After a quick coffee grabbed en route, she found herself sitting across from Ricky DeGraff for the morning's session. He was just as repugnant as he'd been the day before, but today Margot felt especially low on patience, and not particularly interested in stomaching his nonsense.

Andrew was seated next to her, but Margot was the one doing all the talking today. Perhaps not the best idea, given her mood.

"Ricky, what made you decide to become a photographer?"

He shifted in his seat, seeming uncomfortable, though there was nothing particularly provocative about this question.

"I was good at it?" He didn't sound sure of his answer and looked at Margot as if she might be able to tell him if he was right.

"I think you were actually a fairly mediocre photographer, if we're being honest with each other." She pulled out a folder she'd brought in with her and laid out several of Ricky's headshots on the table. Among them were some of the portraits of girls he had killed, which had been an intentional move on her part. "These are all the same poses, the same overexposed lighting. I think anyone with a phone and a home lighting kit from Amazon could probably do what you did. So let's stop fucking around. Why did you *really* become a photographer?"

"To make money." He fixed her with a steady stare, his eyes watery, making them look more oily and fathomless than before. She wouldn't be the first to look away, but she certainly wanted to.

She leaned forward, nudging the photos closer to him with her elbows. She watched carefully as he looked at the images, made sure to see where his eyes focused, and was unsurprised when his attention was drawn to the girls he had killed. He was, in many ways, an extraordinarily predictable man.

"I've seen your bank records. We know you didn't make *that* much money doing this." She continued to stare at him, challenging him with her gaze. His attention was no longer as focused on her as it had been, but was constantly drifting back to the photos on the table.

"You want me to tell you why *I* think you did it?" she asked.

"Sure," Ricky responded, keeping his tone even, though there was some strain in it despite his best efforts. "That should be amusing, anyway."

As if she couldn't possibly know him.

Margot felt like she had lived inside Ricky DeGraff's mind for the last several months. With each photo she looked at, each autopsy report she read, she got closer to understanding him better than he might have understood himself.

"I think you did it because you were lonely."

He lifted his gaze from the photos on the table to look right at her, his expression puzzled. Of all the things she could have said right then, he hadn't anticipated that.

Andrew shifted in his chair beside her, but said nothing. This was a direction they hadn't discussed. For the most part it was assumed that Ricky had become a photographer to give him access to his preferred victim pool. At first, perhaps, just to maintain a level of closeness with such young girls with an established framework of trust. Later because it gave him a way to figure out which girls he was going to take.

Margot was off script now, but she had Ricky's attention.

"I don't know what you mean," he said, his voice strained.

"You didn't have a lot of friends, did you? We certainly haven't been able to find people who are willing to admit they were close with you. None of the other vendors knew anything about you outside the pageant space. So I don't think there was anyone. Not even online, was there? We know about that, too. About all your internet searches. But none of that time spent online involved chatting with anyone. I think you had no friends as a child, and after a while you realized you didn't know how to make any. As an adult, making new connections was harder and harder. So you found a way to insert yourself into the lives of other people. A way to force others to accept your presence, to talk to you, to be nice to you. You loved that there was an element of respect there, too. That people needed you for something."

Ricky's jaw clenched. He pushed the photos back in her direction. "I bet you know a thing or two about not having any friends," he said.

She held her breath for a brief second. She'd hit one hell of a nerve if he was resorting to such petty comebacks, but that was exactly what she'd been hoping would happen. It took all her fortitude not to smile to herself.

She fought the urge to look over at Andrew to see if he appreciated what she had done. Or to cast a glance up at the camera and give a knowing smile to the agents in the film room.

She reeled herself back in. This wasn't a confession. It wasn't a name or a place they could find a body. She hadn't solved the case.

She'd just shown the killer that she was smarter than he gave her credit for.

She did smile at him now, in response to his attempted barb, and some instinct prompted her to lean into what he'd said, to give him something more, even at a cost. "You're right. I didn't have a lot of friends as a kid. I spent a lot of time playing alone with my toys. Maybe that's why I ended up here, sitting across from you."

"Bad luck for both of us," he replied, but she'd noticed the little flicker of interest in his expression when she'd mentioned playing alone. He'd picked up one of the photos he hadn't managed to push away and was now toying with it, his expression almost happy, peaceful.

"Oh, I don't know about that," Margot replied, watching him carefully as she pulled the picture away and added it and the others back into their folder, before hiding them away from him. "I think there's still plenty of time for you and me to get to know each other better, Ricky."

He stared at her, finger scratching the table where the photo had been. He looked as if he couldn't decide if this was a promise or a threat.

In truth, Margot didn't know either.

NINE

They didn't elicit a confession from Ricky DeGraff that morning, but everyone agreed that Margot's off-script approach had done more to get him to open up than any of the talking points they had previously thought to use.

His attitude towards her had been different for the rest of their hour together. Less defensive and dismissive. Occasionally it almost bordered on friendly.

Margot should have found that more upsetting than she did.

The team debrief took several hours. They reviewed the footage of the past two interviews, debating what their next steps should be and reviewing the case notes again. While they were reviewing the notes, she pulled out an old photo of Ricky's mother. She was standing next to a glass-fronted cabinet that was loaded with creepy-looking dolls. The photo had been in Ricky's house when he was arrested, so it had made its way into the case file.

Margot hadn't paid much attention to it at the time because they didn't think Ricky's mother was the source of his parental issues. He was definitely more in conflict with his father. But looking at it now, the woman's thin smile and rigid posture, plus the way the dolls were all locked away, scratched an itch in Margot's brain. During their first interview, Margot had asked him about his father, and Ricky had mentioned that the last contact they'd had had been when his father sent him some of his things. Including a doll that belonged to his mother.

He'd made it sound unimportant, so much so they'd glossed right over it at the time, but, looking at the photo, she wondered if it was worth asking about again.

Between the gruelling debrief and the long drive to and from the prison, Margot was wiped out by the time they called it a day. She was also surprised she hadn't gotten any updates from Wes, not that she'd had any time to message him.

She headed out on her own to find something to eat, ready to decompress and prepare herself for the next day. When her phone started vibrating, she assumed it had to be Wes finally calling her with some news about the missing girl.

The number on her caller ID wasn't one she recognized, though.

"Hello?" she replied, half-expecting a spam robot to answer. Unfortunately, in her job she didn't have the luxury of being able to not answer her phone.

A deep sigh on the other end of the line was all she needed to hear to know it was Wes. She'd know him if it was only a sniffle, a clearing of the throat.

"Wes? Is everything okay?"

A soft chuckle came over the line, though it was devoid of his normal warmth. "No. No, I guess it's not."

"What's going on? Did they find the girl?" Something told her, even as she asked the question, that she didn't want to hear the answer.

Her heart pounded as he was silent for a beat, as if trying to find the right words, before he said, "Margot, I've been arrested."

Margot stopped walking. Her throat felt tight with fear as she whispered, "For what?"

It was such a stupid question, because she knew.

"They found Whitney this morning." His voice hitched, and Margot could picture his face, trying to remain composed when emotions were threatening to overtake him. "She wasn't okay, after all."

Her heart hammered as she tried to think of what to say to him, what to do, and came up with nothing useful.

A girl was dead.

Wes was arrested.

But surely they couldn't believe he would have done it? Didn't they know him?

In her life, Margot had harbored doubts about people she loved, and for good reason. Her father had been a serial killer. Her brother had been an addict. She had trust issues.

But not with Wes.

Never with Wes.

She heard that nagging voice—her father's—asking her, *what if he did it?* She could ignore that question, bury it deep. She knew Wes, knew him better than anyone else in her life. Better than anyone she would ever meet.

Wes would never have hurt a single hair on that poor girl's head.

And she felt a deep-seated anger that the people who had arrested him—people he worked with at the sheriff's department—didn't know that, too.

"What is their evidence?" she asked, her tone bitter. If he had the option to pass the phone to the sheriff, she'd have told him precisely what she thought of his investigative skills.

"It's slim. They knew I gave the girls a ride. I'd already told her parents that much last night. She was the last one I dropped off, and her parents weren't home, so I was the last person to see her alive." He sighed, sounding exhausted. "I didn't—"

Margot sat on the exterior window ledge of a boarded-up building. "Wes, stop. I know." She raked one hand through her hair, and repeated, "I know."

"I just didn't want you to think..."

They both knew what he didn't want her to think.

"I never would. Not you."

There was a pause, and she could almost feel him nodding through the phone line, accepting her at her word. The only person who might have a better grasp on how fucked up Margot's psyche was, was her therapist, but Wes was a very close second. She didn't hide who she was from him. All the ugly bits had been on the surface since almost the very beginning.

"It sounds like all they have is circumstantial. I'm surprised they would arrest you so quickly." He was a volunteer deputy, for crying out loud.

"I think Sheriff Wilder needs to look like he's taking this seriously. He has to know I'd never do this." Wes didn't sound so sure, though.

Margot's hand clenched involuntarily. She was furious for him, and desperately scared.

Under the anger and fear, though, there was something else building inside her.

In the silence that hung between them, Margot steadied herself against the wall and tried to figure out what this meant for their future. They had built a life in Elk Creek, and, while they didn't live right in Willows, they needed to be able to exist there. Even if — *when* they were able to prove that Wes was completely innocent, the damage would be done. He'd be fired as a volunteer with the sheriff. In all likelihood, he wouldn't be able to work at the school anymore.

This could be the end of the life they had spent so much time and energy building together.

Margot was getting ahead of herself.

There were more immediate things to worry about. She switched gears, imagining what Alana would do in this situation. Alana would probably swoop in and take things over, consequences be damned.

"I'll get back as soon as I can." But even as she said it, she knew it wouldn't be immediate. Making these interview arrangements took months, and she couldn't commandeer a private plane to leave when she chose. Andrew was a good man, understanding, but this wasn't just about her. There was a team to think of, and all the work they'd already put into this case. Margot punched her fist against the wall. She'd never felt so powerless.

Wes knew it, too.

"Call Sadie," he said. "She can come and stay at the house while we get this sorted out. And then call that lawyer of yours and see if he can help me. No sense paying him as much as you do and not making use of it." Another hollow laugh.

Margot took a deep breath. This was a good plan. Sadie was Wes's younger sister. She was the only one of his siblings without children, and had a freewheeling lifestyle, even in her late thirties, that allowed her to have a flexible schedule and do her job from anywhere in the world. She had stayed at the ranch in the past and knew how to care for Wes and Margot's menagerie.

Leave it to Wes to be worried about the animals when he was in prison.

Margot doubted her lawyer would be much use in a criminal scenario—not to mention he was based out of San Francisco and pushing seventy—but he would no doubt be able to point her in the right direction of someone who *could* help Wes.

"Are you okay?" she asked, acutely aware that his one call was running out. She knew the answer.

He paused, and she heard the hitch in his breath again.

"No. But I have to believe that after all this time the justice system will get something right."

They had plenty of reasons to doubt the efficacy of the justice system, but they also worked within it and tried to maintain hope that they were working towards some greater good.

Margot would figure out who had killed this girl.

She didn't care if she had to unearth every last secret in the town of Willows to do it.

Enough bad men got away with things.

She wasn't going to let a good one go down for something he didn't do.

TEN

Margot thanked her lucky stars that at least two things went right after she hung up with Wes.

Sadie was home, and horrified by the news of what was happening. She was more than willing to drive to Elk Creek. Margot tried to tell her not to rush. The animals and even Wes could wait until morning; it was getting late to drive all that way. But Sadie wasn't hearing it—Margot could hear the sound of her packing a bag even as they spoke, and she didn't protest; she was relieved to know there would be someone in Wes's corner who could get to Willows before she could. Sadie was smart, stubborn, and most importantly she adored her big brother. She was the perfect person to be there in Margot's stead.

By the time Margot hung up from Sadie, she had a message on her phone from her lawyer—evidently still a workaholic despite his advancing age—telling her that one of the younger partners in his firm would be heading to Willows in the morning to take care of Wes.

Thank God. Now that there were parts in motion, Margot could breathe the tiniest sigh of relief. She might not be able to do anything to help Wes right this second, but she had done everything she was capable of doing from several states away. She didn't have any ins at the SFPD anymore, not after burning so many bridges, but she'd texted a few friends who had gone private since then, asking them to see if they could get any information on the case from *their* sources. It was a long shot, but better than no shot at all.

Next, she needed to find Andrew. When she got back to the hotel, he was sitting at a table in the lobby, a fast-food burger and the saddest side salad she'd ever seen sitting in front of him, barely touched. Margot dropped herself down into the chair across from him.

"I need to go home," she said.

"Good evening to you, too, Special Agent," he said, setting his paper drink cup down beside the burger and wiping his hands in a thin napkin.

"Wes has been arrested." She didn't need to beat around the bush. Andrew knew her personal life details as much as he knew anyone else's. They were all aware who on the team was married, who had kids. When you spent as much time together as they did, it was inevitable that the personal stuff just found its way in over time.

He raised a thick eyebrow as he put his trash inside the takeout bag. Margot suspected he was buying himself some time.

"For what?" he asked, finally.

Margot told him everything she knew. Andrew listened, his face impassive, and once she was finished he gave one nod, then another, both seemingly to himself. "You'll have to forgive me if I sound insensitive, Margot, but is there anything you can do for him there that you can't do from here?"

She had prepared herself for this response, because she knew how Andrew thought, and she knew how her team worked. The work they were doing was important, it was expensive, and it was time-intensive for the whole team. All of them had made personal sacrifices along the way, whether it was time at home, missing events with their kids, or the sleepless nights spent thinking about all those dead girls who hadn't found justice.

Margot knew what he was saying. Her place was here with the team.

She gripped the arms of her chair and forced herself to stay in her seat and not get up and go to the airport, which every fiber of her being wanted her to do right now. She could see the other arguments he was thinking of making. That she already had special privileges, getting to work from home the bulk of the month. That she couldn't insert herself professionally into a case that had such personal stakes for her. That, in that sense, it actually made sense for her to stay away from Willows.

But none of that mattered to her, no matter how sensible or logical it was. Because Ricky DeGraff was in prison. He wasn't going to hurt anyone else, and all they had left to do was find out if there were connections that hadn't yet been made. The girls were already dead.

Wes was very much alive, and every minute he was behind bars was a minute Margot was wasting by being in Montana.

Her phone buzzed and she grabbed at it to see the message.

> In Willows, have spoken to Sadie, about to meet with Wes.

It was the lawyer, who had evidently gotten to Willows that evening instead of waiting for morning. Margot kept forgetting his name, which wasn't fair, considering how far out of his way he was going to help them.

Eugene.

She remembered it suddenly, like the name of an actor nagging her after watching a movie. Eugene Taft. It was an unusually old name for someone her lawyer had called a *bright young man*, but perhaps youth is entirely subjective when you reach seventy.

"I have to be there," she said as evenly as she could manage, hoping Andrew would understand. But she already knew what would come next.

"And you will be, Margot, but you can't do anything for him right now, and if I let you leave, I'm going to need to get our own lawyers involved when you're inevitably slapped with a charge for interfering with a case the FBI is not involved in. And don't tell me you won't, because we both know you will. You'll already have made a call that oversteps. I know you, Margot. It's in your nature to push back against systems you don't think work, and you won't be able to help yourself."

She said nothing, because he thought he was right and wouldn't listen to her, but also because she knew he was right. She was already trying to figure out how to solve this, despite knowing it was the worst possible thing she could do in the situation.

"We only have three days left here. In three days, he'll either already be out, or he'll still be there, and you being three days behind won't change much of anything."

She stared at him, saying nothing, wondering if she might be able to change his mind simply by looking into his eyes and not flinching. That was a skill she had learned from watching her father, and it was one that worked very well in her regular life. No one felt comfortable being stared at. Most people would yield in some capacity just to make it stop.

Andrew Rhodes was not most people.

"We'll try to get through this sooner. I'll get one of the profilers back at the main office to contact your local PD—"

"Sheriff's office."

Andrew winced. "We'll contact them and offer to do a preliminary profile of their potential suspect."

"I'm sure they'll love that," Margot said coolly.

"I will fly you directly to the closest airport, public or private, as soon as we are done here."

Margot had known what it was to hate Andrew in the past. She also knew, from that experience, that it was almost always because he put the job ahead of everything else. Somehow his wife hadn't left him yet, but it was very certainly to the detriment of his relationship with her, not to mention with others around him.

Margot had known Andrew since she was fifteen. Her father had been giving her a driving lesson and, as she turned into their little cul-de-sac in Petaluma, the writing had been on the wall for Ed immediately. The police cruisers. The men in their dark FBI-branded jackets.

They were there to collect a killer.

Ed had jumped from the moving car, leaving Margot stupefied and panicked. She watched her father get tackled by men with guns.

She forgot how to use a brake pedal.

Andrew was the one who had quietly slid into the passenger seat. In a voice as calm as a museum tour guide, he talked her through what to do next. Helping her stay in the moment, stop the car, put it in park.

Margot clung to that memory every time she wanted to throttle him.

She was clinging to it now.

There was, realistically, nothing stopping her from booking a flight or renting a car and driving back to California. But that would take hours. Time that she was useless to everyone. Wes, her team, herself.

She hated to admit it, but Andrew had a point.

Back home, she wouldn't be allowed to see or be with Wes. The best she could do was talk to the lawyer. And she could do that from here. She took a deep breath and sat forward, resting her head in her hands for a moment. She tried to tell herself that it would all work out. Wes would be released. They had no real evidence to hold him longer than forty-eight hours, and any lawyer worth their salt would know that.

But she had also tried to hope for the best when Wes told her the girl was missing, and look where that had gotten them.

The sheriff had jumped the gun arresting Wes, and that was going to make him frustrated in the long run, because no one likes to look stupid, but old-school lawmen like it least of anyone.

She knew that kind of animosity could begin a witch hunt.

They needed to figure out who had done this, and fast. Someone had killed that girl in the time between Wes dropping her off and her parents getting home to find her missing. She'd disappeared in the length of a driveway.

It made Margot's heart ache.

But as she sat back in her seat and looked at Andrew's kind face again, it also reminded her why they had come to Montana in the first place. Because dozens of other girls had vanished from supposedly safe spaces. From small towns, from trailer parks where everyone knew everyone else, and from the kinds of neighborhoods where people might not have a lot of money, but they had *community*. What was Willows, if not exactly like those small towns?

Hell, Margot wouldn't have been surprised if Ricky DeGraff or men like him had worked local pageants in Willows or the surrounding areas in the past. Pageants were a dime a dozen, because there was no shortage of young girls—or usually their mothers—dying to get a sash, a ribbon, or a crown.

Something that said, *you matter. You're important*. Even when the rest of the world seemed to disagree.

Margot had gone through Andrew's entire argument for him, without him having to say a single goddamn word. She stared at him a moment longer, hoping he could see in her expression that she was pissed. Pissed that she wasn't leaving, and pissed that they knew each other so well he hadn't even needed to tell her no. Finally, she shook her head once. "If we get this done early, we leave early."

"Margot, if you can crack this guy in another day, I'll fly you home tomorrow afternoon."

She shook her head, because even though DeGraff was talking, he wasn't saying anything useful yet. That was how these things always seemed to go. The men were in no hurry, and relished the attention too much to turn down more of it.

But Margot knew she could get him to talk.

It was all just a matter of how fast.

ELEVEN

When Margot took her seat across from Ricky DeGraff a third time, she was alone.

Andrew was with the rest of the team in the adjacent room, watching. She knew he would be scrutinizing her work differently today, watching to see what changed, what she did that might blur the line of professionalism. He knew she wanted to leave, and he would be observing to make sure she did her job right.

Margot felt a little offended, but she had gone off script before, so there was precedent, even without the need to get this done and get back to Wes as soon as humanly possible. She had too much at stake personally in finding out about Ricky's victims.

She set a stack of folders on the table beside her and Ricky observed them with mild interest but didn't ask her any questions. He smelled better today, like soap, and she was grateful for that. His hair was still damp. She wondered if he had gone to the extra effort just to impress her.

Then she reminded herself she wasn't exactly his type.

The living doll angle he had revealed the day before was interesting. He had often referred to the girls as *his dolls* in the past, but profilers and psychologists hadn't taken it literally. They'd seen it as his way to not think of the real girls he had killed as being human, thinking of them as inanimate objects instead.

By catching a glimpse into his past, what little of it he had offered them, Margot was beginning to get the sense that there was something else at play.

There was always a chance he was borrowing a page from the old David Berkowitz. Berkowitz, better known as the Son of Sam, had tried to convince the world that his neighbor's dog had told him to commit his murders. This was later revealed to be nonsense, of course, just a man feigning madness.

Perhaps Ricky DeGraff wanted them to believe he was insane, but Margot didn't get that vibe from him.

Not yet, anyway.

"What was her name?" Margot asked, folding her hands neatly on the table between them and locking eyes with Ricky.

He looked away first, cheeks flushed.

Adult women made him uneasy.

Mental note.

"Who?" he asked, looking at his balled hands.

"The doll. The special one of your mother's."

He didn't hesitate. "Mathilda." A faint smile crossed his lips before he flattened his expression and his face became impassive. Margot stored the name of the doll away, knowing that in the other room someone was likely already googling it to see if it was something mass-produced, possibly a brand name, or if this was just something Ricky had come up with to call her.

"Why do you think your father was so worried about you being queer?" she asked, changing tack slightly. She leaned back in her chair, settling her hands in her lap. Her natural inclination was to cross her arms, but she knew this could be interpreted as being closed off, and might make the man across from her less inclined to open up.

Margot fought to keep her mind in the room, rather than letting it wander back to California, where she couldn't be of any use to anyone. She ached for her phone, but it was back at the hotel, since they couldn't bring non-sanctioned devices into a prison. The ache of not knowing threatened to consume her, so she tamped it down, focusing on the man across the table instead.

A man who actually *was* guilty of murder.

And might be guilty of more.

She just needed to figure out the way to crack him, because once she got through his shell, that was where she would finally be able to unearth any secrets he'd been hiding.

This was just day three, she reminded herself. Rome wasn't built in a day, and Bundy wasn't broken overnight.

Well, bad comparison. There was a point where Ted Bundy was *so* willing to talk that investigators couldn't shut him up. He used the prospect of more victims to keep himself from death, until everyone stopped listening.

Ricky wasn't trying to get anything from her, and that made this trickier, because she didn't have anything to bargain with.

She just had to hope she would find a way to make him *want* to talk.

And the sooner the better.

Ricky shifted uncomfortably in his chair. His gaze flicked up to her, then back to his hands, and he took a long moment to make himself comfortable before letting out a long, phlegmy sigh.

"My old man thought a lot of things were queer. Thought it was *gay* to cry, to enjoy cooking or baking, to spend too much time with my mother. Thought it was weird I had female friends but never any girlfriend. Just, y'know, thought I was a bit too strange to understand."

"Are you?" she asked, keeping her tone soft, almost friendly.

"Am I what? A bit too strange to understand?"

"No, queer."

He bristled visibly and Margot thought perhaps she had asked the question too soon. But she was curious. She thought back to their group meeting before coming here. He didn't have all the hallmarks of being a sexual sadist. It made her wonder about his motivations.

She needed to know what made him tick if she was going to be able to connect him to any of their other unsolved homicides.

"What does it matter?" he asked, his voice sharp, cutting. He wanted to push her away with his words because he knew that, if he moved his chair or pounded on the table with his fisted hands, that would be it. Back to his cell. More quiet time alone.

"It's not a bad thing." She scooted closer to the table. "I know your father spent a lot of time when you were growing up telling you it was wrong to be different. That can't have been easy. When he sent you Mathilda, how did that make you feel?"

She would circle back to her question about him being gay, but she suspected if she worked at it a different way she would get her answer eventually. She also knew that having told him a little bit about herself, it took some of the edge off between them. He didn't need to know more than that, but if he understood that she might be able to connect with him on some level, even if it wasn't a conscious understanding, he would open himself up more.

She hoped.

"First I thought he was fucking with me," Ricky admitted. "Like it was a test. Like, he wanted me to call him up and say I threw it out or burned it, and why was he sending me some faggy doll."

The way he said the slur, it was forced, like he was unaccustomed to saying it, but it was something he had *heard* plenty of times. It caught in his throat on the way out, like it was barbed, hurting him the whole time.

"But you didn't throw her away. Or burn her."

He was picking at the dry skin of his thumbnail, and while he didn't reply right away, she knew he had heard her just fine.

"You kept her," Margot urged.

"Of course I kept her," he said, his voice barely more than a whisper. "She's just so... perfect." He let out a little breathy sigh, his cheeks suddenly flush with color. Margot got the uneasy feeling he was aroused. It made the hairs on the back of her neck stand on end.

That hadn't been a part of her plan.

This subject was too interesting not to pursue, though. She didn't want to continue, but this was why she was here.

"Ricky, did you kill those girls because you wanted them to be like Mathilda?"

Ricky offered her a slow smile, his expression almost pitying.

"No one can be like Mathilda. But I didn't want her to be alone. She needed someone she could be with."

"A friend," Margot offered. Something Ricky had never really had.

"Yes."

"She was important to you."

"She's the *most* important thing to me."

Margot tensed, hoping her gut reaction didn't show on her face. Words mattered. People didn't think about them as much as they should, but every word choice *meant* something.

She's.

She *is*.

Present tense. Not *she was*.

"Ricky, where is Mathilda now? Back then, you didn't throw her out. You didn't burn her. Where is she now?"

A slim smile crossed his lips and he rocked backwards and forwards in his chair, the legs making a *thump-thump* noise against the tile on the floor. "She's in good hands."

Margot did her best not to look at the camera that was mounted in the corner of the room, but her eyes darted to it quickly, and back. They were listening, they were paying attention. There was no way they missed it.

"Ricky..." Margot looked at him, but his expression was too lewd, too excited, so she focused on his forehead instead. "Ricky, *who* is looking after Mathilda?"

He raised his cuffed hands to his lips, pressing one finger there as he giggled, mostly to himself. "We don't tell on our friends, Agent Phalen. That wouldn't be very nice of us."

Margot held her breath. Ricky DeGraff had someone on the outside.

Someone who had been around to take his doll before he was arrested. Margot had scoured all the reports, looked at every photo taken of DeGraff's shitty apartment. She would have remembered a doll. Those things were creepy as fuck.

If Ricky had trusted someone enough to let them take Mathilda, then what else did they know?

And what else had they helped him with?

TWELVE

"We've checked his visitor logs over the past decade. There's nothing there," Sydney said.

"Nothing?" Margot raised an eyebrow. "Not a single visitor?"

They were all in a small meeting room they'd rented from the hotel. A pile of pizza boxes sat in the middle of the conference tables they had pushed together, surrounded by greasy plates, crumpled napkins, and a few errant crusts.

Seriously, who didn't eat the crusts?

Alana was drinking a beer, the bottle streaked with condensation. Margot had been nursing the same Diet Coke for the past half-hour. She would have loved a gin and tonic, but she drank to dull her edge, and she didn't feel like being dull right then. She was itching to focus all her attention on what was happening back home, but she also had the low buzz of knowing she was on to something with Ricky, that the puzzle was starting to piece together.

Sydney flushed when she realized everyone's attention was now on her. Margot hadn't meant to sound so bitchy, but she *felt* bitchy about everything right now and there was nothing she could do to keep her tone in check.

When they'd gotten back to the hotel, she had messages

waiting from both Sadie and Eugene. Sadie's voicemails were in her usual chipper tone, but Margot could tell the situation was getting to her.

"I couldn't get in to see him today, but the lawyer seems very smart, and he says it'll only be a matter of time before Wes is out. He said there *was* something unexpected in terms of evidence, something that doesn't look good, but he couldn't tell me what it was."

That had made Margot's stomach sink. What other evidence could there be? A tiny worm of unease had wriggled into her brain when Sadie told her that. Not *doubt* exactly, but just that little whispering voice.

What if.

What if.

Eugene, the lawyer, had been more forthcoming with Margot, perhaps because she was the one footing his bill.

"The evidence is entirely circumstantial, even what they found with the body. I don't see any reason he won't be back home by tomorrow night. Even if he can't go anywhere."

Margot had sunk back onto the bed in relief. Having Wes home was all that mattered. Once he was back on the ranch, they could take whatever the next steps would be to clear his name. She just needed him out of prison, and it sounded like Eugene was working on it.

But *what evidence?*

He hadn't elaborated in his message, but it had been found with the body. Physical evidence? DNA? No, there was no way they'd have been able to verify a DNA match so quickly. Margot had worked on cases with serial killers where the labs had taken almost a week to check for a match. A Podunk small town in Northern California wasn't going to get an expedited test for one dead girl.

That sounded callous, even in her own head, but at the same time it was soothing.

If it wasn't DNA, it didn't matter.

Circumstantial, just like Eugene said.

These were the things she kept telling herself to keep from screaming. To stop herself from stealing a car out of the parking lot and driving through the night to get back to where she belonged. She'd asked Eugene to tell Wes she would be home as soon as she could.

Wild horses might not be able to keep her away, but the persuasive power of the FBI apparently had more pull.

Andrew, perhaps sensing that Margot wasn't fully present or as polite as she normally might be, spoke for her. "I think what Margot is trying, somewhat inelegantly, to say, is that there may not be a *pattern* to the visitors who visited DeGraff. This could be someone who only saw him once. Maybe not at all."

"Can we get access to his mail?" Margot asked.

Her father's mail had been catalogued digitally, but that wasn't true for all killers who got fan mail.

"We've got a request in, they've been stored, but it will take some time to get them. We're having it all shipped back to the office."

So the letters got to go back to California, but not Margot. Didn't seem fair.

"He's an only child," Margot mused, frowning as she rifled through her files. "He also worked alone in his photography business. Everything we know about Ricky DeGraff points to him as a lone wolf type. His kills were for private enjoyment. What else have we missed? Could he have been working *with* someone?"

Greg had his laptop open in front of him. There was a stain on his shirt from where a piece of pepperoni had fallen earlier. He was focused so intently on his computer that his brow was actually pinched in concentration. "Everything we've seen from him and his crimes indicates he was acting alone. He's never mentioned a third party, and there was no part of his profile that would suggest he might have had an accomplice. Even the way he switched to younger girls after Laycee is evidence that he was working alone and needed to be able to physically restrain the girls on his own. If he had a partner, that wouldn't have been a concern." He looked over his laptop screen to Margot, expression almost apologetic. "We never even constructed a list of potential partners. He just didn't seem to have anyone else in his life. He lived alone, he had no work colleagues because he owned his own business, he didn't even seem to have any friends."

"Well, he had *someone*," Margot countered. "Because he wouldn't have given that goddamn doll to a stranger." She shoved the files in front of her aside in disgust, then looked back to Sydney. "Who *has* visited him since he's been inside?"

Sydney, seemingly relieved to have a question she could answer without getting her head bitten off, pulled out a printed document.

"Aside from his father, he had a few press visits, two from someone who was writing a book about him, and one visit from a *spiritual counsellor*." Sydney rolled her eyes. "Name is Sister Mary Callahan."

Greg and Alana shared a similarly baffled expression. "A nun?" Alana asked, setting her bottle down on the table. "The DeGraffs aren't Catholic."

"The mother was Lutheran, but non-practicing. The father was atheist," Greg confirmed.

"Maybe he found Jesus inside," Andrew suggested, though even his tone made it clear he was just playing devil's advocate.

"There's no record of him participating in any church services inside," Sydney confirmed. "He loves the library, but his borrowing history doesn't skew religious."

"Do you have a list?" Margot asked.

Sydney nodded and passed her a thick folder. Margot scanned it. There was too much there for her to read it all. They knew he liked crafting and DIY titles, but Margot noticed that he had borrowed a book on dollhouses over a dozen times. It seemed like a strange book for a prison library to have, but she wasn't surprised that he had been drawn to it. The list also showed a lot of study materials for college courses. Nothing that threw up any red flags.

There were no obviously religious books on the list at all.

"We should go through that more thoroughly, see if there are any other fucked-up doll books he might have been jacking off to." Margot snapped the folder shut. "How did we miss the obvious doll obsession previously, anyway? He used the word a *lot* in his previous interviews."

"It certainly felt metaphorical," Andrew said, his tone curt as he stared at her. It was obvious he was getting annoyed with her bad attitude, but Margot felt like that was his own damned fault. If he had just let her go home, she would have taken her bad attitude with her.

Sydney took the book file back. "I'll review this tonight, see if there's anything that fits that theme."

Alana drummed her long, red fingernails on her glass bottle. "Did you say he met with someone who wanted to write a book about him?" she asked.

"Twice," Sydney replied.

"How many books are there about this case?" she asked, but this time her question was directed right at Greg. Greg had a sort of uncanny ability to know these things off the top of his head.

"To date? Four."

"But only one person visited him, doesn't that seem odd?" Alana asked.

"Not really," Andrew countered. "Typically, those kinds of books don't need a lot of direct insight from their subjects."

He would know. He'd written a bestseller about Margot's father, and hadn't interviewed Ed in the process. However, in this instance his point didn't warrant her being doubtful. He was right —in most situations the author of a book about a serial killer tended to focus on the victims rather than the perpetrator themselves. Most of the time, the author never met the killer. There were exceptions, of course. Ann Rule worked alongside Ted Bundy at a crisis hotline—at the same time as she had signed a book deal to write about his murders should he ever be caught. Margot sometimes tried to imagine if it had ever come up in conversation between them that Ann had a proclivity for writing about crime. Then there was Katherine Ramsland, a noted forensic psychologist who had met with the BTK killer Dennis Rader multiple times over the course of preparing to write her book about him.

Exceptions, though. Not the rule.

They could look in to the author later. Margot was far more interested in what the nun had wanted.

"Can we see if we can get in touch with Sister Mary Callahan?" she asked. "If nothing else, I'd be very interested to know what she and Ricky spoke about."

"Isn't that considered protected?" Greg asked, his tone curious. "Like, isn't religious conversation one of those areas where they don't have to tell us anything?"

"I'm not sure that's quite as cut and dried as it might be with a lawyer," Andrew said. "And nuns can't take confession, so whatever he told her should be fair game, disclosure-wise. It just depends on whether or not she feels like disclosing it."

"I'll look into finding her," Sydney offered.

Margot was looking at the list of victims again, both known and suspected. "He's not trying to recreate the doll," she said. "They all look different. Different hair, different builds. He said he wanted to give her a *friend*."

"He's delusional," Alana offered, shrugging. "He'd hardly be the first serial killer to have a fucked-up reason to kill someone."

"I don't think so," Margot said. "I think he's very lucid. I'm not saying it's *sane* to think a doll is your bestie. But I think he's aware she's a doll. Everything he said today tells me he understands that Mathilda isn't a real person. Did you guys get anywhere on figuring out what kind of doll it was?"

Sydney shook her head. "The name Mathilda doesn't seem to be a brand. We're going to keep looking at dolls from that era, and his mother's, using his description, but they were so common back then that without a picture we would be hard pressed to find something definitive."

Margot sighed. She'd known it would be a long shot, but

finding a doll that looked like Mathilda might have gotten them some extra headway in a hurry.

Her phone buzzed on the table. Eugene.

She looked at the others. "Are we done for tonight?"

Andrew gave a nod, and everyone started to pick up their things, while Margot stuffed her files back into their folders, and then, with an anxious weight in her stomach, answered the phone.

THIRTEEN

"Hello?" Margot was making a beeline for her room, desperately needing some privacy. She wasn't the best at managing her emotions, but usually that manifested itself in her being unnecessarily brusque with people. In this case, she worried that whatever Eugene might have to tell her might make her cry instead, and Margot did *not* cry around other people.

She didn't even like to cry on her own, if she was being honest.

It's weak, the little Ed-shaped voice at the back of her head whispered. *My daughter isn't weak.*

"Ms. Phalen, it's Eugene Taft. I'm here with Wes Fox."

Her heart practically catapulted into her throat as she shut the door behind her, tossed her files on one of the double beds, and sank into a chair by the window.

"Wes, are you okay?" She hated how breathy she sounded, how needy. But goddamn did she need to hear his voice.

"Yeah, I'm keeping it together. Eugene is pretty confident I'll be out of here by morning. He told me Sadie has been stalking him like he's a wounded animal." He chuckled, but Margot could hear that he was exhausted.

"What is this supposed evidence they have that they think merits an arrest?" she asked. There was a hotel notepad and pen on the table and she had picked up the pen without even realizing it. An old habit from her detective days with the SFPD. Always write things down, you never know what might be important later.

It had been a long time since Margot had worked a fresh homicide—she wasn't technically working this either—but old habits died hard.

Wes sighed. "It's my own damn fault. It was raining when we left the school, everyone else had prepared for it, jackets, umbrellas, you know. But Whitney..." His voice hitched and the raw emotion from saying her name was more than enough to convince Margot of his innocence even if she hadn't already been sure. He was crushed that this poor girl was dead. He loved the kids he worked with. "Whitney didn't have anything, so I loaned her my jacket. She was still wearing it when they found her."

Margot leaned forward and rested her head in her free hand. As circumstantial evidence went, it wasn't ideal. A jacket had DNA on it, and DNA would certainly have transferred in some capacity to the victim.

"Did any of the other girls see you give Whitney the jacket?" she asked.

"I think so, there was a large group of us leaving together. Whitney was already wearing the jacket when we got into the car."

"Was it marked with your name?" She had to wonder how the local police had figured out it was his so quickly. It wasn't like she went around drawing "WES" in big black Sharpie letters in all of his clothes.

"It was my coach's jacket," he clarified.

Then that made sense. She knew the blue windbreaker he was talking about well. It was somewhat flimsy and had the school's name and crest on the front, and COACH in large letters on the back. His last name was on the shoulder.

She had teased him endlessly when he'd worn it the first time, suggesting that branding the hottest coach in school as *Fox* was just begging for trouble. He had told her none of his students would even know that foxy was a thing, they were all too young.

Margot had sprouted a few new grey hairs that day.

"Surely that's not sufficient evidence to get an arrest."

Eugene must have sensed she was speaking to him with this, as he took in a breath and said, "Under normal circumstances you would be right. I think the local sheriff was a bit jumpy, saw something he considered to be a slam-dunk piece of the puzzle, and they decided it was enough to move forward with a warrant. I've been talking to the district prosecutor, and he knows full well this isn't enough to take a case to court, let alone make any charges stick. In my opinion they're just looking for a way to save face for the local law enforcement before they release Wes. I have already asked them to make an official statement when he is released that indicates the mistake they made in arresting him so quickly, but whether or not they decide to admit to anything remains to be seen."

Yeah, Margot knew there was fat chance of that happening. Small-town law enforcement didn't appreciate outside input, whether it was in the form of larger agencies coming in—something she had seen time and time again when the FBI tried to help resolve cold cases—or lawyers meddling in local affairs.

She'd met the sheriff in Willows multiple times. Jim Wilder was a nice man—even if Margot did not align with him politically—and she believed he had the best intentions when it came to protecting his community.

But that kind of approach could make someone turn a blind eye to the truth because he was too focused on what he *wanted* to be true.

Which meant a killer was walking free, and Wes was in jail, all because of stubbornness. She wasn't sure what made her angrier: that someone could believe Wes was capable of murder, or that in doing so they were putting so many others at risk.

Margot knew that there were two likely scenarios. The first—and most likely—was that Whitney *had* been killed by someone she knew. Nine times out of ten, murders were committed by someone the victim was familiar with. While people liked to focus on—and oddly sometimes romanticize—the idea that serial killers lurked around every corner, that simply wasn't the case. When people were killed, the reason behind it was usually personal.

But Margot couldn't ignore the other possibility: that poor Whitney had just so happened to fall into the path of a killer. This person could have just been passing through Willows on his way to broader hunting grounds, which would make him hard to identify, or he could be local to the area.

Margot and Wes would have heard if there had been any other murders in the vicinity. Part of the reason they had moved to Elk Creek was because of how low the crime rate was, and how far removed it was from the darker parts of their lives. They'd wanted a break from all of that, a different way of living where Margot could walk outside at night without constantly looking behind her.

There had been no homicides in the area in decades.

So either this was a killer on the move, or it was the first of potentially many.

But in a small community, that kind of killing was risky. Even Ed Finch had known to move to surrounding areas.

Margot shook her head, trying to cast off this line of thought. It had to have been someone that Whitney knew. A parent or family member. An ex-boyfriend perhaps. Or current boyfriend.

Her detective brain had a thousand questions, but she knew this wasn't the time.

And it wasn't her case.

"I'll try to get home tomorrow," she promised.

"Please don't worry," Wes protested. "As much as I want to see your face right now, you've been working on that case for eight months. I'm *fine*. I'll *be* fine. Sadie is here. Eugene is here. As much as I love you, we both know if you were home right now, you'd probably be slapped with harassment charges for sitting in the sheriff's driveway until he let me out." He laughed, and for the first time in days it sounded genuine.

"I love you," she said, and wished Eugene wasn't in the middle of this conversation. "I want to be there for you." She wiped a hot tear that slid down her cheek.

"I know you do, Margot. I know you're dying to stick your nose in this and solve it all on your own. But we need to let this play itself out the right way."

He sounded like Andrew, but his tone was gentler, more teasing. He was right, of course, the same way Andrew had been right. If she was home, she would be making a menace of herself.

She both loved and hated how these men knew her, knew that it was in her bones not to rest until an injustice had been righted.

"I'll be home in a few days," she promised. "Please keep me updated, no matter what the change. And Wesley," she scolded, using his full name as a teasing inside joke between them. "Don't you dare let Sadie leave you alone until I get back."

He laughed again. "If there was any woman in my life who could challenge you for being the most stubborn and headstrong, it would be my baby sister."

Margot smiled, wishing she could talk to him longer, but knowing it was more important for him and Eugene to have the time.

"Good," she said. "Maybe *she* can solve the murder."

FOURTEEN

Margot dreamed of dolls.

She was no stranger to a good nightmare every now and then. She had seen enough dead bodies, enough human horror, to have a different nightmare every day about corpses.

But that was a part of her life she was usually able to compartmentalize. Yes, bodies were upsetting to look at. Seeing the capacity for evil in the world was a miserable thing. Yet, that wasn't what Margot had nightmares about.

Usually, it was things she could not control. Fires at the ranch where all the senior dogs and cats couldn't get free. Something bad happening to Wes. Her brother calling her to tell her Cruz was dead. Those were the things that made Margot sit up at night in a cold sweat. Made her get out of bed and make sure no candles were burning and that the oven was off. Reach across the pillow to make sure Wes was still snoring softly beside her. Text David just to *check in.*

It had been a good long time since Margot had dreamed of something surreal, but when she finally fell asleep that night after torturing herself with an hour of checking local news feeds from back in California for the story of Whitney's death, she'd dreamed about dolls.

The dolls lined a long, seemingly endless hallway, rows upon rows of them, higher and farther than the eye could see. They all stared down at her with their dead glass eyes, each with a small smirk affixed to its painted lips.

They watched her, and somewhere in the distance she could hear laughter.

And then crying.

As she walked down the hallway, she felt certain the dolls were turning their heads to watch her pass. And the further she got, the less fake the dolls looked, and the more human they became. Only then did Margot realize they were little girls, their dead eyes white, unseeing. Flies moving over their mottled cheeks, their texture changed forever by death.

Even though Margot knew the appearance of death intimately, this still rocked her. She felt like she was seeing a body for the first time, and those animal instincts to scream or run or vomit rushed back to greet her.

You never really recover from seeing a dead body.

Even if it's a body of someone who has died in a natural way, there's something unexpectedly harrowing about meeting Death face-to-face like that, and the realization that the person who had once inhabited that body was gone and only the shell of them was left behind.

You could *tell* when someone was dead, there was simply no mistaking the physiological change. Margot wasn't sure if she believed in the soul, or in the afterlife, but she knew that there was a force that animated all living beings, and you could see its absence when it wasn't there.

She was staring into that void when the little girl in front of her opened her eyes.

That was when Margot awoke, panting and soaked with sweat.

She glanced at the clock on the nightstand. It was barely after five in the morning. Too early to start looking at the case notes again, definitely too early to call Eugene to find out the status on Wes.

But sleep, she knew, was not an option either. There would be no drifting off again now, not after that dream, and not now that she was up and felt like a whole world of problems was sitting on her chest, sucking the life out of her.

Margot was, by nature, inclined to try to solve problems. That was what a detective did. And even though she was no longer a detective, those old habits died hard.

She kicked off the sheets and changed into gym clothes. Years ago, the mere idea of going to a gym would have made sweat start to bead on her brow and her heart rate kick up a few notches. She had made do with the grimy, ancient equipment in the lowest level of the precinct, and that was all she did in terms of exercise.

Going to a public gym would have been establishing a routine, and the old Margot tried to limit routines as much as possible. If someone was going to kill you, she knew, they would often try to learn your habits first. Did you have a favorite place to get food? Did you stop at the bank or grocery store on specific days? Did you go to the gym every night? Back then, she believed routines created vulnerability.

She'd believed that because her father taught her to believe it.

And he'd been a serial killer, so why *wouldn't* she take his advice about protecting herself from people like him?

But since Ed had died, since she had left the SFPD, she had learned the quiet joy of routines. Every morning, she fed the animals at the same time, because animals did not care about your hang-ups, they just wanted to get fed. She enjoyed walking her own property, drinking her coffee outside, going into Willows once or twice a week for groceries.

Routines were *nice*.

She had also learned that most of the hotels they stayed at had a gym. Nothing fancy, but enough that, when the stress of these interviews was starting to gnaw at her, she could throw on leggings, a baggy Giants T-shirt, and some running shoes, and take a thirty-minute run on a treadmill to let her mind focus on that instead.

While she considered herself much less anxious and paranoid

than she had once been, she had never quite been able to wear headphones when she exercised. It was one distraction too far, and she still couldn't understand how people just walked around on busy streets wearing headphones, completely oblivious to the world around them and who might be watching.

Margot would never be *that* comfortable.

When she got to the hotel gym, she found the small space welcoming enough. Plenty of mirrors on the walls so she wouldn't be surprised by anyone entering, decent, new equipment, and the whole room smelled of lemon-scented cleaner instead of old gym socks. Definitely an improvement from the last place they'd stayed.

She was also surprised to see that she wasn't alone.

Alana was already there, doing a committed leg press, in a matching bright red exercise set that looked as if it must have been very expensive, but was worth every penny for how well it fit the woman's toned physique.

"Morning, Margot," Alana greeted her, as if the ample weights on the machine were doing nothing to faze her. They probably weren't. Alana was a gym rat, so Margot shouldn't have been surprised to see her here.

"No pool?" Margot asked, knowing that a swim was generally Alana's preferred morning workout. She even lived in a building in San Francisco with tenant access to an Olympic-sized pool. Margot had an old cattle trough they sometimes filled with water in the summer if the heat got unexpectedly bad. Otherwise, the closest they got to a pool on the ranch was a plastic kiddie pool the dogs played in that she and Wes sometimes set up lawn chairs next to and dipped their feet in.

"Pool has tourist hours," Alana scoffed, extending her legs effortlessly. "Like I can wait until ten o'clock to do laps. Absolutely not."

Margot smiled. She waited a moment, watching Alana breeze through her workout, and felt a little jealous of her friend's physique and ability. Margot felt every minor insecurity that went along with turning forty and realizing that those extra pounds hung on a lot harder now than they had when she was in her twenties. She was still in good shape, but now she needed to work for it.

Alana, on the other hand, while it was obvious that she *did* work for it, had the body of a twenty-five-year-old beach volleyball player. Margot couldn't help but sometimes feel a little... *less than* when she was in the same room as her.

It was the kind of slightly unfair comparison she had managed to avoid for years while working homicide, because she had been the only woman in her precinct the entire time she'd worked there. There were other female homicide detectives in San Francisco, but none of them had worked with her team.

Now she was working with multiple women every day, and it certainly changed the way Margot had to work and think. She'd had to have such a boys' club mentality to work alongside the guys in her department, and now she had to reassess how she worked with others. The FBI was not the SFPD, and that had taken some getting used to.

Margot was just getting her treadmill set up when Alana came to claim the one beside her.

"You know, you're the only person I've ever known who could talk to Andrew the way you do and get away with it."

Margot scoffed, starting her speed at a gentle jog. "I wouldn't say I *get away* with much. If I did, I'd be home right now."

Alana shook her head, then matched Margot's pace, though Margot felt certain she could easily go much faster.

"That's not what I mean and I think you know that." Alana was looking forward at the video of a coastal beach that was meant to mimic her outdoor running environment. Margot had chosen to look at her running stats. Still, even though Alana wasn't looking right at her, Margot could feel the weight of being closely observed.

She wondered, briefly, if Alana was ever profiling her while they spoke.

"I think I probably get a little more leniency because of our history," she admitted. This was honest, unfiltered. There was no way that Andrew *didn't* feel a little differently about Margot because of what they had gone through together. That was the kind of unusual bond that couldn't be forced or faked. Sometimes they hated each other, and Margot was certain he got more pissed with her than he let on, but at the end of the day there was a connection there that bonded them as deeply as family.

"You know, there was a rumor when you joined the team that you and Andrew were having an affair."

Margot staggered, almost falling off the treadmill before she managed to regain her balance. Her heart was racing as she slowed the treadmill down to a walk just so she could look at Alana without killing herself by accident. "Who said that?"

Alana raised her hands. "You know how those fresh-faced kids on the team could get sometimes. A little bitterness, a lot of jealousy. Everyone wanted to be Andrew's favorite, but that particular rumor hung around for a little while. I'm not sure if they realized the implications of it. Like, I wondered sometimes if they thought Andrew was fucking you because of your connection to Finch? I'm not sure they really thought that one through beyond you being attractive and him letting you talk shit to him." That last bit made her smile.

"For the record," Margot said, "I have never and will never sleep with Andrew Rhodes."

She glanced around her, because, if this were as terrible a moment as it felt like it was, it would have been the perfect time for Andrew to walk in and overhear her. But no, it was just her and Alana.

"I know. That doesn't make your dynamic any less interesting. Sometimes you act like father and daughter so much that I have to do a double take. I'm surprised anyone would assume a romantic relationship, when to me it's fairly obvious you view him as an alternative father figure to what you had been given."

So Alana *had* been profiling her. This was a little too close to the truth of Margot's own feelings about Andrew to just be a lucky guess. She would have been lying if she said there hadn't been moments when she was a teenager that she'd dreamed Andrew would marry her mother and things would all get better.

But a small, nagging part of her also blamed Andrew, because without him and what he'd uncovered, maybe her family never would have fallen apart.

Obviously that notion was foolish, because, even if Andrew hadn't figured Ed out, Ed was still a killer. He was going to get caught or go out refusing to get caught at one point or another. Or he'd pick the wrong house, the wrong victim, and instead of another body added to his count there would be a bullet in his head and cops at Margot's door in the middle of the night.

No, there was never going to be an outcome for the Finch family that wasn't rooted in tragedy.

"He's complicated. I'm complicated." Margot inched the speed back up so she was jogging, hoping the effort might put an end to the conversation. "I think it's just a powder keg of complications sometimes. That's probably why there's only one of me on the team." She scoffed.

Alana slowed her treadmill down, watching Margot carefully even though Margot refused to look at her.

"There's no one else like you out there, Margot."

As Alana slipped on her sleek headphones and focused on her workout, Margot couldn't help but wonder if that had been a compliment or an insult.

And just what had Alana gleaned from all this extra attention?

Margot didn't think *anyone* needed to know her that well.

FIFTEEN
WILLOWS, CA

Present

He should have left.

Get in, get out, move on.

He'd done what he came to do, but still, something about this little shitty town was fascinating to him.

He wasn't staying there—this wasn't his first rodeo. Everyone knew that, in small towns like this, outsiders stuck out like a sore thumb. A random man at the diner or the run-down little motel skipping town right after the body turns up? They'd be looking right at him.

No, he was just fine sleeping in his truck, down a dirt road about twenty miles south of town. He guessed it used to be a driveway just based on his minimal explorations. There was a shitty little bungalow down the way, but the broken windows and rotted porch told him it had been a good long time since anyone had lived there.

And because it wasn't a county road, no one should be rapping on his windows at night, telling him to get on. No one should notice him, or his plates. His car was nondescript enough. A late-nineties Ford, black. It wasn't old enough to get the attention of vintage car fans, not new enough to stick out in a place where no one could really afford to drive a new truck.

Blend in.

It might be the most important rule of them all when it came to not getting caught.

But then again, *get out* was the second rule, and he wasn't obeying it right now at all.

Every one of his well-honed survival instincts told him to cut and run. But he'd been interrupted with the girl. Things hadn't gone according to plan. He hadn't been able to hide her the way he'd normally like. To take his time with her pose. He'd just had to leave her there. And that wasn't the point of any of this.

While the ones he chose were incidental, the planning of all this had taken him years. For all that work to be interrupted felt agonizing. Insulting. He was better than unfinished efforts. What was he even doing if he was leaving the work incomplete?

He'd been careful not to stop anywhere *in* Willows two nights earlier, which meant, thanks to time and a little safe distance, he could go into town today and be a new face after the fact. No one would connect him to the girl, and he could get a sense of what was being said.

He loved to hear opinions on his work.

He wanted to know how it made people *feel*.

After leaving his truck parked next to a shuttered hardware store, he walked a few blocks to the town's diner. The town was big enough to have a few fast-food chains, but he liked to find something a little more local, somewhere the old-timers would be getting their morning coffee, shooting the shit, usually just a little louder than they ought to be. That was when a prime seat in a middle booth, the daily paper unfolded in front of you, could turn you nearly goddamn invisible, and really let the truth come out to play.

As soon as he walked in, the sheriff was obvious enough, in his khaki uniform, his hat parked next to him in the teal leatherette booth. The man took a seat a few booths down, smiled politely but not too friendly-like at the waitress. If she'd been a bit younger, he might have laid on the charm, but she was in her forties, and women like that just paid too goddamn much attention to things. So nice, but not too nice. Tip well, but not too well. Don't do anything to stand out.

She'd remember a prick, but she'd remember a charming big spender, too.

"Do you have a newspaper?" he asked, after ordering a coffee and the basic breakfast special.

"Local, or you want the *San Francisco Chronicle*?" She must get asked this a fair bit.

"I'd take 'em both if you have'm, ma'am," he said. The accent was subtle, not his true speaking voice, but also not specific enough to make her ask about it. She nodded at him and moved away from the table, returning a moment later with two newspapers, one much thinner than the other.

He set that one aside, though the front-page story was all for him. He didn't want to seem too eager to get to it, and so he perused the San Francisco news first. No murders had made the front page of the *Chronicle*. There was a story about the former chief of police making a new appeal for a retrial. He'd been trying for years, but the damning testimony of a noted crime boss—Emmanuel Riga—had sealed the man's fate.

Riga, whose tentacles tickled every taint on the West Coast, had gotten three years' house arrest for his involvement.

The dirty cop was in gen pop at San Quentin.

Guess when they say *lay with dogs and you'll get fleas* it was true enough in his case.

The man skipped ahead, bored with the crime and political stories, focusing instead on the sports section, because that's what guys did, and he just went with the flow. The Giants season was winding down with the approach of fall. It would take a miracle, and perhaps the disappearance of the Padres off the face of the planet, if the Giants hoped to sniff the postseason, but stranger things happened.

After his food was delivered and his coffee refilled, he neatly folded the San Francisco paper and set it aside.

Having done the necessary song and dance to appear as normal and boring as possible, he chewed his bacon—more underdone than he would have liked—and turned his attention to the front page of the local newspaper, a slim edition called the *Willows Courier*. The news was all about him.

Local Girl Slain—High School Coach Detained for Questioning.

This little detail irked him.

Someone else getting credit for his work? No, that simply wouldn't do, would it? He didn't want to get caught, that wasn't the point of this, but he wanted people to talk, to wonder.

He wanted them to fear.

No one was going to be afraid if they thought their killer was behind bars.

After reading the article, he was more annoyed by the shoddy police work that had clearly gone into narrowing their suspect pool. Only one man, and the last one to have seen the girl? Yet he was a volunteer deputy and local coach? The lack of imagination was staggering.

So was this town's willingness to believe the worst in their own.

He poured a dash of hot sauce on his eggs, then shifted his focus from the newspaper to the discussion happening at the booth in the corner, just close enough he could hear without it seeming like he was listening.

"—had to let him go this morning. That lawyer was right up our asses. The DA issuing that statement was a real goddamn shame. Going to make him eat his words if we find out Fox did it."

The sheriff was the one speaking. He had no hair to speak of, excluding a ring around the back of his head from ear to ear. His paunch pressed against the table of his booth, uniform buttons straining to hold the extra girth added by his morning meal. He had one of those faces that could be any age from forty to sixty, and an unhealthy tan that suggested he'd spent a life in the sun and never once considered sunscreen.

Rugged, he might be called.

The back of the head of the person he spoke to had dark, curly hair, a little unruly, like it hadn't been brushed that morning. He had hunched shoulders, a thin frame.

"Sir, do you think it's possible that Wes... er, that Fox didn't do it? We *know* him, sir."

The man was surprised. The voice was feminine, high-pitched. He'd made a quick judgement based on the hair—and the likelihood that all the law in this town would be men—and assumed this deputy was as well. He was intrigued. She was so slight of build.

The sheriff grumbled. "Don't you get foolish on me, now, Cassidy. I know we all liked him, but there's *evidence*."

"Circumstantial evidence," the woman replied. "I'm sorry, I don't want to overstep, but... I guess..." Her voice drifted and she stopped and regrouped. "I guess I just don't want us to put all our eggs in one basket."

The man smiled at the evident annoyance in the sheriff's face. He wasn't accustomed to being talked back to, it was clear, and especially not by a subordinate woman.

The waitress magically appeared at their table, potentially sensing the rising tension, and asked if they wanted anything else, before leaving the check with them and topping off the sheriff's coffee. The deputy didn't speak up again, but the man wished she would.

Because she wanted to give *him* credit.

And all he wanted was to be acknowledged for his work.

SIXTEEN

Over breakfast Margot had reviewed some of their more promising cold case leads, and she kept circling back to one in particular. A little girl named Maddie Moore, who despite her poor upbringing had managed to capture the attention of the nation when she had vanished in the mid-nineties. Ultimately, her story got buried when a much wealthier, much more interesting young pageant star was found dead in the basement of her own home, sparking decades of speculation and no arrest.

Maddie's case went cold, but was largely forgotten, strange considering the splash it had made initially.

Maddie's body had been found about three weeks after she had been taken from her family trailer. Her parents had both been at work and the teen babysitter—who had long been suspected of involvement—had fallen asleep. While the teen girl allegedly snoozed on the couch, young Maddie went outside to play in the yard.

Maddie was eight at this time, and it was an especially hot day in Nevada. She wanted to play in the sprinkler. So she'd changed into her bathing suit—this was confirmed by the small heap of clothing left on her bed and the parents acknowledging her favorite bathing suit was gone—and headed outside to play in her front yard on her own.

When her mother returned to the trailer after work, the babysitter was still asleep and the lawn sprinkler had been running for hours. There was no sign of Maddie. The trailer itself was set back from a main road and not immediately close to any neighbors. No one remembered seeing Maddie. No one saw anyone take her.

The girl's body was found about ten miles from her home. She wore a dress that Maddie's parents didn't recognize, and her bathing suit was never found. She was left at a playground, seated on a bench, and it was only sheer luck that an early-morning dog walker spotted the body before any children did.

Margot looked at the photos of Maddie, the sweet dress, the perfectly styled hair, and the glazed, haunted expression on her face. She looked just like the girls in Margot's dream last night. It was uncanny. It made her come back to the photo over and over again with growing certainty that Ricky DeGraff was Maddie's killer.

The only problem was, Ricky had an alibi for the day of Maddie's disappearance. Airtight, multiple witnesses. He'd been *in* Nevada, but he'd also been photographing a teen pageant two hours away. After his arrest he'd been high on the list of suspects, but there just hadn't been a way to tie him to the crime and so he'd dropped out of the discussion.

Now, Margot wasn't so sure.

If Ricky trusted someone enough to leave Mathilda with them while he was in prison, had he trusted that person with his living dolls, too? Had he had someone help him take these girls?

If so, it opened up a whole new pool of possibility, because there were other crimes they had dismissed due to alibis, or Ricky being out of state. But if he had someone helping him, bringing the girls to him, that changed everything.

As Margot took her seat across from him, she tried to get a read on him just by looking at his face.

He had delicate features, if she could look past the scruff on his face, the pale complexion and gaunt cheekbones. She'd seen photos of him when he was younger, and he had the kind of appearance one could almost call feminine. She suspected that was part of what made him so approachable as a photographer on the pageant scene. Ricky was certainly not scary to look at.

Or at least he hadn't been when he had all of his teeth and regular civilian clothes.

He wouldn't have looked out of place going door-to-door and trying to introduce people to the Book of Mormon.

She could also see why his father prickled at the possibility of his son being something less than *manly*. A pretty boy who liked dolls? Ricky's dad came from a generation where the worst thing your kid could be was gay.

Margot tried to imagine Ricky in his booth at a pageant, smiling at the mothers as he told them the different portrait packages he offered. Margot knew his work was okay, in a Sears Portrait Studio kind of way. But that's exactly what those moms wanted. Soft-focus pictures of their little angels, filtered to the heavens, looking like they might be six or sixteen.

Ricky glanced up at her then, actually meeting her gaze, and it startled her out of her reverie.

He might look harmless on the surface, but she saw that thing in his eyes that she saw every time she sat across the table from a killer.

Emptiness.

Where there should have been something, anything, reflecting back at her to let her know there was a spark of humanity inside them, there was just a blankness. A void.

Margot shuddered involuntarily, and Ricky looked back at his hands.

"Ricky, I want to ask you about someone today, someone specific, okay?" She started mild, not accusing him of anything, almost inviting him to join her in the conversation.

"Okay," he said, and picked at an already red hangnail on his thumb. His cuticles, Margot noted, were ragged and bloody in places. Not that cons were getting weekly manicures, but he seemed to be focused on how dry his hands were, which made her wonder if Ricky *had* enjoyed having his nails cared for in the outside world.

"I know you care about your dolls very much, Ricky," Margot said, leaning forward against the table. "You took very good care of them, just like your mother told you that you should, right? Be gentle with them, don't get their dresses dirty, be careful not to drop them. Are those the things your mother told you about Mathilda?"

The faintest smile ticked at the corner of his mouth and he stopped picking his nails, let his hands rest in his lap. He scooted his chair closer to the table, the wooden legs making an awful squeal on the tile as he did so. Margot schooled her expression so she didn't flinch, but him moving closer made her want to back away.

Sometimes, getting to the truth in these situations relied entirely on how she approached the killer in question. Some of them wanted her to be direct, even mean. They liked to have someone meet them on their level, to give back a little of the toxicity they were putting out. Margot almost preferred those situations to the alternatives, because then she got to treat the fuckers the way she thought they deserved to be treated. Cruelty meeting cruelty.

But then there were guys like Ricky. Guys who were a little softer, despite the things they'd done, who needed a gentler touch. These situations seemed like the easier ones to an outside observer. Butter the guy up, be nice to him, and you'll get what you want eventually.

The problem with that, as peachy as it sounded, was that Margot didn't *want* to be nice to convicted serial killers.

"What else did your mother tell you?" Margot asked.

Ricky's father had tended to be the focus when people asked him about his childhood in past interviews. Most of the experts—even the ones on Margot's own team—had believed that it was the father whose oppressive and verbally abusive behavior towards Ricky had shaped him into becoming a killer.

Margot wasn't so sure anymore.

Ricky rested one hand in the crook of his elbow and held his arms as if he were cradling a baby. "She told me they weren't for playing with, they were for admiring. She said such beautiful things, they were meant to be looked at, appreciated, but not fooled around with. Too precious, too breakable."

Margot thought about everything she knew of his victims, and knew that this was her way in. "But your dolls, they didn't do what you wanted them to do, did they?" she asked. "They didn't sit still for you to enjoy and look at. They couldn't be quiet, or do what you asked them to do, isn't that right?"

He kept his gaze on his own hand in the crook of his arm. "All they had to do was play along."

SEVENTEEN

Twenty Years Ago

This one wouldn't stop crying.

He was no stranger to their tears, but all the wailing was going to be a problem.

"Hush. *Shhh*," he hissed at her as she kicked at him, knocking one of her patent leather Mary Janes to the floor. "Oh, now look what you've done."

He resisted the urge to slap her, though it took all of his willpower. All she needed to do was listen, to sit still and listen. But the way she was behaving, he knew she'd never make suitable company for Mathilda. She was likely to flail around and knock his angel on the floor, and the mere thought of that happening made Ricky's blood boil.

He'd thought this girl would be such a good pick when he first took her photo. Her hair was lighter than he would have liked, but he also didn't want Mathilda to feel like the new arrival was stealing her spotlight. The last time he'd brought home a girl with dark hair there hadn't been enough contrast. Mathilda hadn't even looked at him for a week afterwards. He knew the mistake was his, and he'd punished himself.

It was a shame, too, because that girl had been very well behaved. She had done all of her crying quietly, and even changed her own dresses when he asked her to. He would have liked to keep her a little longer.

Mathilda's needs always came first, though, that was the number one rule in the house.

All of this was for her, after all.

The new girl hauled back and slapped Ricky in the head when he tried to put her shoe back on, and this time his impatience got the better of him.

He grabbed her by both shoulders and lifted her off the bed, shaking her so hard her head snapped back and all his hard work doing her hair was undone.

"Stop that. You stop that right now. You're in my house, and you're going to behave like a good girl while you're here. If you're a good girl, the best girl, then when this is all done, I'll let you go home, do you understand me?"

The girl was still in his arms, her body feeling limp and heavy. For a moment he worried he had shaken her too hard. Then she let out a little whimper, her body trembling.

"I want my mommy," she said, and though the screaming was done now, her voice was small.

"I know. I know." He made shushing sounds at her, setting her back on the mattress. "And your mommy wants you to be the very best girl, just like she's told you to be."

"Mommy said I shouldn't talk to strangers."

Ricky sat on the bed beside the girl, folding his hands in his lap. "Well, Maddie, you and I aren't strangers."

"W-we're not?" Her lower lip trembled, but she was no longer throwing a fit, and that was something Ricky could deal with.

"No, we're not. We're going to be very good friends. And you're going to be *best* friends with a dear friend of mine."

"I am?" She seemed confused, but also curious, and that curiosity was something he could work with.

He nodded vigorously.

"Do you promise to be a good girl?" He stood up again, and this time the girl watched him carefully for a moment before nodding.
"Yes."
"Would you like to meet my friend, Mathilda?"

EIGHTEEN

"Can you take a look at a photo for me, Ricky?" Margot asked.

"One of my dolls?" he replied, his voice so hopeful it made Margot's skin crawl.

"That's what we'd like you to tell us. You see, the thing is, I don't think you've been entirely honest about your collection. Have you?"

He looked from the folder on the table to Margot, then back again. "Can I see?" Ricky sounded pleading, almost desperate. His hands were back in his lap, but his body was stiff with tension, practically vibrating.

Margot opened the Maddie Moore file and took out a photo of the girl all done up for a pageant. Her cheeks were rosy with blush, and her blonde hair was piled in elaborate curls on top of her head.

Ricky's lip momentarily curled when he looked at the photo. "I didn't take that."

For a second, Margot thought the *that* he was referring to was Maddie.

Then she realized what he really meant.

The photo. The picture of Maddie was a professional shot, likely taken at an event, but the signature watermark Margot had come to recognize from other photos he had taken wasn't there. One of his competitors had shot this.

"No, I suppose it's not one of yours, is it?"

She took another photo from the folder, this one a candid taken by Maddie's mother, Jean. It was from a different pageant, and Maddie wore a sparkly purple dress with a wide tutu skirt. She was drinking from a juice box, but leaning forward almost comically to avoid getting juice on her dress.

Margot set another photo beside that. This one showed Maddie on her front lawn, jumping through a sprinkler. She wore the same bathing suit she had disappeared in.

She watched Ricky's face to see how he reacted to each of these new photos. The disgust from the first portrait was gone. In its place was a sort of hazy curiosity, like the way someone might reflect on a family photo album and know the faces but not remember Aunt So-and-So's name because it had been so long since their paths had crossed.

Margot let him have a moment, mulling things over. Ricky moved the two candid photos on top of the offensive portrait, and then Margot put down a fourth photo.

This was a crime scene photo from the morning Maddie's body had been discovered. There was something haunting about it—it was almost a portrait itself, with the soft morning light lending a false warmth to her nearly blue skin. Her pretty dress was covered in a handful of brown leaves that had fallen from the overhead trees that night. Her mouth, unnaturally glossy, was slightly open, and she seemed to stare right through the camera's lens, because her eyes no longer saw anything.

Ricky stopped looking at the candids and turned his attention to this new photo.

Once again, so fast it might be missed, that little hint of a smile ticked up the corner of his mouth, and she knew she had him.

She allowed herself one quick look at the camera in the corner of the room. They probably couldn't even see Ricky's expressions from there, wouldn't have realized the moment of recognition when it happened, but Margot had.

"You remember her, don't you?" Margot asked. She intentionally fidgeted with the folder, and he turned eager, hungry eyes towards it, as if hoping there might be more treasures inside.

"Such a pretty dress," he mused, and then, realizing she wasn't going to give him anything else to look at, turned his full attention back to the crime scene photo. "Who took this?"

"A crime scene photographer. One from Carson City, I imagine." Maddie's family had lived on the outskirts of the city, where things had a much more rural feel to them.

Ricky picked up the photo, the chains on his cuffs clattering on the tabletop. "He has an eye for it, you know? The beauty? He really captured her."

"Ricky, when you were questioned about the disappearance of Maddie Moore, you told local police you were working at a small event in Winnemucca, almost three hours away."

"I was."

"But you know this girl, don't you?"

He touched the photo again, gently, reverently. "Of course. She was close."

"Close to what?"

"Perfect."

Margot took a breath. "Ricky, did you kill Maddie Moore?"

"I had to. She was *almost* perfect. But not quite." He let out a sad sigh. "I thought I'd need to get rid of her right away."

"Because of all the attention?"

He scoffed, and looked right at her, briefly meeting her eyes. His expression made his thoughts obvious: he was better at avoiding the police than that. And he was right, he had been.

"Why couldn't you keep her?" Margot asked.

"Mathilda didn't like her. I thought, at first, that once she had settled down, once she started acting like a good girl, she might be perfect. And when I told her she could go home if she behaved, she was so good, proper. I thought I could trust her with Mathilda one day. But she wasn't good enough."

"Were any of them good enough?"

Ricky smiled, then, and it wasn't a subtle smirk, it was a genuine, happy smile, one that was unmistakable to anyone in the room. It was a horrific thing to behold.

"Only one."

"Which one?" Margot tried to think of his known victims, of the list of candidates they had come with; she wanted to be prepared for whatever he said next. "Which girl was perfect, Ricky?"

He looked back down at the photos of Maddie and pushed the stack back across the table.

"The one who is still there."

NINETEEN

Margot was waiting for the rest of the crew in the lobby, pacing, anxious to get to the airport and back to Wes, when her phone rang.

Sadie's face appeared on the screen, and Margot scrambled to answer before it went to voicemail.

"Sadie, is everything okay?"

"Hi, Margot," Sadie replied, unresponsive to Margot's obvious worry. "I just wanted to let you know there's good news."

Margot waited a beat, hoping the news would be forthcoming, but Sadie didn't immediately say anything.

"What's happening?" Margot urged. Sadie was lovely, but she was never in a *hurry* for anything. Talking to her was the human equivalent of a calm Sunday afternoon, but that tranquility didn't fit Margot's current mood.

"Eugene has put the legal fear of God into local law enforcement. Wes is getting released right now, and we should be back at the ranch in an hour or so. Eugene just wants to do a quick debrief. I'm pretty sure he's even convinced the local DA that a public statement needs to be issued about the premature and unfounded arrest of an upstanding local citizen." Margot could hear the smile in Sadie's voice. "He's going to be fine, Margot, I promise. He's in good spirits, I talked to him just a minute ago."

Margot closed her eyes in relief. She wished Wes had been the one telling her all this, if only so she could hear his voice instead of anyone else's, but she also appreciated Sadie giving her the news as soon as it broke. Chances were good she'd have been in the air before Wes could get in touch with her, and signal was never a guarantee while flying.

"Thank you, Sadie, truly. We're on our way to the airport now, I'll be back as soon as I can."

"Mmm," Sadie said, the sound loaded with a lot of unspoken things. "We'll be here."

The flight back to San Francisco that afternoon was tense, and more quiet than usual. They had cut the trip short, because the revelation of Maddie Moore's murder had given them part of what they'd come for.

But it had given them more, as well.

Ricky hadn't elaborated on what he'd meant when he said *the one who is still there*, but the words clung to Margot like cigarette smoke, feeling thick in the back of her throat.

There was a girl out there who might not be on any of their lists.

They could have stayed and asked Ricky about more unsolved homicides, because there were more they had wanted to know about, but this little plot twist meant they had to pivot.

Margot's hunch was right; someone had been helping Ricky pick up his victims.

Whoever that was, he had entrusted Mathilda with them; what was more, they might have the body of a missing child. She believed there was a victim out there waiting to be found, but they needed to find the person Ricky had been working with to get there.

Finding that person mattered more than probing the inner workings of Ricky DeGraff's mind. They would come back and interview him further once they'd spent time finding his accomplice and Maddie's body.

Margot knew that another part of the reason they were going back to California to regroup was her, and she was grateful to Andrew for making this the plan. Because she needed to get home if she was going to be any good to her team.

At least she wouldn't now have to go to the sheriff's office and dig up her old bad cop routine.

Wes was back at the ranch, and the relief of knowing he was free was enough to almost push her over the edge.

But she could wait to cry until she was with him.

Sadie had told her he was fine, but she still found that hard to believe. It was impossible for someone like him, who was so good, and so morally *right*, to be unaffected by having anyone believe he was capable of this. He needed her, and she was lucky that Andrew understood that enough to call an end to their trip.

A debrief was scheduled for the following day, with Margot joining remotely.

It took all her self-control to stick to the posted speed limits on the drive home, though even there she skirted the acceptable wiggle-room that almost all California motorists had learned as second nature. But as she neared Elk Creek, her heart pounding more and more wildly the closer she got, she knew she had to be on her best behavior. The last thing she or Wes needed was her getting pulled over for something as stupid as speeding and bringing further attention to their little family.

She pulled up the long, dusty driveway to the ranch, and spotted Wes's SUV parked out front beside Sadie's forest-green Subaru with a Pride flag bumper sticker and one that said *Give Greenpeace a Chance*. Margot hadn't spent time with Sadie since Christmas and, while she could already smell the patchouli, she was very much looking forward to seeing her not-quite-sister-in-law.

Margot didn't bother to get her bag out of the car, though out of habit she did bring in her laptop case, because it had been beaten into her year after year that data privacy was the most important part of her job. That and the bag was also filled with case files containing gruesome crime scene photos, which certainly should *not* be seen by any local hooligans who wanted to rifle through her car for loose change.

Not that that was likely. No one locked their cars out here.

She was barely on the first step of the deck when the screen door of the house opened and Wes came out, with Sadie close at his heels. Margot dropped her laptop bag on a porch chair and threw herself at Wes.

He let out a little grunt when he caught her, wrapping her tightly in his arms and giving her long, red ponytail a tug. "God, you're a sight for sore eyes, aren't you?"

A pack of small dogs—and one large German Shepherd with one eye—swarmed around their legs, eagerly nudging snouts into their calves as their tails wagged furiously. One cat, Lucy the large calico, batted several of the dogs away, because she was in charge of the entire ranch, and she let Margot know that her absence was unwelcome by reaching both front paws up Margot's leg in a stretch, then digging her claws into her thigh.

Margot winced, but refused to let go of Wes, despite all the other demands for her affection. When she finally pulled back, she looked at him intently. "Are you okay?" She brushed her hands over his cheeks, scanning his face for any signs that he was different. He had two-day-old stubbled growth the same dark blond as his hair, and the lines around his eyes crinkled when he looked at her.

He looked tired, but he was still her Wes.

"I'm fine. I promise you they weren't waterboarding me or anything. Deputy Cassidy kept sneaking me extra food. I don't think anyone there—except maybe the sheriff—actually thinks I had anything to do with it. And even him, he just wants an easy answer to give people who are scared."

"But at whose expense?" Margot grumbled, pressing a kiss on

either cheek before she finally remembered they were ignoring Sadie. She broke away from Wes to greet his sister.

Sadie looked good. She looked a lot like Wes, with the same dark blonde hair and a perfectly symmetrical face. All the Fox siblings had been blessed with wonderful genetics; it was almost unfair they should all be so attractive. Sadie looked like she had just left a New Age cult in Santa Fe, with a flowy dress and her hair wrapped up in a brightly printed silk scarf. Dozens of bangles competed for attention on her wrists and a collection of evil eye pendants dangled from her neck. As she hugged Margot, Margot breathed in the familiar scent of incense and a sage-scented deodorant that was probably branded as all-natural.

Sadie could have been a cliché, the butt of a joke, but there was something about the serene way she moved through life, untethered but grounded, that made all of her outward displays just make sense somehow. She was who she was, even if she looked like she was going to try to sell you crystals or read your aura at any moment.

Margot took in a long breath of Sadie's soothing scent before letting her go. "Thank you. A million times, thank you."

"Of course, you guys can always count on me." Sadie smiled, though it wasn't quite as bright and brilliant as it was when she was actually happy. The last couple of days couldn't have been easy on her, so Margot tried not to take it personally, but it was hard not to imagine that Sadie was judging her for not rushing home.

Margot was judging herself, so she would be in fine company.

"You guys got to leave early," Wes commented, cutting through the tension a little. "Does that mean you got what you were looking for?"

Margot could feel the pinch of an incoming migraine behind her eyes. "Yes and no. We got him to admit to one of the murders we suspected him of, but we're also pretty sure now that he might have had an accomplice helping him collect the girls, someone we missed this whole time."

Sadie shifted uncomfortably, reminding Margot that casual

discussions of child murder weren't really pleasant for normal people. Especially given the circumstances of Wes's recent arrest.

"But let's not talk about my case right now. What did Eugene say about your situation?"

"Well, defying all odds, the local prosecutor did make a statement to the press that my arrest was premature and there was no physical evidence to connect me with the crime. He didn't go as far as to say I was innocent, and I'm on indefinite leave from the school, but at least I'm home."

Sadie opened the door to the house. "Let's talk about this inside," she muttered, looking down the empty driveway as if someone might appear at any moment to rearrest her brother if they heard him discussing the case.

Margot collected her laptop bag, gave an annoyed Lucy a stroke, and then ushered the whole animal welcome party back inside. Dog nails clattered across the hardwood floors as they all followed Wes towards the outdoor dining room on the back porch.

Sadie brought out a pitcher of iced tea, something she and Wes would never think to have if they were on their own, and Margot took a glass gratefully as she and Wes settled in beside each other on the outdoor sofa. Lucy curled up beside Margot on the couch, close enough to keep an eye on things but just out of reach to be petted. She slow-blinked when Margot looked over at her, so at least she wasn't too mad about Margot being gone. When Lucy got truly ticked off, she would pee on a guest room bed, which inevitably meant Margot and Wes might not immediately discover it.

Sadie sat in a rocking chair and sipped her drink, watching Margot and Wes carefully. Margot knew she wasn't imagining the change in Sadie's usual demeanor towards her, and she expected she probably deserved Sadie's version of a cold shoulder.

She just hoped her sister-in-law would get over it now that Margot was back.

"Tell me everything we know," she said, tucking her feet up under her. "The reporting online was sparse and very vague. I sent out some feelers to old contacts, but the sheriff's office is keeping this very tight-lipped, so they couldn't give me much more than what the press did."

Wes gave Sadie a quick look. "You okay with this?" he asked.

"Not normally, but in this case I've already heard it all, so go ahead."

Sadie was the kind of person who would rescue a wasp trapped in her house, so the work Margot and Wes did was so far removed from her comfort zone that she usually just asked how the dogs were whenever she checked in, rather than asking about work. When Wes had been coaching that made things easier. Sadie never wanted to know about the cases Margot was working on, which was fine, because Margot didn't like to discuss them any more than she had to.

"Whitney Eflin was sixteen." Wes paused. Margot had to remind herself this wasn't just any victim, this was a girl Wes had known personally; even though he wasn't the usual softball coach, he saw her every day at school. She squeezed his hand, waiting for him to be ready again. "She was a good kid, smart. Honor roll, cheer squad. She was also really small, just over five feet, maybe ninety pounds. Great for cheer, I gathered, but it also meant..." He drifted.

Margot could fill in the blanks. No matter how athletic Whitney had been, it would have been damn near impossible for a girl that petite to fend off a grown man who outweighed her and had malice on his mind. Even most of the teen boys at the school—if it had been one of them—significantly outweighed the girl. If someone had wanted to hurt her, her best chance would have been running.

But if someone had snuck up on her? She wouldn't have had a chance.

"Talk me through the evening." Margot redirected the discussion, hoping that just going through the facts could refocus his attention away from how sad this all was. She was sure she had probably seen Whitney in the past, though she couldn't recall meeting the girl in the photos on the news. Margot had been to enough events in Willows, including a rare football game—though those were too busy for her taste and triggered some of her old anxieties—so it seemed likely that Whitney might have crossed her path at some point.

It was all too close to home, and that was evident in Wes's response.

"We finished practice at about seven, it was starting to rain, getting dark. Most of the girls brought their cars—including Whitney—but hers wouldn't start. So I offered to drive her and the two girls she had come with home. Whitney hadn't come prepared for the weather, so I gave her my jacket. The two other girls—Savannah and Chloe—apparently reported that to the sheriff when asked. It was no secret, I did it in front of them. The other girls had their own jackets. Savannah and Chloe both lived closer to the school, so I dropped them both off by about seven fifteen. Whitney's parents have a farm about five minutes from the outskirts of town. I dropped her off by about seven twenty or shortly after that. She mentioned when I pulled into the driveway that her parents weren't home yet. I made sure she had her key, told her I'd help her jump her car in the morning. It was just too rainy, and the other girls needed to get home before their curfews. Then I watched her get to her door and unlock it, then headed back home. That was the last I saw her."

"What time did you get back home?" Margot asked, knowing the police would have asked this as well, if they were smart.

"Just before eight. I stopped at the McDonald's because I didn't feel like cooking." Before Margot could ask, he continued, "Yes, the receipt was on the passenger floor of my car. Yes, I paid by card. I think a lot of that helped Eugene get me out."

Margot let out a little sigh of relief. So not only was all the evidence against him circumstantial, but he had strong evidence backing up his alibi. There would almost certainly be video footage of his SUV in the drive-thru. And they had security cameras on the house—those would back up his arrival time and show he hadn't left again.

It was appalling that, with so much in his favor, the sheriff had still gone ahead with the arrest. Anger churned in Margot's stomach, making her feel physically queasy. When the real killer was found, that initial fuck-up was going to look terrible for the department. Everyone knew the first forty-eight hours were the most vital to an investigation, and the local cops had tossed those away looking at an innocent man.

What bothered Margot the most was knowing that if Wes hadn't been the one they'd locked up, he would have been free to actually *help* them. This case might look very different if things had happened that way.

But she couldn't dwell on what hadn't happened, she needed to focus on the facts. Whitney was dead, and someone who wasn't Wes Fox had done it. They needed to do whatever was in their power to help figure out who that person was, so attention could finally be shifted off Wes.

Margot also wasn't stupid. She knew she wouldn't be allowed anywhere near the investigation; the conflict of interest was evident a mile away. But she could speak to the sheriff in the morning about Andrew's offer to have an independent FBI profiler look over the case details and help them narrow down who they were looking for.

"Do you know any of the details of what happened to her?" Margot asked. She darted a quick glance at Sadie, whose expression had become noticeably more queasy.

"I'll go start some dinner," Sadie offered, pushing herself up out of her chair. The jangle of her bracelets followed her out of the room. Margot heard the rattle of condiments against the fridge door.

"She hates me now," she said with a sigh.

"She could never hate you, Margot. My family loves you, you know that. I just think she doesn't understand, that's all."

"Well, maybe she's right. I'm a dickhead for not coming back right away."

Wes snorted. "You weren't allowed to, and I told you not to."

"When have I ever listened to you?" she countered.

Wes smiled and leaned in, kissing her softly. "You would have been miserable if you'd come back sooner. You would have wanted to help, and you would have been a huge pain in everyone's ass. And while I love you when you go into problem-solving mode, I think it all went about as well as we could have hoped. You solved a murder, I'm home. Sadie will get over it."

This only validated Margot's concern that Sadie was mad at her, but she hoped that she might come to understand the situation as Wes did.

She wasn't holding her breath, though.

But maybe that was because in *her* family people took their grudges to the grave. Wes seemed confident that Sadie would let it go sooner rather than later.

"Tell me what you know about the murder," Margot urged. This was familiar territory for her. Something she could navigate comfortably.

"I know what Cassidy told me, though she probably shouldn't have said anything. And I know what Eugene was able to glean. Between the two of them, that's probably a mostly complete version of the truth, but if the sheriff is being smart, he'll be holding something back that we don't know about."

Margot snorted. "If the sheriff was smart, he never would have arrested you in the first place. So I'm not going to keep my fingers crossed that he's smart enough to withhold vital pieces of evidence."

"I don't think that line of thinking is going to get us anywhere." He smiled softly.

"You're too nice. It makes me look meaner by comparison," she complained.

"I'm pretty sure you spent the entire first year of our partnership calling me a dick."

"In fairness, that might have been unconscious flirting on my part, but also, you *were* kind of a dick when we started working together."

"All this buttering me up isn't going to get you the details you wanted on the case," he reminded her.

She held up her hands in a mock surrender. "Go ahead."

"From what I've been able to gather, even though Whitney went into her house—I saw her—she must have either left again, or possibly let someone in. If it were me betting, I wouldn't be surprised if she tried to walk back to the school to see if her car would work. She seemed very upset about it not starting, the other girls had to calm her down. From what I've heard, I think her father is pretty strict, and she was probably worried he would get mad at her for leaving the car at school, or possibly take her car away completely. You know how teenagers can get about their car. If she thought she might lose it, I wouldn't be surprised if she walked back in the rain."

Margot mulled this over. "It's a possibility. It's also possible she might have called someone she knew, a boyfriend maybe, to pick her up and drive her back over to the school. Give her a boost."

Wes nodded. "I definitely considered that. I don't know if Whitney had a boyfriend. But she was a popular girl, so I can't imagine she would have had trouble finding someone willing to help her. It wasn't that late."

"Do we know what the coroner had to say about her time of death?"

Wes shook his head and raked his hands through his hair. "I have no idea. I can't think it was too late at night though. After her parents got home and found her missing they called a bunch of her friends, and I guess no one mentioned driving her back to the school, or at least not from what I've heard. No one knew where she was. They went around looking for her, and just before midnight someone found her bag on the side of the road about three miles from the school. Right by that big old cornfield the Raffertys own."

Margot knew what he was talking about, because corn wasn't a widely grown crop in Northern California, so the field was unique enough to stand out.

"They found her in the corn?" Margot asked.

Wes nodded again, looking more exhausted now than he had even a minute earlier.

"What had happened to her?" Margot asked, lowering her voice to keep their conversation from drifting into the kitchen.

"If I was looking at this as a case I wasn't connected to, just based on what I've learned, I think she probably left her house after I dropped her off, and something happened to her along the way. No one saw her after I did, from what I've gathered, otherwise I don't think they'd be leaning so hard on me as a suspect." He paused for a moment, shook his head, and then took a deep breath before he started again. "She was assaulted. And she was stabbed. But they haven't told me the rest of the details. I don't know what happened to her, not really. But I know she died alone and afraid, and I was the last person to see her, and I couldn't stop that from happening to her."

Margot squeezed Wes's hand. "Don't do that to yourself," she said, though she knew it was an impossible thing to ask. She'd spent decades asking herself how she never knew her father was a killer.

The guilt clings to you, even when you don't deserve it. That was just the price you paid for living through the worst.

"We're going to figure out what happened," Margot said. "We used to solve cases like this all the time. We just need to take a step back, look at it objectively."

Sadie returned, carefully carrying three plates of sandwiches, reminding Margot they would need groceries if that was all Sadie could muster for dinner. "*We* should leave this to the professionals."

Margot accepted a plate and bit her tongue. She worked in a special offshoot of the FBI's BSU, tracking cold case homicides and talking to serial killers. How, exactly, was she not a *professional?*

Not to mention the decade or more she and Wes had both spent with the homicide department.

"I'm going to call Leon," Margot said.

Their old colleague Leon Telly was long retired from the police force, but he was a licensed private investigator, using his innumerable talents to earn a little extra money for things his pension didn't cover. He had the good fortune to be able to pick and choose his cases, and Margot suspected he would be willing to look into this for them. She hadn't wanted to bother him with it before, knowing he'd only worry with Wes being in jail. But now that Wes was out, he seemed like a good person to loop in.

Wes looked as if he might argue. Sadie actually opened her mouth. Margot was the one to backpedal on her own. "All right, I can see the Fox death stare working at me from both sides of the room. I won't call Leon. Yet. But can I at least talk to the sheriff to offer non-biased FBI support? I think we can all agree that if you weren't involved in this, I'd be making that offer anyway. Hell, I think the town would expect it."

Wes finally yielded to her on this one. "I don't think he'll accept it, but it's the right thing to do."

"Are you sure you're okay?" she asked.

Wes pushed his sandwich around on the plate It looked delicious, with thick cuts of bacon and fresh tomatoes from their garden, but he didn't appear to be interested in eating it.

"No. But I'm better now that you're back."

It was as close as he would come to saying it had been hard here without her.

The pit in her stomach that had been growing since he'd first called her from jail continued to gnaw.

Something was very wrong in Willows, and she wasn't going to let it happen under her nose.

TWENTY

Margot found some relief the next morning in doing her usual ranch chores. The sun was barely up when she got out of bed, and she let Wes continue to doze. He hadn't been able to sleep in their home for two nights; he deserved to get as much rest as humanly possible.

Sadie was also still asleep, judging by the soft sounds of snoring coming through the closed guest room door.

Margot, who had not had a moment alone that week, headed outside to feed the chickens, followed by her entourage of rescue dogs and Lucy the cat taking the lead as usual. Lucy was the only cat with indoor–outdoor privileges. She had proven over time that she only wanted to be outside with people, and never ran away or chased birds, so Margot let her tag along with the dogs.

The morning air was crisp, a welcome feeling on her skin. Margot loved the way cold air smelled. Snow was uncommon, though it could show up in December and January. But something about a bracing morning reminded her of the years she had spent growing up in the Midwest. While that hadn't been the happiest time in her life, she *had* enjoyed more varied seasons.

Now, she just enjoyed the way it felt to stand outside and

breathe fresh air, have it fill her lungs, and not have a lingering sensation in the back of her mind that something might go wrong.

The chickens began to chatter with one another as soon as Margot let them out of their roost, and the chatter became squabbling once she poured their feed onto the dry earth. She loved these silly little birds, who cared about nothing except what was in front of them to eat. It was a simple life, and one they seemed to have no complaints about.

That was what Margot wanted here, too. A simple life. And now she had to worry about it, to wonder if what was happening to Wes might mean she could lose this.

It was a thought too dark to stick with this early in the morning. She watched the hens peck near her shoes and tried to push away her worries for a little longer.

The ranch had come with a variety of buildings, most of which Margot and Wes didn't need, at least not at this point in their lives. The more animals they got the more she wondered if the big, aging barn could be used for more than storage. The outbuildings with their faded wooden siding, turned grey by weather and age, had been a blessing, especially the work shed with insulation and electricity that Margot had converted into a feed shed, complete with a fridge for all the medication the dogs needed. The more seniors they had adopted, the more room their special foods and medicines started to take up, until it had become too much for the indoor fridge to reasonably handle.

Margot enjoyed the excuse to get outside twice a day; it let her walk around the property under the guise of getting her steps, when what she was really doing was an elaborate check that all the buildings were locked, and nothing looked out of place since the last time she'd gone.

She was *better*, but old habits died hard.

Margot continued her rounds, feeding and cleaning, and was just in the outdoor feed shed getting the dog's dishes ready, mumbling softly to each of them as they wagged their tails around her, when she heard the sound of tires on gravel on the front drive.

She paused, glancing at her watch.

It wasn't even seven. No one should be coming to visit this early.

Her pulse hammered as she imagined the sheriff's office Jeep pulling up, coming to try to take Wes again. While she knew, logically, this wasn't likely, she couldn't help the nausea that rose in her stomach at the thought.

She had just stepped out of the shed, wiping her hands on her jeans, ready to pick a fight with whichever poor deputy she was about to confront, when the sound of gunshots rang out.

Margot's hand immediately went to her hip, where of course there was no weapon. As the second shot echoed in the still morning air, she grabbed Lucy, who had frozen beside her, puffed up and frightened, and ran back to the shed. The dogs, who had started to bark wildly at the unexpected sound, followed her, and she shut the door, closing everyone in. There was plenty of whining and Lucy had dug her claws into Margot's forearm as she gripped her tight, drawing blood. Still, Margot didn't dare let go of the cat. She huddled on the wooden floor of the shed, tucked under the bench where she doled out food and medications. The small bar fridge beside her hummed, but there was no more gunfire.

For a moment, Margot couldn't form a sensible thought.

She was back almost eight years in the past, huddled under a café table, listening to people scream outside. Gunfire from a sniper rained over the street. Despite knowing in her very soul that the man who had terrorized San Francisco all those years ago was long dead, there was an animal part of her brain that said differently.

You're being hunted.

They're here for you.

She whispered nonsensical things into Lucy's fur, the pain in her arm from the cat scratches pulling her back to the present moment. Margot's body was shaking, which did nothing to comfort the animals. The dogs whined.

She heard the distinctive sound of breaking glass, but it wasn't the glass in the shed. It was further away, in the direction of the house.

Wes.

She scrambled up, terror for Wes and fury over her space being violated commingled in her gut, telling her to get out there and see what was happening. But her logic center—and the part of her that had once survived that sniper attack—told her to stay exactly where she was.

She crouched down again and after what could have been only minutes, but felt like a solid hour, she heard the sound of tires spinning in the gravel of her driveway, then a revving truck engine receding.

She waited and listened, but there was only silence beyond the continual whining of the dogs. Finally, when she felt like she could stand without collapsing, she opened the shed door and headed outside. The morning air felt more still than usual, and the sky had barely turned pink, let alone blue.

"Margot?" She heard Wes's voice, calling for her from the house. He must have awoken to the sound of the gunfire and found her gone. An invisible weight lifted from her shoulders. He was okay. She thought she might be crying.

"I'm here," she said as she rounded the front of the house, Lucy still clinging to her, the dogs clamoring after her as if they were afraid to let her out of their sight.

Wes was standing on the porch, still wearing his plaid pajama pants and a battered old 49ers T-shirt with a robe over it. His feet were bare. He was holding a rifle, though it was pointed down to the porch floorboards. Sadie was inside, hugging a robe tightly around her as she peered at them through the screen door.

Margot had never been so relieved to see two people before in her life, and she ran to Wes and buried her face in his shoulder as he wrapped an arm around her.

"What the fuck happened?" Wes asked fiercely. Margot knew his anger wasn't directed at her. Now that he knew she was safe, he was letting himself fully invest in his fury.

"I don't know," she admitted, her voice trembling. She took a breath to steady herself before continuing. "I was around back feeding the dogs when I heard the first shot. I locked us all in the shed. Was that glass breaking?"

"Kitchen window," Sadie confirmed, glancing back over her shoulder. She looked frazzled, her hair in a messy bun on top of her head, pillow creases on her face. Her expression suggested she was just hoping this was a nightmare and she was going to wake up soon.

Their kitchen faced the front driveway and adjacent kitchen garden, so if someone was in the driveway it would be the easiest target. Margot would see what they'd thrown later. For now, she just wanted to figure out where the bullets had gone.

"Did they hit anything?" she asked, her gaze raking the front porch. There were no obvious signs of damage and the only thing she could see were the new deep tire ruts in their gravel.

"I don't think so," Wes said, setting down his gun beside one of their chairs. "It looks like they were just shooting into the gravel."

"We have to call the sheriff," Margot said.

She saw his expression shift to a momentary grimace before he grudgingly nodded. The sheriff's department might not be on their holiday card list at the moment, but if people were coming onto their property and shooting at their house, then they *had* to report it.

"I'll call them," Sadie said, and vanished from the door.

Margot realized that she was still holding Lucy, who at least now seemed calm. Margot set her down on the porch.

"Is everyone accounted for?" Wes asked, looking at Margot's entourage.

"The rest of the cats are inside, all the dogs were with me." She scanned the yard, as if there might be animals present she wasn't aware of. The chickens, if they'd been bothered at all, were already back out clucking and pecking, completely unfazed.

No, Margot didn't think this morning's visitor had intended to harm any of their animals.

Or even them.

Now that she could think more clearly, she felt deep in her bones that this had been a warning.

You're no longer welcome here. Leave or this will get worse.

Margot stared down the driveway as if she could see beyond it to whoever had done this. She wasn't going anywhere.

TWENTY-ONE

Margot couldn't decide if she was offended or relieved that it was Deputy Florence Cassidy who pulled into their driveway about twenty minutes later. The sun was up now, and it was looking to be a stunning day.

Margot had expected the sheriff himself to arrive and already had her hackles up when the Jeep pulled in. But when she saw Flo's petite figure emerge, she had to let all her animosity out in a long exhale. While she currently didn't harbor any tender feelings towards local law enforcement, she knew through Wes that Flo was on their side, as much as anyone in the area was likely to be.

Flo was shorter than Margot and Wes, coming in at about five foot six tops, even with her heavy work boots. She wore the department-issued khaki uniform, tailored within an inch of its life to fit her small frame. But despite being slight of stature, Flo managed to command respect, and that was how she'd managed to become one of only two paid deputies in Willows, while the others—like Wes—worked on an as-needed volunteer basis.

Flo's father, Duncan Cassidy, had been the sheriff before Jim Wilder had been elected. It was a local opinion that the only reason Wilder had won election was because Duncan Cassidy died, and even then he still got twenty percent of the votes.

"Morning, Ms. Margot," Flo greeted her warmly. "Morning, Wes."

Wes had taken the rifle back inside while they'd waited. They had also taken stock of what went down inside, and while they couldn't find any bullet holes in the house, they had found a brick with a note attached to it—very clichéd—on the kitchen floor.

They'd left it where it was without reading the note, on the off chance the police might get some physical evidence from it.

The security cameras had been operational as well, but thanks to the dim morning light they could only see that it was a big black pickup truck that had come in. Faces were a little hazier. Still, Margot had a fairly good hunch she could narrow down who had been driving.

While trucks were a dime a dozen in the county, shit-disturbers were a bit easier to make a list of. And someone willing to drive all the way from Willows just to shoot in their dirt and throw a brick through their window... well, the list was short, no matter how unpopular Wes might be at the moment.

"Morning, Flo," Margot greeted her.

Flo's cheeks flushed. "Deputy Cassidy while I'm on duty, Margot, if you don't mind."

Margot's first instinct was to snark back that perhaps Flo should call her Special Agent, then, but she bit her tongue. Her hostility had another target, and Flo didn't deserve to bear the brunt of it.

"Of course, you want to come in and see the kitchen?"

Flo made a general gesture to the parking area at the front of the house. She had avoided driving over the big ruts left by the truck. "Why don't you just walk me through what happened here first."

Margot filled her in, since she was the only one who had been awake when things started happening. Wes interjected with what he'd been able to see from the upstairs window, as did Sadie when she came out to join them. Everyone had the same description of the truck, a newer-model Ford, black. There appeared to be at least two people in the cab, though neither Wes nor Sadie could see into the back row of seating. One person got out, while another fired from the passenger window.

The gunshots—upon reviewing the security footage—appeared to have been aimed into the driveway, and Margot pointed Flo in the general vicinity where they did, indeed, find three bullets in the soil, and three shell casings where the truck had been.

Flo collected everything with a dutiful attention to detail, photographing the evidence and then bagging it and marking each bag.

"Seems like they were just trying to spook you," she observed after prying a bullet out of the dirt.

"Job well-fucking-done, then," Margot grumbled.

They headed as a group into the kitchen, where Margot had shut the doors to keep the animals from wandering in and stepping on all the broken glass. Flo took a few more pictures before gingerly stepping onto the tile, bits of glass crunching under her heel even as she did her best to avoid them. She donned a pair of gloves before picking up the brick—a move Margot was impressed by and admittedly hadn't expected—and then opened the note attached.

"Bit theatrical," Flo mused.

"Zero points for creativity," Wes agreed.

Flo looked down at the piece of paper in her hand before setting the brick back on the floor. She was frowning.

"What does it say?" Sadie asked from the doorway, where she was keeping curious house-members at bay.

Flo turned the note around to show them, grimacing as she did.

KILLER.

That was it. No threats, no wordy rants. Just one simple word that said it all.

Margot looked at Wes, who was transfixed by the paper. As she watched him, aware of her heart pounding, she realized he hadn't thought about all this. About the consequences. She'd been dreading this since he first mentioned his arrest, because Margot knew how people reacted in situations like these.

There was a reason—beyond just changing her name and moving—that Margot didn't have any of the friends she had been so close to when she started high school, people she'd sworn when she'd been only fifteen would be in her life forever.

She'd seen the way people changed when they learned about her father; the way they pulled away from her, and how suddenly she became the villain, even though she understood that, in a sense, she was just another victim.

They didn't see it that way. People looking in from the outside never did. They saw only the simplest answer, the worst-case scenario, and they reacted to it the only way they knew how. With fear, and anger, and judgement.

Margot had seen all of this coming because she'd lived through it. But he never had. He, despite all he had seen in his life, still believed there was some inherent goodness in humanity.

Margot had been disabused of that notion long ago, though she'd been trying to adjust to Wes's way of thinking in recent years.

Still, she went to him, put her arms around him and whispered, "It'll be okay. They'll figure it out, and it'll be okay."

When it had happened to her, their family had run. They'd changed names, changed states, done everything possible to start fresh. But this place, this ranch, this was Margot's true fresh start, and she would be damned if she was going to let it go without a fight.

"Deputy Cassidy, I think we both know that Wes had nothing to do with what happened to Whitney," Margot said, when she could finally beat down her anger enough to form words. "And I know I can't personally help you prove that, because of my connection to Wes. But I have access to people and tools that can help you find whoever did this. *Please* don't let jurisdictional pride let that girl's real killer walk away to do this again."

She looked imploringly at the smaller woman, and could see the uneasy position she was putting Flo in. She didn't care.

The tense silence was broken by Margot's phone ringing. The unexpected sound was enough to make her and Sadie jump. She glanced at the clock on the kitchen wall and realized with a jolt that she was late for the debrief meeting about DeGraff.

"Just think about it, please," Margot asked. "I know the sheriff might balk at the suggestion, but my team are very good at what they do, we have a world-class criminal profiler working for us, and the FBI prides itself on independent and unbiased assessments. If they think Wes matches the profile, they won't hesitate to report that. But we both *know* he's not who you're looking for. And if we don't find that person, shit like this morning is just going to keep happening. Except maybe next time they won't just shoot at the driveway. Maybe next time it won't be a brick, it'll be something on fire. None of us want to see that happen in our county, do we?"

Flo nodded, swallowing hard. "I'll talk to him. I won't make any promises, but... I can at least talk to him." She glanced around the kitchen. "As for this, I will take this very seriously. Can you email me a copy of that security video?"

Margot promised she would, and they walked Flo to the door.

Before she left, Flo looked at Wes. "I'm so sorry this is happening, Wes."

He nodded. "I know. Me too."

"I promise we'll catch this guy." Flo offered a gentle smile.

Margot didn't smile back.

Because she knew if they continued the way they were, this murder would become just another cold case, and she was not letting that happen.

TWENTY-TWO

While Margot did get a brief reprieve from her morning meeting—extenuating circumstances being what they were—she had to promise to join the rescheduled meeting that afternoon.

The morning was spent cleaning broken glass—Flo had taken the brick and note—and boarding up the broken window. Under different circumstances they would have called someone locally to come fix it, but the general level of trust Margot felt towards the local community at the moment was sub-zero. Wes was confident that, as soon as they could get a replacement window, he could install it on his own.

He might not be a born handyman, but he was pretty sure that an hour alone with the window, YouTube, and some intense focus would get the job done.

Margot had no doubt.

When she settled into her office a few hours later with a coffee and a slightly calmer view on life, she joined the online meeting with her team. Her office was the only room in their house with new locks. Not because Margot felt the need to protect her cases from Wes—he was welcome to peruse them if his curiosity ever got that piqued—but she wanted to ensure that the rare guests who visited didn't wander into her workspace instead of the bathroom next door.

By necessity, Margot's work lived at home with her, and that meant the large bulletin board beside her desk was often covered in gruesome crime scene photography. It was just part of getting the job done. Once she knew the crimes inside and out, she was better able to get into the head of the person who had committed them.

The cold case unit was a rare creature inside the FBI. While they operated adjacent to the BSU—the Behavioral Science Unit— their involvement in cases looked very different to that of their BSU colleagues. In the BSU, an agent's involvement in a crime might consist of only an hour or a day. They were brought in to look at things through an untainted lens, with no personal or emotional connection to the case, provide their professional insights either individually or with a larger group view of the details, and then move on to the next.

In the cold case unit, they got much more involved. Where a BSU agent might never know the outcome of a case they provided their expert opinion on, Margot's group saw things from a different perspective. Margot got to know the killers better than they might even know themselves, learning tidbits about their lives that the people who originally hunted them had no access to. It meant she was able to speak to them with a better understanding of who they were, because their unsubs—unknown subjects—weren't unknown at all.

It was the victims who might remain a mystery.

Margot, in her five years of working cold cases, had worked with BSU agents consistently, and their dispassionate detachment was always a fascinating thing to her. Years as a homicide detective had trained her not to feel anything personal towards victims, but in that position, as with her current one, she could do her best to see a case through from beginning to end. Her BSU colleagues might do a profile one day and then never ask or wonder what had happened to that case ever again.

Margot simply couldn't do that. She had a strong sense of

connection and responsibility towards the victims, and there was a drive in her to see things finished that meant that particular line of work could never suit her, whereas what she was currently doing was kind of the perfect fit.

Anyway, that was what she told herself as the online meeting began and the familiar faces of her colleagues popped onto the screen. She knew this was all for her benefit and if she was there in person, it wouldn't be necessary, but as she noticed Greg cramming a burrito into his face while he waited for the meeting to start, she suspected a few of her teammates probably appreciated an excuse to sit at their own desks for an hour.

When everyone who had gone to Montana was on the call, Andrew cleared his throat to signal that it was time to get things going.

"Margot, I hope all is well. If you want to send your security camera footage to us, we can have someone enhance and brighten it if you would like." He offered this the way other bosses might say, *Go ahead and expense a lunch on us.*

Margot wasn't going to look this particular gift horse in the mouth. "That would be great, thank you. I've also offered to connect the sheriff's department with the BSU for a profile, but I haven't heard anything back about that yet, and I suspect hell might freeze over before I do."

"Well, one solvable problem at a time, I suppose," Andrew offered.

"Thank you," she managed. She knew she should feel more gratitude, but she was exhausted from the stress of the morning, which had never fully manifested as shock, but would certainly have her looking over her shoulder in the mornings when she went out to feed the chickens for the next few weeks, if not longer.

In the back of her mind, she heard her father say, *This is the price you pay for having a predictable life.*

She swallowed back an acrid taste in her throat and tried to blot out that nagging idea. At least she'd have something new and exciting to talk to her therapist about this week.

They dove into the DeGraff case without further mention of Margot's harrowing morning, and while she was glad not to dwell on it, she was also amazed at this team's ability to move from one horrible thing to the next. No time to talk about a shooting, there was a serial homicide to discuss.

One interesting tidbit that Sydney and Harper—their resident tech wiz—had dug up was that the nun who had gone to visit DeGraff in prison, Sister Mary Callahan, did not exist.

Not that she never *had* existed, but that she had left the fold since her visits to DeGraff.

They were working on figuring out what her new—or previous—civilian name was, but so far it was something of a dead end.

Margot knew the team so well that, as she watched her colleagues' faces, she could practically see what they were really thinking about as they broke down their parts of the case. Alana was trying to remember if it was arm day or leg day at the gym. Greg—still picking at his burrito whenever he wasn't speaking—was wondering what to make for dinner when he got home. Sydney was too alert, too attuned. She was wondering what Andrew was thinking every time she offered an insight.

Andrew was wondering if he had Margot's full attention, when in fact he had nobody's.

"DeGraff's father is still alive," Greg offered, wiping a dab of guacamole from the corner of his mouth. "The house where DeGraff grew up was sold decades ago, so no such luck checking there for any artifacts of his childhood, but who knows, his father might still have something."

Margot wasn't sure why she had assumed both of Ricky's parents must have been dead, but it was still surprising to her to learn that Rick Sr. was still alive. She might have known and forgotten, since it was such a minor detail in the research, but she scolded herself for glossing over it.

"Where is he?" Margot asked.

"He's actually local. Or local-ish." Greg pulled something up on his own computer to confirm before he spoke. "He's living at a care home in Fresno."

There was a long beat while everyone processed this.

"Margot, you and Alana can go," Andrew said. "Tomorrow?"

Margot gave him a hard stare and was about to protest. To remind him that her life was a bit too complicated right now for road trips to Fresno. But she knew it was pointless. Everyone had personal bullshit going on. Everyone had issues they would rather be dealing with than this. Despite the fact that her problems felt huge, she also knew the same might be true for others on the team, and they weren't bringing their issues into the workroom.

"All right," she agreed, hoping her tone didn't bely how pissy she felt. "Alana, I can pick you up en route."

It would be an early fucking start to the day for her but, again, that was a complication she had created for herself. At least she could probably pick up a new kitchen window in San Francisco on her way home.

"Sounds good. I'll get you a good Philz fix since I'm sure those philistines up north have nothing even remotely worth drinking."

This made Margot crack a smile.

"You may save a life or two," she said. "Thank you."

"Margot, can you stay on the line for me once everyone else is gone?" Andrew asked. She got the very distinct guilty feeling that one might associate with being asked to speak one-on-one with a principal or teacher, but she nodded her agreement and waited for everyone else to end their connection.

Once it was only her and Andrew, he took a pause before speaking. She saw the way his thick brows briefly knit together in frustration or stress, before he schooled his expression into something much more stoic.

She genuinely had no idea what to expect from this private discussion, and was aware her anxiety was unusually high, something that often made her start scanning the room for exits.

To calm herself she glanced out the window that overlooked her backyard, where the chickens pecked at the earth, and nearby someone was running a vacuum, likely to make sure the kitchen floor was clear of the last of glass.

"Margot, I hope you won't misunderstand me. You're one of the most professional people I've ever worked with, even when the case you were working on was as personal as it got. You never let that get in the way of what you were doing."

She snorted, because she felt like Andrew might have a selective memory regarding some of the sessions she'd had with Ed. Because of her father's ability to push her buttons just so—and she his—things often got explosive and deeply unprofessional. But perhaps he was overlooking that now because of the positive results they had had in finding Ed's missing victims.

She also knew he wasn't really talking about Ed.

He wanted to remind her she had to compartmentalize.

And that's when she realized he had picked her to go to Fresno intentionally. Alana could have gone with Greg, with Sydney, with any other member of their team who knew Ricky and this case just as well as she did. But he had picked *her*, wanted *her* to drive the nearly six hours each way. Was it just to test her? Did he want to see if she would complain?

He didn't know her very well if he thought that was the case, because she had already seen how willing he was to bend to her needs, and that was not very far at all. Complaining would do no good. He cared enough to adjust meeting times, to offer assistance, but he wasn't going to pull her off the case, and maybe this was his way of reminding her of that.

"You don't have to worry about me," she said, because she knew this was the only answer he was looking for.

"I hope not."

Margot bit her tongue.

Sometimes, despite all the hours she spent immersed in the reality of how cruel human beings could be to each other, she still found herself surprised by the pain a well-meaning friend could inflict without even trying.

TWENTY-THREE

By the time the next morning dawned, too early and not at all bright, there was a text waiting on Margot's phone from Alana.

> Convinced Rhodes driving from here to Fresno was stupid. Secured us the plane for the afternoon. Might as well use it if we have it.

Margot might have normally argued that an in-state visit wasn't worth wasting the fuel of a flight on, but she already had to drive almost three hours to get to San Francisco to meet Alana and, if using the plane meant she could get home sooner rather than later, she wasn't going to look a gift jet in the engine.

She still had to be on the road before dawn, which normally wouldn't bother her. But as she did the morning chores with a headlamp on, she couldn't help but feel like she had a bright target on her forehead if anyone was watching her yard. That might have typically made her chide herself for being paranoid, but this week had been anything but normal, and she was willing to forgive herself for being a little extra on edge.

She fed the outdoor animals and prepared the special dishes each of the dogs would need, setting them all out on the front porch at their preferred location. She was so focused on her morning chores that she almost didn't notice Sadie sitting on the porch until the swing creaked slightly as she adjusted her weight.

Margot let out a little yelp of surprise before calming her breathing. "Sadie, I thought you were still sleeping." She glanced around, wondering if Wes might also be up, but he had been dead to the world when she'd left their bed that morning, and she hoped he still was.

"Sorry, I wasn't trying to scare you, just having trouble sleeping." Sadie was wrapped in the patchwork quilt from the guest bedroom to stave off the surprisingly cold morning air. When Margot had first come outside it had been chilly enough to see her breath.

Margot turned off her headlamp to avoid blinding her sister-in-law and sat down on the top step of the porch, adjusting to the near-darkness. A Maltese that reminded Margot of her first dog, Betty, settled in beside her and put her head on her lap. Margot had named her Bea, to continue an unplanned *Golden Girls* naming trend. At Margot's feet, a scruffy terrier named Yahtzee lay across her toes.

Lucy patrolled the porch for a moment before settling into one of the empty chairs. If Margot had been dog-free, the cat would have come to her lap, but Lucy only tolerated the dogs, she didn't particularly like them.

Margot watched Sadie for a moment as the animals settled. She could tell she wanted to say something, but she wasn't going to push her into it, largely because she knew it would be uncomfortable to hear, and she was trying to avoid any more tension in her week.

"You're leaving again," Sadie said, though this had already been discussed at dinner the night before. She didn't phrase it like a question, just a statement.

"I have work," Margot said, shuffling her tennis shoes in the dirt and gravel at the bottom of the porch steps. This frustrated Yahtzee into moving elsewhere, though that was only about a foot away as he waited for her to stop fidgeting.

"Don't you think what's going on here is more important?" Sadie asked. The porch swing rocked gently. While Sadie's tone wasn't angry—she almost sounded the way a kindergarten teacher might when asking a small child a leading question—Margot still felt the accusation in it.

Obviously being here was more important.

But what could she *do* here?

She bit her lip as she considered how to answer. She was effectively being torn in two directions, one a test from her boss, the other where she would much rather be. She couldn't expect Sadie to understand her choice, but she knew that Wes did. He might want to have her close, but he also knew it was probably better for everyone involved if she had a way to distract herself.

Otherwise, she was likely going to drive around the entire day until she spotted a black truck that looked like the one on their security camera footage and took justice into her own hands out of pure spite.

There were people here who knew who she was, beyond Ms. Phalen, then FBI agent. Her history was part of the public record now. She hadn't changed her name when they'd moved, and she had been part of a very popular streaming documentary about Ed Finch. So anyone who had a propensity for watching true crime shows, or was even remotely attuned to the small-town gossip mill, would know that Margot was the daughter of a serial killer.

Normally that wasn't the sort of thing she wanted people to know when they thought about her.

But if those little pricks who had shot at her house showed their faces again, she would be more than happy to let them wonder if she was her father's daughter.

Sometimes the idea of violence was a lot scarier than an actual threat.

"This case you're working on," Sadie said. "He's already in jail, right?"

Margot knew what she was implying. That there was no rush, no immediate need for Margot to leave. Except that was no longer the case, now that they believed Ricky DeGraff likely had an accomplice.

"When we were interviewing him, he gave us reason to believe there was someone else who helped him." Margot didn't get into more of the specifics, knowing Sadie didn't want or need to hear them. "That means there could be someone at large who either assisted him in preparing for his crimes, or potentially even in the execution of those crimes. That makes this case very important for us to resolve. Quickly, if possible."

The porch swing creaked. The sky was light enough now that Margot got a better look at Sadie, whose knees were pulled up to her chest, and who was looking out into the yard rather than at Margot.

"I can't pretend to understand it. Not what you do—or how you can sleep at night after doing it—but *he* gets it. And I know it's important work, I hope you don't think I'm implying otherwise."

"I know."

"It's just hard for him. When you're not here."

Margot nodded, picking up a large piece of gravel and tossing it across the driveway. She could see the divots near the gate where the bullets had hit, and they made her stomach clench.

"It's hard for me when I'm not here, too," she said. "He's the most important thing in my life, Sadie."

They were both quiet for a long minute.

Finally, Sadie swung her feet off the bench and headed for the house. "I just hope it's worth it. What you're doing."

The door shut behind her with a faint slapping sound.

Margot looked out into the purple-tinged light of pre-dawn and wondered.

Was it worth it?

It was a question she was never sure she had the answer to, even five years and dozens of closed cases later.

Because even for all the good they were doing, there was always a cost.

And she'd never felt that cost more acutely than right now.

TWENTY-FOUR

As Margot drove out of Elk Creek, she knew it was probably for the best she was getting a change of scenery. She passed a battered brown truck on the side of the road, a man apparently taking a brief nap in the front seat, and in the moment she saw it her heart went into her throat.

Threat, her inner alarms insisted. Her hands tensed on the steering wheel.

But it was too old a truck.

Too brown.

It was just a truck. And there were thousands of them in the county. She couldn't go through her whole day reacting to every truck she saw as if it belonged to their attackers.

She ignored the brown truck in her rearview and picked up the coffee Wes had made her before she left, a move that forced her to release her death grip on the steering wheel. It was perfect. Always perfect. She tried to focus on that simple joy, and a playlist of upbeat music to take her south to San Francisco.

For a moment, she was clutched by a sudden panic that she had forgotten to lock the shed. It was so strong, so fierce, that she almost wanted to turn around.

But she scolded herself. Wes was home, he would have to go to the shed for the evening feeding and medication routine. Even if she *had* forgotten to lock the door—which was unlikely—he would do it for her.

She swallowed the lump in her throat.

The more distance between herself and Elk Creek, the more Margot was able to focus. She had no idea what to expect from their meeting today with Rick DeGraff Sr. Last night she had reviewed their existing notes on Ricky's father, but they were scant. They knew more about what Ricky had said about his father than what Senior had to say about Ricky. It seemed that following Ricky's arrest he had been very tight-lipped and had withdrawn from public view.

It made sense, in a way, that he would end up in a different state. Margot could appreciate that desire to move on, to move away. It was funny that he hadn't changed his name, because sharing a name with his son couldn't have made it easy for him to escape the legacy he had created, but she imagined that an old-school type like him would be stubborn about something like that.

He had the name first, after all.

As she parked at the airport, where she was meeting Alana—no need to stop at the office first—she wondered if he would speak to them at all, and whether there would be anything useful in his insights.

Ricky painted a picture of a man who hated his son, who might have sensed something different about him and wanted no part of it. Margot didn't know if Ricky *was* gay, or if that was just the worst-case scenario for his father. It ultimately had little to do with the murders themselves if he was or wasn't. But Senior might know if Ricky had any close friends, anyone he would have trusted with secrets like that.

Trusted enough to help him kill.

Alana was waiting beside the jet, two cups of coffee in hand. She looked ready to report on Paris Fashion Week in her eggplant purple suit and sky-high heels that Margot couldn't have walked in, let alone worked in. Margot sported her typical uniform of dark-wash denim, a linen button-down, and one of only two blazers she owned.

The FBI didn't pay well enough to keep Alana so well dressed, which made Margot suspect there was some generational wealth at play that Alana didn't talk about. There had been more than one complaint from other departments about Alana's attire, implying it was distracting. But Alana wasn't stupid, and she knew the FBI code of conduct like the back of her hand. Nowhere in it did it say she wasn't allowed to wear heels.

Margot had only seen Alana run in her stilettos once, but once was enough for her to never doubt the other woman's abilities. She could probably complete the Quantico training course in them, unless she didn't want to risk ruining them.

Alana smiled and handed Margot a still-hot coffee. "You look like hell," she said warmly.

"I'm always going to look like hell standing next to you," Margot countered.

Alana tsked and they headed up the steps into the jet. "Just looks like you haven't had much sleep. You doing okay? How's Wes?"

She sounded genuinely interested, and even a little concerned, which Margot found touching.

"It's all kind of a sliding scale of shit, you know?" She shrugged and sipped her coffee. It was good—Philz couldn't *be* bad—but it wasn't the way Wes had always ordered it for her, and that made her love him just a little bit more.

It also shot a sharp stab of guilt through her. She shouldn't be here. She should be home with him.

"And where on the sliding scale are you?" Alana had pulled out her laptop, though they wouldn't be in the air that long. There was always work to be done, cases to review. DeGraff might be their current focus, but there were at least six other killers they were exploring in the background as well. New targets, new potential crimes to solve.

New monsters for Margot to sit across from.

She wondered, sometimes, about the burnout of it all. Thanks to her proximity to the BSU over the previous five years, she had seen plenty of agents come and go. Even on their team, a lot of up-and-coming agents only lasted a year or two before heading off to a different specialty, one that wouldn't keep them up at night in the same way.

As someone who had left and then decided to come back, Sydney was a rare outlier.

Margot realized that violent crime, and serial killers especially, was a niche that went one of two ways. Either you worked it for a few years as a stepping stool to something different, or you did it for the rest of your career.

Margot had joined the Bureau specifically to work this kind of case, but that didn't mean she didn't sometimes think about what it would be like to leave. She was in the system now, an actual agent, but all the allowances she'd been given were only in place because of the team she worked for. The FBI didn't really have a lot of work-from-home options.

You could quit, a voice told her, and she honestly couldn't tell if it was her voice or Ed's. But whenever the thought emerged, she couldn't help but listen to it for a moment or two.

Could she? Could she ever really shake this?

There was something so easy about the idea of it, but part of her hesitated to embrace the thought.

Wes had left law enforcement, and—until this week—he had seemed the better for it. Maybe she *could* leave, start truly fresh. What if the reason all these bad things kept happening was because of *her*. Was she the one who kept bringing misery and despair to their doorstep? And if that was the case, then wasn't leaving the only right thing to do?

"Margot?"

God, there she went again, spacing out. She pushed her thoughts of quitting her job onto a far distant back burner.

This job was the only thing she knew at this point. Leaving would just make her feel more lost than ever before. She was tired, that was all. Tired and anxious, a deadly combo.

She sighed. "On the sliding scale? I don't know, not in the pits per se, but it's been pretty shitty."

"How visceral." Alana leaned back in her seat, holding her coffee and looking at Margot in a way that felt inescapable. Margot shifted uncomfortably. She hated to be perceived.

"I feel like it will be a win if I get through this week with no one else shooting at my property or accusing my partner of murder. I don't think that's too much to ask."

Alana gave her a soft smile. "The truth always comes to light eventually."

"Right, but in our line of work that can mean decades. I'd prefer it not take decades to clear Wes's name."

Alana shrugged and returned to her laptop. "I could always help, do a little independent exploration."

"The sheriff's department are being kind of stubborn about sharing files."

While Alana continued to look at her laptop, Margot couldn't help but notice the little smirk at the corner of her mouth. "There are ways around that."

Margot stared at her for a long moment, not sure if she was kidding or not. Not sure if she wanted to know. While Margot had no doubt that the security protecting the sheriff's department's documents was unlikely to be any match for the FBI, she also had no idea Alana had that specific skillset up her sleeve.

"Let's put a pin in that one for now," she said cautiously. "Though I am both impressed and terrified by your willingness."

"Friends look out for each other."

This took Margot aback. She sometimes forgot that people might actually consider her to be a friend. Or consider themselves to be her friend. Alana *was* her friend, in as much as Margot let anyone in to be her friend. And more importantly, Alana had always known the truth of who Margot was from the moment they first met, and that hadn't deterred her from wanting to get close.

That was a rare gift.

"Thank you." She meant it, too, and not just for the offer.

In Fresno, a rental car was waiting for them at the small airport. Margot appreciated whoever had the foresight to make that rental, because she had left her brain in bed that morning and it was only just now catching up with her.

About fifteen minutes later they were in the lobby of the Ruth Weir Rest Home, a single-story building made of red brick with neatly trimmed bushes outside. The residents all appeared to have individual units with small patio spaces outside, and a few had decorated with potted flowers—still going strong late in the season—but that was the extent of the décor outside.

After a brief meeting with the nurse at the front desk, and a chat with the home's managing director to confirm the FBI was supposed to be there, it was agreed that they could speak to Rick Senior, but only if he wanted to.

Margot and Alana paced the lobby, and Margot looked at the old oil paintings on the walls, of serene landscapes and birds that would have been more at home in Florida.

The nurse returned.

"He's just woken up, but he's willing to talk to you." She didn't move or indicate a direction they should go. She seemed to want to say more. "I should warn you that Richard can be... prickly. And especially so right after he's woken up. He may be a bit rude, I'm sorry."

Margot actually smiled at this, because no matter how rude Senior might be, he wouldn't even come close to being the most odious person she would speak to this year.

"I'm sure we've met with worse," Alana said, mirroring Margot's own thoughts.

"And..." The nurse drifted for a moment. "Well, he has some issues with women in authority roles. We have a lot of trouble with him and female doctors." She raised her hands helplessly. "Just be prepared to meet some friction, that's all."

"Thank you for the warning," Margot said, and caught Alana's eye as they followed the nurse to a room at the end of the hall. She knew Alana well enough to know she would be looking forward to this. The nurse opened the door for them and headed in. "Richard, the two FBI agents are here to talk to you."

"You just told me five minutes ago. My goddamn memory isn't failing, just my fucking legs."

The nurse, who was maybe thirty years old tops, clucked her tongue at him like he was a little boy.

"Sorry, Rachel, send them in."

Rachel waved Alana and Margot in, giving them their first look at Richard Senior and his space. As Margot had guessed from the exterior of the building, there was a door on the far wall that looked as if it went outside, but all the windows facing the light were covered in thick curtains, making the room look dingy and dark.

Richard Senior was sitting in a wheelchair near the covered main window. He had a tray of breakfast food sitting on a small table beside him, and there was a TV on, the volume muted, showing a notably right-wing news station.

The nurse excused herself and shut the interior door with a hushed *click*. Next to Senior was an old loveseat, with a fuzzy camo blanket over the back and some unexpected throw cushions that looked as if they had been hand-embroidered. Margot wondered if those had been the work of Ricky's mother when she was still alive.

On the wall was an array of taxidermized animals. A deer head, a pheasant, a large fish of some kind.

Senior must have caught her looking because he gestured towards the collection. "I was a pretty decent hunter back in my day. Before..." He didn't finish his sentence, and Margot wasn't sure if he meant before his legs stopped working or before his son was discovered to be a killer.

"Those are all yours, then?" Alana asked, making it sound like she was genuinely curious.

Senior nodded. "Ayup. I had more, but they only let you bring so much with you in a dickass small place like this." He wiped the front of his shirt, where a collection of toast crumbs had settled. "You're FBI agents?" He couldn't hide his incredulous tone, but at least he wasn't actively insulting them yet. Rachel had braced them for worse than what they were getting so far.

"We are," Margot confirmed. They had made plans for this visit with the care home in advance, but apparently that information had not trickled down to Richard Sr.

"Hmm." He mulled this over, his attention briefly captured by the TV, before he waved his hand to the loveseat. "Well, sit down, I guess. I'd offer you a drink, but I ain't got nothing 'cept water, so unless you want tap water, you're on your own."

"We're fine," Alana assured him.

"Get on with it then. I suppose you want to talk to me about Ricky." He said this in the exact way he might have if they were his neighbors wanting to complain about a dog that had been pissing on their lawn too often. He was cool and almost detached when saying his son's name.

"We were in Montana to speak with him earlier this week," Margot said by way of confirmation.

This grabbed his attention away from the blonde woman on his TV set. He reached to his side table instinctively, fingers feeling for something, but finding only a toast crust, he recoiled.

Margot suspected he was on the hunt for a cigarette, but the building was covered in no-smoking signs, and the room had no lingering stink of nicotine. He was probably a lifelong smoker who had been forced to give it up to move in here. Probably a big reason he was so crabby to the staff.

She almost wished she could offer him one, but it was impossible.

"Aw hell," he grumbled, pushing away his breakfast tray with annoyance and knocking a coaster to the floor as he did so. Alana picked it up and placed it on the coffee table.

"How was he?" Senior asked after a moment's pause. He didn't look at either of them, a move that was almost a spot-on impression of how Ricky had consistently avoided Margot's gaze during their interviews. Now that she was really looking at him, she could see the similarities in their features. While Ricky didn't favor his father in most ways, she saw little glimpses of him around the mouth, in the sag of his shoulders, even the shape of his eyebrows.

As she looked around the room, she noticed a framed wedding photo next to the television, obviously Senior in his glory days with Ricky's mother. Ricky, it turned out, was the spit and image of his mother, the same dark hair and sharp bone structure.

There were no photos of Ricky anywhere in the room.

"He's doing as well as can be expected," Margot said.

"Bet he talked a lot of shit about his old man," Senior scoffed. "Never had a kind word to say about me, and that's the God's honest truth."

Margot debated how to answer. "He said you two had a difficult relationship. That he was closer to his mother. But he did say he appreciated the parcel you sent him after she died." Margot was testing the water here, because Ricky hadn't specifically mentioned how he'd gotten Mathilda, but it seemed likely that Senior must have been involved in getting it to him, since it seemed like Ricky was not a frequent family visitor by the time his mother died.

Senior took this in, fingering one of the buttons on his plaid shirt. If Margot wasn't paying so much attention to him, she might have wondered if he had stopped listening to them. But he was listening.

He was just a man who chose his words very carefully.

"Been a long time since I've seen him. I went, you know. To the prison?"

"We know," Alana said. "You were in his visitor records."

Senior shuffled in his chair. "Just a couple times. I don't think it did either of us much good. It was hard to see him like that, even though I know it's where he belongs. Ain't a damn thing anyone out here can do for a mind like that, if you don't mind me saying."

Margot nodded. "You're right." Perhaps she shouldn't have agreed so readily, but she suspected that Senior was the kind of man who appreciated it when people told it like it was. She figured he might warm to them faster if they didn't tiptoe around him.

"You mind if I ask how you ladies became FBI? Seems like a man's job to me." There was nothing particularly venomous in his tone; if anything, Margot thought the question was genuine. She caught Alana's eye and nodded for her to go first.

"I studied criminology in university, as well as a lot of computer classes. The FBI was really behind the curve when it came to technology, so it helped me find my place in cyberterrorism first, then I moved onto criminal profiling," Alana said plainly, not bragging, just laying out the facts.

"I was a homicide detective for about a decade in San Francisco before I was recruited by the FBI," Margot said.

"Women FBI." Senior let out a little huff that might have been a laugh or might have been disgust, Margot couldn't quite tell the difference with him. "Will wonders never cease."

"Richard, we have some questions for you about Ricky if you don't mind—it shouldn't take us too long and then we can leave you be," Margot said. The room felt stuffy and a little too warm. She wanted to open the blinds and let natural light in, but that didn't seem to be Senior's preference.

She found that the longer they sat there, the more difficult it became for her to breathe. The air was stale, and Margot had started to pick up on lingering smells, like burnt meat and a potent laundry detergent.

"Sure, if I can help, I'll help, but I gotta tell you, ladies, I don't know much about what went on in that head of his."

"Does the name Mathilda mean anything to you?" Margot asked, wanting to plow ahead and get back outside.

This question hadn't been meant as a difficult one, but she saw

Senior rock back in his chair almost as if he'd been struck. "Where did you hear that name from? Ricky told you that name?"

"He did," Alana confirmed but didn't elaborate.

Senior stared at his knees. "Mathilda was Ricky's baby sister."

Of all the things Margot had expected him to say—most of them about the doll—she hadn't been expecting this. Nowhere in Ricky's files had there been any mention of a sibling.

"What happened to her?" Margot asked softly, knowing it was unlikely that the story had a happy ending just based on Senior's reactions thus far.

"She died. Five months old. Just one of those freak things." He scratched his stubble, and Margot got the feeling he wasn't looking at them this time because he didn't want them to see the pain in his face.

Alana gave Margot a quick look. They both seemed to be wondering the same thing, but it was Alana who finally gave voice to their mutual concern.

"Mr. DeGraff, you don't suppose there was any chance that Ricky had some involvement in Mathilda's death, do you?"

Margot wasn't sure how he'd respond to this. Anger? Shock? She watched him carefully, but he just sighed as he shook his head.

"No. No, I thought about that for a while after. Not right after it happened, mind you. Ricky was only five at the time, and he'd been so in love with his baby sister. Always talking to her, wanting to hold her, play with her. He would sneak into her room sometimes just to watch her sleep. But later, you know, much later after everything happened with him, it made me stop to think about it. I don't think he could have done anything to her."

Margot was less certain. Children might not be born evil—or maybe they were; it was a question no one could ever really answer definitively. Children *could* be born psychopaths, though. What flipped the switch in their brain so they turned from a safe psychopath to one who murdered people was something even the experts on her own team hadn't figured out yet.

She wasn't sure she had the same certainty as Senior about

Ricky's innocence, but it did give her new questions to ask if she had to continue her interviews with Ricky.

"Sir, Ricky told us that the doll you sent him, the one from his mother, he told us her name was Mathilda."

"That fucking thing." Senior almost spat these words out. He adjusted his chair slightly, wheeling it backward, then forward, a fraction of an inch so it seemed almost as if he hadn't moved at all.

"Do you know the doll we're talking about?" Alana asked.

"Of course I do. Now, you have to understand, my wife, she loved those awful things. She didn't have a lot of money growing up, but she was given some godforsaken doll when she was a little girl, and she *loved* that thing. When she was older, after we got married, she collected them. Found them at garage sales, flea markets. That one, though, that one she got from an estate sale, and she tried to explain to me over and over again how valuable it was, and what a bargain it was, but I didn't care, I just paid for it. But you should have seen the way she and Ricky looked at that thing. She told him all about it, when it was made, how much it was worth. And she would let him hold it, but only while she was watching."

"Do you remember if she got the doll before or after Mathilda died?" Margot asked.

"After. Maybe a year or so. I would have bought her anything to make her smile in those days, didn't care if I thought it was stupid." There was a flicker of real emotion across his face, and Margot could tell that, while Ricky painted his father as authoritarian and perhaps abusive, that might not have been the entire truth.

Margot knew that the saying goes, there are three versions of every story—yours , mine, and the truth. It was very possible that Ricky conflated or embellished his father's actions, or outright lied. But it was also possible that Ricky had been telling the truth about Senior, and his father just looked to the past with rose-colored glasses that didn't include his own abuse.

What he was telling them about both Mathildas, though, was

an interesting revelation and offered a lot more insight into Ricky than the killer probably had into himself.

"You don't happen to have a photo of that doll anywhere, do you?" Alana asked.

Margot expected Senior to brush this off immediately, but instead he looked pensive, and eventually pointed to a lower shelf on the unit that held his TV. "Can you pass me that brown album?"

Margot got up from the loveseat, collected the battered album, and handed it to Senior. He flipped through the pages thoughtfully, his shaggy gray brows knit in concentration. Alana, who was sitting closer to him, had edged forward in her seat ever so slightly, obviously hoping she might see something relevant as he flipped the pages. Either that, or she was just morbidly curious to get a glimpse of the childhood of a killer.

Sometimes, you couldn't help but look at the car wreck.

Senior stopped turning the pages and peeled back the sheet that held the photos in place. He withdrew a single picture, his fingers trembling slightly as he held it out to them. "I guess you might think I'm a bad father. I'm sure that's what Ricky said. I got rid of most of my photos of him after the last time I went to see him. Stopped telling people I had any kids if they asked. It was just easier. Maybe that makes me a coward, I don't know. Maybe I *was* a bad father. He had to turn out the way he did for a reason. But I know I never killed nobody. So how did he get that from me? He certainly didn't get it from his mother."

For a moment this seemed to be a rhetorical question, until Senior looked at Alana. "You studied this, didn't you? Tell me, FBI woman, what did I do to deserve this boy?"

He thrust the photo into Alana's hands. It was a picture of a young Ricky, maybe nine or ten, standing beside his mother. The woman looked exhausted, but was smiling, her arm wrapped tenderly around her son, who was looking up at her like she hung the moon.

In her other arm, a doll was cradled gently, like it was a child.

With Ricky and his mother side by side it was easier than ever to see the resemblance between them.

Alana seemed to sense that Senior was still awaiting some answer to his question. "While some serial killers show definite history of abuse, that isn't necessarily the only way someone commits these acts. We know now that psychopaths are most likely born and not created as a matter of their environment, though environment does shape the path someone might ultimately go down." Alana looked to Margot for help as she realized that what she was saying probably wasn't comforting at all.

Margot took over the task from Alana. "Sir, there's no way to predict what will drive someone to kill. The Bureau has done extensive research, talking to many people like your son, to try to establish root causes. But the truth of the matter is, while there are patterns we can see emerging through those histories, some people are just driven by a compulsion we can't understand. From what you've told us today, I suspect even Ricky might not understand where his compulsions came from. He just acted on them."

Margot *did* have a much better idea of what may have triggered Ricky to become who he was, but she didn't need to tell Senior her theory. What could he do with that information? Nothing. His daughter's death was an accident. Hopefully. And it seemed very likely that Ricky started doing what he did to fill the vacuum Mathilda's death left in his life.

For his father, though, that information could only cause pain.

"So it wasn't my fault?" Senior asked.

This was one of those questions that couldn't be answered with the truth, because the truth was too fluid to know for certain. Ricky certainly had enough animosity towards his father to indicate that relationship was an issue for him. But whether it was a trigger? They would never really know for certain.

"It's unlikely," Margot said, offering a gentle smile. When the truth was unknowable, a kind lie was usually the second-best option.

Senior sat back in his chair, blinking hard as he looked away from them. Margot felt like they should leave before he started to cry. He wouldn't want them to see that.

Alana took out her phone to take a photo of the picture Senior had given them, but he waved his hand at her. "You can keep that," he said, his voice thick with emotion. "I don't need it anymore."

TWENTY-FIVE

Margot and Alana both buried themselves in work for the flight back to San Francisco, but every sentence Margot read seemed to blur as she struggled to fight against the exhaustion she was feeling. It had been bad on the way there, but now she felt like her eyelids weighed a thousand pounds each. Every part of her body felt tired.

But there was work to be done, and no rest for the wicked, as they say. The photo, and Senior's insights into Ricky's past, had been unexpectedly helpful in terms of building a better profile of Ricky himself, but Margot wasn't sure it got them any closer to finding his potential accomplice.

They'd managed to ask a few last questions before they'd left, but he was insistent his son never had any close friends. He didn't bring people over as a teenager or young adult, and was never invited anywhere, either.

Had he met this person on the pageant circuit? That seemed the most likely, since it was the only place he was socially active as far as Margot could glean from his files. But what was the likelihood of two child predators working the same pageants?

She didn't even have time to finish the thought before she realized, horribly, that the answer might be higher than she wanted to think about. The harsh reality was, wherever there were children, there were people who would gravitate to those spaces for nefarious reasons. They had recently sat in on a seminar about online child predators who were following kid-themed accounts on social media platforms. Margot would never look at the number of saved videos on a post the same way again. It was stomach-churning what even seemingly innocuous content could spark in dark minds.

Margot had warned her brother and his ex about keeping her nephew Cruz as offline as possible.

Back at headquarters, they reconvened with everyone working the DeGraff case to share what they'd learned.

"But nothing in terms of his accomplice?" Greg asked, sounding crestfallen.

"It was going to be a long shot that DeGraff Senior would know anything useful, and I think he's given us a lot of food for thought for next time we talk to Ricky," Alana replied defensively.

"Let's see if we can figure out a brand type on the doll. If there's a chance that Ricky's friend on the outside might not be that reliable, he or she might have sold it," Margot suggested. "DeGraff Senior suggested it was a pretty valuable collectable even back when he bought it for his wife, and those kinds of things tend to increase in value. Maybe Ricky let it slip that the thing was worth money and their friend on the outside figured he'd never know if they sold it."

Andrew nodded. "It's a good suggestion. We can also share the photo with some online doll collector Facebook pages or forums. Reddit could be useful."

"I can work on that," Margot offered. It made sense for her to focus on things she could do offsite, while the others made calls or hunted down other potential leads.

"All right. We've got a lot of work to do still, but this was really nice field work by Agents Yarrow and Phalen, thank you both."

Margot appreciated that he didn't say, *thank you ladies*. Not that Andrew would ever have done this. But something about

Senior's astonishment at their being women was still rankling her, and she was relieved not to get any of it at the office. She just felt sensitive for no good reason at the moment.

God help her if it was perimenopause.

As she left the meeting she saw a text on her phone from Wes, letting her know that he'd managed to find a window their size at a specialty store in San Francisco as long as she could pick it up before six. Thankfully, with meetings winding down for the day, Margot would be able to get there with a little time to spare.

"Margot, a word?" Andrew asked before she could make a beeline for the elevator.

Twice in one week? That didn't bode well.

She sighed inwardly before nodding and following him to his office.

The task force generally existed in a state of chaos, with folders and pictures scattered everywhere in the office, but Andrew maintained one of the tidiest spaces Margot had ever seen. His desk had no loose papers on it whatsoever; anything he might be in the process of reading or signing was neatly sorted into a tray system on the corner of the desk. The only personal details were framed commendations hanging on the wall, and a single framed photo on the bookshelf of his wife and kids.

Margot took a seat across from him.

"I reached out to Sheriff Wilder directly today," he said bluntly.

She didn't know what to do with that information at first. She was annoyed he'd done it without telling her, but there was also a not-so-small part of her that felt an enormous sense of relief that he'd taken the burden off her.

"Thank God," she said. "Alana was offering to hack their database for me."

"I'm choosing to hear that as a joke."

"That's your right as an American," she said with a smile.

Andrew's mouth formed a thin, unamused line before he spoke again. "Now, he was as stubborn as you had suggested he would be, but I gather a more soft-hearted voice may have intervened to convince him to accept the offer."

Margot was stunned that Deputy Cassidy had actually managed to twist the old man's arm, but she would take it.

"I appreciate you letting me know, thank you," she said, pushing her chair away from his desk.

At least now that they were being looped in, there was a good chance that someone would be able to point them away from Wes and towards their real killer. She assumed Andrew would pass the files on to the BSU to avoid conflict, or maybe to one of the members of the team who she didn't work closely with.

"Before you go, do you mind just waiting here for a moment while I go deliver something to Alana before she leaves?"

Margot raised a quizzical brow at him. This conversation was over as far as she was concerned. What else could he possibly want to discuss?

He opened a drawer beside him and placed a thick folder on the desk. Margot would have had to be blind not to see Whitney's name on the front.

"I'll be keeping this copy of the files the sheriff sent over for my own records. We've already shared them with the BSU and someone there is working the case." He laid heavy emphasis on the word *copy*, and stood up from his desk. Considering he was meant to be delivering something to Alana, he had nothing in his hands when he left the office.

Margot sat there for a moment. It seemed quite clear that Andrew meant for her to take that file. She just couldn't for the life of her understand why he would do something like that.

And then, as she stared at it wondering if this was some kind of test, his reasoning clicked, like a lightbulb coming on over her head.

She had been distracted, her mind elsewhere, ever since she'd learned of Wes's arrest. Andrew must have known that with her mind divided by two things she wasn't fully present in the DeGraff case, which was where she needed to be if she was going to help them solve the new mystery he had thrown them. The DeGraff case was no longer just a simple task of marking a cold case closed. Now they had the new curveball of figuring out who he had been working with.

And, in Margot's mind, there was still the question of whether his first victim might have been his sister, despite what Richard Senior believed.

Andrew needed Margot's head in the game.

He was letting her have all the information available on Whitney's case so she could sate her agonizing curiosity there. He knew her too well. She wouldn't be able to work it—the conflict of interest would be enormous—but at least she would *know* what was going on.

As she slipped the folder into her bag, she had to wonder if, in this situation, knowledge was power, or ignorance was bliss.

TWENTY-SIX
WILLOWS, CA

Four days ago

He didn't pick specific people. He believed that if he was prepared, and had taken all the right steps, the universe would reward him with the right person at the right time.

Was it really so different from believing that your soulmate would walk into your life if you just opened yourself to the possibility of love?

He didn't believe in soulmates, that kind of romantic nonsense was for women and miserable men. But he did believe that if a person set themselves up for success, they would get what they deserved in the long run.

That thinking hadn't failed him to date.

What it did mean was that there was a lot of waiting, planning, preparing before he got to enjoy the payoff for all his hard work. He'd spent *years* honing his skills to the point where he knew he could be as lethal and invisible as necessary. He'd visited places across the country to observe, to understand how they worked, and to leave behind whatever he might need to complete his work.

That was a mistake so many others made. Get pulled over for something stupid, a broken taillight, a stop sign they missed, and their behavior tweaks something for the officer. They look in the back and find all the tools of the trade.

He wasn't stupid.

The first time he'd done it, he hadn't been prepared. He'd just let the urge take him. What a simpleton he'd been at the start of this journey, thinking his own strength and smarts would be enough. It was, as it turned out, not easy to commit the perfect crime.

He certainly hadn't the first time.

But he also hadn't gotten caught, because a secondary truth in all of this was that you didn't always *need* to commit the perfect crime. Police were only human, after all, and if you left a puzzle just confusing enough behind you, they would spend so much time chasing their tails the man could be in another state before they realized they'd been barking up the wrong tree.

Because the police liked easy answers. It was the husband, the boyfriend, a jealous co-worker. The police wanted murders wrapped up in tidy little bows, packages they could understand. They *wanted* the killer to be a known quantity. Strangers were too scary, too much like giving credence to the monster under your bed or in your closet. It was easier and safer to assume that all evil was explainable.

He didn't fit into that tidy story they told themselves, and that alone was a reason he often got away with it.

The first time he killed someone it wasn't even a girl. He liked girls, preferred them. He wanted to see what their pretty little insides looked like, what happened to their faces when they realized they were never going home alive. *That* was what he craved and looked for.

But as it turned out, the hunger inside him that wanted all those dark and nasty things, it wasn't as particular as he was.

He'd seen the boy standing at a bus stop, and what happened next was as natural to him as breathing.

Pull over.

Smile.

Offer a ride.

Smile.

Ask questions until you know they're comfortable.

Smile as you pull out the knife and let it sit between you on the seat.

Breathe in the delicious and cloying smell of fear.

The man had made mistakes that first time, but not enough to matter. Not enough to get caught. And he'd learned from it, too. Learned that it was better to leave all the evidence behind, never take anything with you.

He had learned not to look for a specific victim, because that could lead to him being too focused and missing an opportunity elsewhere. The universe would provide. A college co-ed walking home from a party. A lone woman closing down a little ice cream shop in the middle of nowhere.

A girl walking along the highway on her own in a small town.

"Where are you headed?" he'd asked, the rain pelting down on her much-too-large jacket. A school emblem on the chest and the word *Coach* on the back. He didn't think it was hers.

"I have to go back to get something out of my car. I left it at the school." She'd shuffled from foot to foot, uncomfortable in the rain.

God, but she was a pretty thing, her little heart-shaped face and curly hair. Her eyes were both brown and green, but he wouldn't have called them hazel.

"Why did you leave your car at the school?" Smile.

"It wouldn't start."

"Well, I've got some jumper cables in the back. Why don't you hop in, I'll take you to the school and help get that car started for you in a jiff?" Smile.

This girl knew what she'd been told as a child. Be wary of strangers. Be careful of men you don't know. But she had also been raised in a small town. There were no strangers, only people you hadn't been properly introduced to yet. Plus, it was cold, and she was soaking. There was something in her expression that spoke to worry. Fear. But he didn't think it was him she was worried about.

Finally, after a moment of consideration, she said, "What's your name?"

"Eli," he said, the lie coming almost as easily as his real name might have. "What's yours?"

"Whitney."

"Well, all right then, Whitney. Now that we're not strangers anymore, let's go fix that car of yours, shall we?"

He wondered, as she got into the truck beside him, giving a faint waft of a baby powder-scented perfume as she buckled in, if a baby zebra would walk right into the mouth of a lion if the lion just smiled enough.

TWENTY-SEVEN

Margot was glad she'd remembered to pick up the new kitchen window on her way home. The exhilaration of having Whitney's case file in her bag was so overwhelming she had to resist the urge to open it in her car before leaving the office. All she wanted to do was get home and read it; she hoped she might be able to see something in the pages of notes and photos that the local law enforcement had missed.

Because they were so focused on Wes, she could imagine there were glaring bits of evidence that pointed elsewhere that they had chosen to ignore. She also realized it wouldn't be as simple as that, but she wouldn't *know* anything until she was able to lay it all out in front of her.

Bringing home the window was an excellent way to distract Wes. It wasn't that she wanted to hide the files from him. But it might cause problems for him if he knew what was in them. And she didn't want him knowing things he couldn't possibly know unless he'd killed Whitney—or seen the file.

Margot understood that there was no real way to disassociate from a case like that. Wes had been an incredible detective, but he was also a man with a big heart, and she didn't think he needed or likely wanted to see the photos and reports about what had been done to Whitney, especially knowing that he'd been the one to drop her off at home.

That kind of guilt might be more than he could bear, even if he wasn't necessarily willing to admit that to himself.

Margot could be impartial.

She knew Wes hadn't killed the girl, and that was all she needed to know. The rest was just the work she did on a daily basis. She solved murders, that was her job, it was the one thing in this world she knew she was good at. *Great* at, even.

Margot picked up pizzas about twenty minutes from Elk Creek, since no one in the house would be keen to make dinner this late in the evening, and she could hardly suggest they drive to Willows for a bite somewhere local. Even in her desire to show the town they weren't guilty and had nothing to hide, she didn't have the energy for that kind of side-eye whisper party. No food in Willows was worth that.

Margot was aching to get into her office and have a look at the file, but she also knew that taking time to sit and eat with her family was important. It was something she needed to remind herself of, because the workaholic part of her brain would stop her from even eating if given the opportunity.

She set the table with proper plates, even though they were just eating pizza, and as she did, Sadie whipped up a simple salad, using the ingredients in Margot and Wes's fridge that were on the cusp of being unsalvageable. That was another reminder to Margot of the simple life things that were slipping through her fingers. When was the last time they'd picked up groceries? They would need to soon, but the anxious part of her didn't want to deal with that.

Perhaps she could ask Sadie to help, since no one in Willows knew who she was.

She was thankful the animal food was ordered online, so they only needed to deal with the post office boxes in Elk Creek to get that.

As they sat around the table, a few candles lit in the middle, it was hard to ignore the plastic sheet taped to the window, or the fact that none of the cats—who normally loved to be wherever their people were—would set foot in the kitchen.

"How was your trip?" Sadie asked, picking a mushroom off her pizza and putting it automatically on Wes's, something she had likely been doing since they were children.

Perhaps it was Margot's own guilty conscience, but she couldn't help but think it sounded like Sadie's question was barbed.

Must have been nice to get to run off on a private jet while we were here picking bullets out of the driveway.

At her core, Margot knew this niggling voice in her head didn't belong to her sister-in-law. It might not even belong to Margot herself, but she still felt defensive.

"It wasn't a pleasure trip. We were interviewing the father of a serial killer." Even to her own ears this sounded too harsh.

"Hey, she wasn't implying anything," Wes said protectively, though in typical Wes fashion his tone was calm and steady, something he'd honed through years of experience with the moments Margot's temper got the better of her.

She hated herself in that moment. Hated that he had needed to learn to tiptoe around her, like she was a wild animal he didn't want to get bitten by. Most days that wasn't who she was, but there were times she couldn't seem to help what came over her.

Like father, like daughter, the familiar voice cooed.

She wanted so badly to snap at Wes in that moment. To be angry with him for choosing his sister over her, even though she *knew* she was in the wrong. There were just times when rationality left the building entirely, and all that was left was raw *feeling*, like an exposed nerve.

Margot stared at the pizza on her plate rather than looking at either of them. She took a steadying breath, then said, "I'm sorry. This week has been a lot."

"For everyone," Sadie said, as if Margot didn't know, and as Margot glanced up at her Sadie's eyes flashed almost in a challenge.

She was a strong-willed person, and Margot knew she didn't respond well when people were unkind to her.

Like Margot was being.

She wasn't used to being on the receiving end of Sadie's ire, but it was her own fault.

"You're right," she replied, channeling a response she thought might make Dr. Singh proud. "I'm sorry I reacted that way. My trip was... valuable," she added, hoping it was true. Wanting to make it seem as if it had been worthwhile for her to once again not be here when she was needed.

Her guilt gnawed at her, and it made her angrier at them both in turn. It was safer for her not to speak at all. Once she could turn her attention to the case, all this bitterness would fade away. Her anger needed an outlet that wasn't her family, and focusing it on a killer seemed like the perfect solution.

They spoke very little for the rest of the meal.

After they'd eaten, Sadie and Wes set to work changing out the kitchen window—a good thing, too, because the night was supposed to cool off quite a bit, plus Margot wasn't ready to test her hard-won trust of humanity with a night spent sleeping in a house with an unsecured hole in the side of it. She excused herself and slunk off to her office.

She wouldn't have been much use with the window, anyway. Too many cooks in the kitchen, so to speak. Sadie and Wes were both handier than she was, having been raised by a father who had a wood shop and DIY'd almost everything around the house.

Margot could have given a TED Talk on how to avoid making yourself an easy target for a serial killer, but her father hadn't passed down any other useful life skills to her. He used to take her brother camping sometimes, taught him weird survivalist shit, but he hadn't done the same for her. At the time it had rankled her, but now she was almost grateful that she didn't have memories of her father explaining how to stalk animals and move unheard through the woods.

She shuddered at the thought.

After closing her office door, she pulled out a Miles Davis record and set it on the turntable under the window. Wes had found the whole setup at a garage sale a few years earlier, and now whenever he ventured to thrift stores or just happened to be out shopping and found records he thought she might like, he brought them home.

Margot had never thought of herself as a jazz person—she hadn't actually listened to a lot of music for most of her life because the idea of not hearing something coming bothered her too much—but late in life she was coming to find there were a lot of things she took pleasure in. Miles Davis was one of them.

Plus, the sounds of *Kind of Blue* helped dampen all the hammering and sibling bickering coming from the kitchen.

She settled in at her desk, put on her reading glasses, and opened up the purloined file.

There, the story of Whitney Eflin's death started to fall into place.

There were several crime scene photos in the file, which Margot set aside for the time being, wanting to go over the county medical examiner's report, the details from the first arrivals on the scene, and all the witness statements they'd gathered already.

She looked through everything in the file, then looked again.

Beyond Whitney being found with Wes's jacket beside her—not on her, not covering her—and him being the last person to see her alive, according to witness statements from the other two girls he dropped off, there was no other evidence to point to him. Nothing.

There were no hair or semen samples. It was still too soon for DNA to come back with matches, although there would be traces of his DNA on her from the jacket, undoubtedly; but even that was still only circumstantial.

Both the other softball players he had dropped off had reported they saw him offer Whitney his jacket and confirmed it had been raining very heavily at the time and there was nothing unseemly about the gesture beyond "Coach just being a good guy."

Other members of the coaching staff, including the regular softball coach, all reported that Wes was never inappropriate with any of the kids he coached, never said or did anything to raise red flags with the other teachers. More than one of them insisted in their interviews that the sheriff had the wrong guy.

Margot felt a deep sense of relief knowing that other people were on their side in this. Though, the question remained: for how long? If there were no other suspects, no other options, then sooner or later they'd all start asking that nagging question that she'd heard at the back of her own mind.

What if.

Especially when they learned his DNA was on her. People with no background in forensics or policing could hear that and only assume the worst. Little did they know they were all sprinkling bits of their DNA all over their homes, families, and possessions every single day.

What people didn't understand scared them, and they needed to find a different target for the town's fear before those lab results came back and gave them more reasons to focus on Wes.

This place was supposed to be their happily ever after, goddamnit.

Once she had a good grasp on the case files, and a good idea of what to expect from the scene, she pulled out the photos, laying them out across her desk.

Margot had seen some terrible things in her career. She was no stranger to a bloody crime scene, or horrific, graphic things. But the day she stopped feeling that initial twinge of repulsion was the day she would hang up her badge forever.

Looking at the photos laid out in front of her, she winced.

It was obvious that both Flo and Eugene the lawyer were being reserved about the details of what they had shared with Wes. Because this wasn't just a stabbing, it was an evisceration.

There was really no other way to describe it. Whitney had been fileted.

There was a deep slash horizontally across her lower abdomen, then a long upward slash from there up to the gap between her breasts.

Margot's analytical brain kicked in then and she noted that, while the cuts looked clean and precise, the person doing the cutting was definitely not in a job that involved postmortem work, like a mortuary assistant or a funeral home worker. The cuts on Whitney's body were counterintuitive to how those fields were trained.

She didn't think the person who had cut Whitney open was in the medical field either. Those cuts, just based on an initial examination, were too deep and choppy to be from something as delicate as a scalpel. The careful nature of the lines was likely from someone who had a lot of experience slicing things open, but not professionally.

A hunter.

In more ways than one, Margot supposed.

Narrowing down who in the area had hunting licenses wouldn't help them at all, though it might help eliminate Wes.

Of course, someone who knew how to hunt, and how to gut a deer, might not necessarily have a current hunting license, especially if he had moved on to different kinds of game.

The fact that the jacket had been tossed aside and no efforts had been made to cover Whitney told Margot that whoever had done this didn't feel shame or guilt for what they had done. Sometimes killers might cover the face or eyes of their victims because they couldn't stand the idea of the victim seeing what they were doing.

This person didn't care.

He might have even wanted to see that expression on Whitney's face before she died.

This was either a person who knew her well and harbored some intense ill-will towards her, or he was someone who didn't care about her at all. A stranger. Someone who just wanted to look at her while he tormented her.

Margot's mouth was dry. She put down the picture she was looking at.

There were plenty of little things she knew now that she hadn't known before. Whitney wasn't sexually assaulted, but she had been mostly undressed. Probably because it was easier for the killer to do what he wanted to her without being encumbered by clothing. Her underwear was in place but not her bra.

Margot took off her glasses and rubbed her eyes.

The record had long since ended and the room was filled with the repeated static of the vinyl spinning. It had been a while since she'd heard any hammering or swearing. She should probably go check on the window installation.

But for a long time she just sat, listening to the white noise from the turntable and staring at the photos in front of her.

It was a relief, in a way, to know with such absolute certainty this wasn't Wes and no part of the crime would create a profile that matched him.

Unfortunately, that made way for a much harsher reality.

A true monster had done this to a teenaged girl. And it was either a devil they knew or a devil they didn't, but no matter which option, the same thing was true at the end of the day.

The devil was still out there.

TWENTY-EIGHT

Margot had never been to a pageant in her life, and she didn't watch the adult pageants on TV. Were they even on TV anymore? She didn't know.

Her mother thought pageants were anti-feminist, and while her father hadn't expressed opinions, knowing what she knew now Margot had to believe he wasn't a fan. Then again, the opinion of a noted woman-killer wasn't really relevant to her.

She and Greg stood in the lobby of the Petaluma Princess Pageant, and she was both appalled and strangely fascinated by the world unfolding around her.

The high Margot had felt after getting Whitney's file was long gone. Both reading it and looking at her new kitchen window that morning had stripped her of almost all her energy to function.

She knew what this feeling was, the creeping, insidious weight of it. Depression was a tricky thing, kind of like a tattoo you get in a place you can't see. It was always there, but sometimes it took you by surprise.

Right now was *not* a good time for all her carefully constructed defense mechanisms to fail her. She didn't have the luxury of taking to her bed to rot. There was work that needed to be done. And unlike when she'd last let herself go under, after her mother died, Margot now had people who relied on her. She couldn't fall apart without tremendous consequences.

The air in the convention center smelled strongly of hairspray and sugar. Beside her, Greg looked more queasy than fascinated. Margot tried to concentrate on the scent to keep herself awake and focused, and found that it was surprisingly effective.

The pageant had categories for ages from five to eighteen, so the number of girls in the convention hall was much larger than Margot had expected. The pageant, according to a pamphlet she had picked up at the door, was one of the longest running in the state, going back to the early fifties, which meant it had been happening the whole time Margot lived in Petaluma. She tried to remember if she'd ever heard any of the girls in her school talk about competing, but her memory of those days was hazy, and she had spent a lot of her adulthood forgetting.

Little girls in sequined dresses, with hair teased so high Dolly Parton might say it was a bit much, were walking by in groups of three and four. Margot might have assumed there would be more of a cutthroat sense of competition between the children present, but so far this just seemed to be another way for girls to make friends.

The mothers, on the other hand, were obviously keeping an eye on their kids, and if it seemed like anyone was having too much fun, or was at risk of wrinkling a satin one-piece or leaning their towers of hair against anything, they would swoop in and whisk the girls back to seating areas set up through the lobby.

"I've never seen anything like this," Margot said, her gaze sweeping the room, trying to imagine a childhood where this sort of thing was happening almost every weekend. It had to lose its lustre after a while.

"I watched *Miss Congeniality* once," Greg said, as if this was in some way relevant to the current situation. "That's all I know about pageants."

"Well, thank God the FBI isn't trying to put us undercover here." Margot gestured towards their ensembles. "I don't think we exactly blend." She was wearing jeans, a hunter green T-shirt, and a leather jacket. Blazers were for in-office only. She felt stupid wearing them on cases. Greg, who Margot was sure only owned one suit, was wearing khaki pants, Converse sneakers, a button-down white shirt, and a sports coat one size too big for him.

The latter, she suspected, was because he thought it made him look older.

Greg, inching into his thirties now, was always going to look like he was sixteen as far as Margot was concerned. The mussed red hair and freckles just gave him a permanently youthful vibe.

The lobby was so filled with people that no one seemed to notice how out of place the two of them were. Aside from all the moving parents and children, there were about a dozen different merchant booths set up all around the large open space.

Margot saw a stall selling hair extensions and decorative bows and hair clips. Another was offering custom and pre-made gowns, with at least a hundred ice cream-colored samples hanging from rolling racks and a little booth set up for the girls to try things on.

Another booth advertised singing and dance lessons.

Then Margot spotted what she was looking for on the far back wall. A booth set up with several drop-cloth backgrounds, and big studio lights. A banner sitting in front of it read *Like Magic Photograph* and there were samples of portraits on smaller stand-up banners in front of the booth.

Margot nudged Greg, who was fastidiously looking at his feet to avoid being caught looking anywhere else. She felt a little bad for him, the veritable fish out of water that he was, but Alana was otherwise occupied and when the team had realized there was a local pageant that weekend, it seemed sensible to go, get a lay of the land, better understand the environment they were working with in the DeGraff case. It was strange to be back in her hometown.

They needed other avenues to explore, in case all the online searching for the doll brought them nothing. Andrew had suggested this might be a good place to gather basic intel on the circuit. Perhaps if some of the vendors had been around long enough and had worked out-of-state events as well as local ones, they might even remember Ricky DeGraff. Margot wasn't holding her breath for that one, but a lead was a lead no matter how insignificant it might seem.

Still, poor Greg was going to need to learn to move around with more confidence, otherwise his awkward attempts to avoid sticking out were going to be the very thing that drew attention.

"Let's go talk to some of the vendors," Margot suggested.

Before they could even move two feet towards the booths, however, a woman in a too-tight dress with a bouffant hairdo and the scent of Elizabeth Taylor's White Diamonds hanging around her like a potent force field stepped in their way.

Her smile was forced, intense, and the look in her eyes was nearly feral.

Margot took a step back.

"Hello, y'all," the woman said in a Texas accent so concentrated it might as well have been flavored like barbeque sauce.

Greg immediately seemed disarmed by her, but Margot had a pretty good read on the situation. She gave back a fake smile of her own, one that she knew from previous feedback was more *terrifying* than it was *warm and inviting*.

The smaller woman blanched for a moment, but she also wasn't the type to be a pushover, Margot could tell. This was someone who was accustomed to getting her way and having everyone in the room pay attention to her when she spoke. Margot could see they were either dealing with the person who was in charge here, or the person who believed she *should be* in charge. Either way, they wouldn't be getting any further until they figured out the riddle to keep this sphinx at bay.

"How can I be of service?" the woman asked, indicating she did not believe she could be, and they best be moving on.

Margot flashed her badge long enough for it to be read, then slipped it back in her jacket. No need to draw undue attention. Any kind of police badge was going to make people assume something was wrong. An FBI badge made them think things were *really* wrong.

This woman was no exception. She blanched when Margot's badge appeared.

"I'm Special Agent Margot Phalen, this is Special Agent Gregory Howell." She looked to Greg, and he nodded at the woman, his smile more effectively convincing than Margot's had been. Of course.

"I'm Bev Townsend," the woman said, offering each of them a limp handshake. Her skin was so soft it almost felt wet. Margot took back her own hand as soon as it was polite to do so. "Is there anything the matter?" Bev's tone was hushed, conspiratorial.

She wanted to know what was going on because it would make her an insider. Margot knew the type well. This would be a story she would tell for the next decade, about the time she was instrumental in an FBI investigation.

Whatever worked.

"Do you recall the Ricky DeGraff pageant murders?" Margot said, matching Bev's conspiratorial tone. This also wasn't really a topic they needed people listening in on if they could avoid it. The word *murder* was insidious, and would spread over the entire floor in no time flat if they weren't careful. Margot knew the gossip would become unavoidable as soon as they started asking questions, but if she could at least get through one or two interviews without everyone in the building knowing why they were there, it would be nice.

Bev's eyes went predictably wide, darting from side to side as if she was worried about who might be nearby. Margot wasn't sure if she was concerned about young ears, or more worried that someone might try to butt in and steal this story from her.

"Well, yes, of course. That whole thing was quite a shock. Of course, that monster never worked one of *our* pageants."

Like the organizers of the pageants DeGraff had worked at were being remiss in not asking screening questions like, *are you a serial killer?*

"No, of course not," Margot said. "And of course, he's been in prison quite some time now."

"Where he belongs," Bev replied curtly.

"We certainly agree with you there."

"But if you're involved in the DeGraff case, why would you be looking into a pageant he's never been to before?" Bev's tone projected a little paranoia, mixed with insult.

Greg surprised Margot by speaking. "Ma'am, we're from the San Francisco office, and we're working a series of cold cases we think might be connected to DeGraff. While we know he hasn't worked your venue in the past, it's possible some of your other vendors may have interacted with him. We were just hoping to have a quick word with them, and also to better understand what the pageant world feels like, operationally."

By the time he finished, his cheeks were flushed. But there was such an endearing, aw shucks quality to Greg that, as Margot watched in fascination, Bev's whole demeanor changed. She clutched her hands together over her heart, leaned in as he spoke, even nodded along. She was *rapt*.

Greg hadn't even said anything that interesting as far as Margot was concerned, but this woman certainly didn't care. She was hanging on Greg's every word.

"Of course, of course, I understand completely. It's certainly a tightknit group that does these shows. You two come with me, I'll make all the introductions, make sure no one tells you any fibs." She gave Greg a little wink and Margot had to stifle a laugh.

But Greg, as socially awkward as he often was, seemed to have realized that Bev was completely swept up in him. "That would be incredibly kind of you... Now is it Ms., or is it Mrs. Townsend?"

She swatted his arm with a little giggle. "Are you trying to ask if I'm a married woman, Agent Howell?"

There was a wedding band and a sizeable diamond on her ring finger, so she was very clearly married, but Greg let her flirt, and Margot could have kissed him for it.

"Just want to be polite," he said.

"You can just call me Bev, okay?"

Margot noticed she did not clarify that she was married. If Bev was someone she was profiling, that would have been an interesting thing to flag. Since Bev was just a means to an end, Margot let it go.

Bev took them around like she was a paid escort. While she walked them through the lobby, she explained how pageants worked, the judging process, the prizes, and what made the circuit so competitive. Margot might not have thought much of Bev in general—she was just the kind of person Margot disliked instinctively—but the woman was certainly a bottomless pit of knowledge about pageants.

She had been, she told them, a runner-up for Miss California in the statewide preliminaries for Miss America. Margot didn't know the difference between Miss America and Miss USA, but based on what Bev told them Miss America was the better of the two. Something about scholarships instead of modeling contracts. Margot didn't understand how any of this was related to scholarships, but there were obviously a lot of things she didn't understand about the pageant world.

In that sense, they were lucky to have Bev around.

She introduced them to the vendors, but even in those initial meetings it became obvious that this was something of a dead end in terms of real leads to follow. Many of the vendors were so young they could have been participating in the pageants when DeGraff was doing his circuit, and those who were old enough to remember the murders had only worked in Northern California at the time.

Still, they dutifully went from booth to booth, and Margot was ever-so-slightly glad to have Bev along making the introductions. It seemed to soften the initial blow of having to talk to the FBI.

The last booth they approached was the Like Magic photo booth, where a lineup of little girls wearing more makeup than Margot had ever put on in her life were queued up to have their photos taken. Clouds of hairspray made the air around the booth almost unbreathable, and, out of sight, Margot could hear a mother commanding, "Smile. Suck in your belly. No, Destiny, *smile*."

Margot shared a quick look with Greg, who appeared queasy from the smells surrounding them.

There had been a hot dog cart outside when they entered, most likely to lure in spectators, because Margot doubted any mother here would let her child indulge in something so potentially messy. But once they got through this, she promised herself that she and Greg deserved a fully loaded hot dog out in the fresh air.

A girl sporting a bedazzled cowboy hat, her baby-blue satin outfit festooned with fringe, exited the photo area, accompanied by a woman who was wearing a bright pink sweatshirt with PAGEANT MOM on the front. The pair breezed past them and headed for the main conference room, where the judging would soon begin.

Another woman emerged, tall and willowy, her silver hair cut into a pixie. Despite the color of her hair, she had a youthful face, and Margot didn't think she was much older than forty.

The woman paused when she saw the three of them, and Bev waved her over.

After looking at the long line waiting, she seemed to debate ignoring them before she approached, looking slightly peeved at the demand on her time.

"Sam, these are FBI agents." Bev lowered her voice to a whisper for the last part, tying Sam into their conspiracy. "They just have a few questions." Bev swept a hand towards Sam, inviting Margot and Greg to proceed.

Margot couldn't wait to get out of there.

"Sam, is that short for Samantha?" Margot asked, politely fishing for the woman's full name.

"Well, it's not short for Samwise," the woman huffed, digging in the waist apron she was wearing and handing Margot a glossy business card.

Sam Reed.

"Sam, we're working on the Ricky DeGraff case." Margot

watched the woman's face carefully, and for the first time that day she saw something interesting.

All the other vendors and people they had spoken to were either too young to clearly remember the case, or they remembered it and their first reaction was one of disgust or horror.

Sam was different. When Margot said Ricky's name, Sam's eyebrow went up, but her expression wasn't the same as everyone else's had been. She didn't seem appalled or frightened. She was just curious.

"Ricky DeGraff? Isn't he in prison already?"

"He is," Margot confirmed. "But we have reason to believe there may be additional crimes he committed that were previously not connected to him."

Sam's expression was stoic. "How interesting. And how, exactly, can I help with that?"

"We have been asking if anyone here may remember DeGraff—since he did the pageant circuit, we thought there might be some crossover."

Sam thoughtfully considered this, thumbing the pocket of her apron, before finally letting out a little huff.

"Yes, I knew Ricky," she said finally.

Margot tried to tamp down some of the excitement that had flooded into her body. Just because they finally had someone who'd known him didn't necessarily mean anything.

"How did you know Mr. DeGraff?" she asked.

"I used to be his assistant."

TWENTY-NINE

The convention center's small cafeteria was blessedly empty because judging had gotten underway in several categories and most of the girls had headed into the conference rooms.

Those that weren't in this batch of performances were practicing their dance routines and struts out in the main lobby, the sound of Britney Spears' song "Lucky" was playing on a loop, and even through the walls it was starting to make Margot feel like she'd taken a short trip to hell.

Sam Reed sat across from Margot and Greg at a plastic table. They all had a coffee in front of them, but Sam hadn't touched hers and her knee was bouncing under the table, making the whole thing vibrate.

"Can you tell us more about your history with DeGraff?" Greg urged, seeming to notice that Sam's attention really wasn't with them.

They'd let her finish shooting all the waiting girls she'd had in line, but it was clear she wanted to be anywhere else.

Margot watched her closely. She had the kind of face that would never be called *pretty* exactly, but might have been noted as *handsome* in a Jane Austen novel. She had sharp, arresting features and strong bone structure, but everything was just a bit much. She was an interesting person to look at, though.

"Look, I'm not really sure what you're hoping to get out of this. For a very short time I was Ricky's assistant. I was seventeen at the time, and I worked with him for one summer because I was planning to go to art school to study photography. I thought that spending a summer with a real photographer would give me some insights into how the whole thing worked."

"And did it?" Margot asked.

Sam scoffed. "I had these big, ambitious dreams of being a landscape photographer, of camping out in the Utah wilderness to get those perfect *National Geographic* shots of sunrises and wildlife, the things that win awards and people hang in their houses."

"What happened?"

"Ricky happened." Sam sipped her coffee, and a small part of Margot wondered why she had waited so long. "I don't want you to misunderstand what I'm saying. Ricky never laid a hand on me. Never hurt me, never said a single threatening thing to me. When I heard what he'd done, I was shocked. I didn't believe it. So don't get it twisted. What Ricky changed was the entire professional trajectory of my career. He showed me that in life, in real life, passion has to come second to money. When I was seventeen, I thought that was such a radical, capitalist thing to say. I rejected it. But then he asked me, *how are you going to pay for all that gear? How are you going to afford all those trips?* He just knocked some common sense into me."

"Sounds a little depressing," Greg said quietly.

Sam shrugged. "Maybe. But it's the reality of things, at least in this country, isn't it? You have to have an income if you're going to have a dream. I ended up leaving art school early, starting my own photo company. Ricky was supportive, he gave me some great wisdom, showed me how to work the pageant circuit, how to make the moms trust you, how to upsell the packages. I wanted to photograph mountains, but it turns out the money is in soft-focus headshots of pre-teens." She finished off the last of her coffee.

"During your time with him, did DeGraff ever ask you to assist him with anything other than photography?"

Sam fidgeted with her cup. "I'm not really sure what you're implying, but if you're asking if he and I had some kind of relationship, we didn't. I'm pretty sure I'm not Ricky's type, if you know what I mean." She gave them a meaningful look, and it didn't take an expert profiler to understand what she was implying.

"I was actually wondering if he ever enlisted your help, maybe with private photoshoots, things he did at his house?"

This time Sam looked genuinely confused. "Ricky didn't do shoots at his house. He said I could probably get away with doing that sort of thing, but for a man, he thought parents might find it a little strange, even with the proper setups. He was very thoughtful like that, always worried about how things might be perceived."

This gave Margot a pause. "Did he ever invite you over to his house?"

Sam wrinkled her nose. "No. That might have been a little unseemly for him, I guess. He really worried about what people thought of him. A lot."

Margot wasn't so sure it was perception that Ricky was worried about.

She suspected it was more likely he didn't want anyone to see who he really was behind closed doors.

"Did Ricky have any close friends, or friends he might have mentioned or introduced you to?"

Sam was distracted. Her gaze kept drifting back towards the open doors of the cafeteria. The Britney song was no longer playing, so perhaps it was time for one session to end and another to begin. More people would be waiting for photos.

"No," she replied finally. "He had a different assistant before me, I don't remember her name, but I think he said she also went on to start her own company, so maybe check other female photographers on the circuit? I heard a rumor she found Jesus and left pageants completely, but no one puts a lot of stock in rumors like that, it's just catty bullshit. Look, I want to be helpful, but I really don't know much. Do you mind if I get back to work? Every minute I'm here, I'm not there." She jerked her chin towards the doors, where small voices were getting louder and laughter echoed through the halls.

"Yes, you can go. We'll call you if we have any additional questions."

As Sam slipped back into the noisy lobby, Margot watched her go, more curious than anything else. She drummed her fingernails on the tabletop for a moment before finally pushing back her chair.

"Greg, I think you and I deserve a hot dog. My treat."

Whether Greg actually wanted the hot dog or not, he nodded his agreement and followed her back outside. While they inhaled deep lungfuls of clean-ish Northern California air, Margot's phone buzzed in her pocket.

She assumed it was Andrew either checking in on their progress or letting them know if something had been found back at the office, but instead it was Wes.

Wes never called while she was working. He always sent texts.

She answered with her heart in her throat, barely able to get out a, "Wes?"

On the other end of the line his voice was tired, and, more than that, Margot could tell he was angry. "Margot, you'd better get back here."

"What's going on? We're just in Petaluma."

Wes replied bluntly, "Someone burned down the barn."

THIRTY

Margot thanked God she and Greg had driven separately to the pageant, because it meant she could head right home without worrying about abandoning him at the convention center.

She texted Andrew before she pulled out onto the highway, and it took him less than three minutes to call her back.

"You think this is related to the situation up there?" he asked, getting right to the point.

"I don't see that it can be anything else," she answered, trying to focus on the road when all she wanted to do was pull over and start screaming. Why was this happening to her? Why was her family, her property the target of such violence?

She knew why, but it was still a hard pill to swallow. When people had turned against her born family in Petaluma it made sense. Ed Finch had been guilty. Ed Finch was a monster. In a way, Margot almost felt like they deserved the hate they were getting. Ed was locked up and people had nowhere else to direct their rage. It didn't make living with it any easier, but she *understood* it, even as a teenager.

This, though, this she couldn't understand. Wes wasn't a killer, he was a free man. The DA had apologized for his arrest. There was a *pile* of concrete evidence that he was completely innocent, and no one seemed to care.

They saw an easy target, and they weren't being shy about letting her family know they were no longer welcome.

That people were driving all the way from Willows—fifteen minutes of time to think, to reconsider—and were still singling them out, told Margot all she needed to know.

These people didn't care about logic or reason. They didn't care that someone *else* was out there, someone who had actually killed Whitney.

It was so much easier to dig their claws in and keep this going to the bitter end.

But Margot didn't know what that end was.

Wes in prison?

Them moving?

Neither of those things were going to happen.

"Can I do anything? Talk to the sheriff about getting you protection?" Andrew offered.

"For all I know one of the volunteer deputies could be the one doing this," Margot replied. "No, we have to handle this on our own. I'll keep working remotely tomorrow; Greg can fill you in on what we learned today."

"Margot, forget work right now. You're important to this team, and we need you, but I'm worried about you. Your safety and the safety of your family matters more than a case."

She almost snapped back that he hadn't been worried when her partner was in jail. The case had been more important then. But she managed to restrain herself. Andrew was being uncharacteristically kind to her and she didn't want to look the gift horse in the mouth.

"Thank you," she replied. "I'll let you know what's going on when I know more."

A little over an hour and several broken speed limits later, she pulled into her driveway. The volunteer fire department's truck was still there, but the fire itself appeared to be out. Smoke curled into the air, but there was no active fire once Margot got out of her car, her stomach somewhere in her shoes, her mouth hanging open in shock. She made her way up to the small huddle near the edge of what had once been their barn, though she barely remembered taking a single step.

Now it was the shell of a barn; the hundred-year-old beams, though thoroughly charred, still held stubbornly in place, but the peeling red exterior had been almost entirely burned away.

Wes and Sadie were sitting on the front steps, staring forlornly in the direction of the destroyed building. Margot would join them just as soon as rational thought was back in the forefront of her mind. Right now, all she could feel was a helpless kind of fury that could only manifest itself in screaming, crying, or hitting things.

She took several deep breaths to remind herself that this, much like the brick attack, could have been worse.

While she and Wes had talked about rescuing larger farm animals because they had an empty barn and plenty of land, they hadn't yet gotten that far. They'd done some work fixing up the interior of the barn to make it livable if they decided to take those next steps, but there had been no one living in the barn. Even the cats rarely went in it. She'd have to do a head count, but for the moment she refused to believe there were any feline fatalities. She simply *couldn't* let that be a possibility.

All of the cats liked to be within viewing distance of one of their humans at all times. They were always in the house unless Margot or Wes was outside. The chicken coop was across the yard from the barn, and it appeared the only other building that had sustained damage was the workshop shed where she kept all the dog food and medications. Even there, it looked to mostly be smoke damage that had charred the grey exterior.

Margot took a deep breath, trying to soothe herself, though her hands were balled into such tight fists she could feel her nails digging into the flesh of her palms.

She walked away from the fire crew, who were all focused on

making sure there were no hot spots left in the wreckage that might flare up again, and crossed the gravel driveway towards Wes.

He was wearing jeans and a button-down plaid shirt, like perhaps he had just been getting ready to do the evening yard chores when he realized what was happening. His cheeks and blond hair were streaked with soot.

He got to his feet the moment he saw her coming, and, once they met, halfway between the house and the fire truck, he wrapped his arms around her, squeezing tightly. She wasn't sure if this was meant to calm her, or comfort himself, but she yielded to it gladly, melting into him. That familiar clean, soapy smell was tinged with smoke, but it was still Wes, still home, and she felt the vengeful tension she had been carrying give way.

Her eyes stung, but she chose to tell herself it was from the smoke in the air and not because she was crying.

The loud voices of the firefighters faded away, and Margot let herself just *be* in Wes's arms for a moment.

Finally, she sniffed, swiped at her eyes, and gave him a quick kiss before letting him lead her back to where Sadie was sitting. Her sister-in-law was staring at the smoldering wreckage of the barn, her jaw tight.

"Why would they do something like this?" she asked, though it seemed like it was more a question to the universe than to either Wes or Margot.

"They want me to leave," Wes said flatly, sitting back down on the step beside his sister. He put an arm around her and pulled her close, pressing a gentle kiss to the side of her head before rubbing her arm as if to warm her.

"Maybe you should leave," Sadie said.

Margot felt immediately defensive, but, before she could speak, Wes shook his head. "No. If I go, they just get the proof they want that I'm guilty. This is my community. This is my home. I'm not going anywhere." Margot knew he was waiting for his temporary suspension from school to lift, that he wanted to go back to work when this was all done, but she personally couldn't imagine working alongside people who could have imagined he was capable of murder.

"But what if next time it's the house? What if next time it's Margot, or it's you?" Sadie's voice, usually so calm and steady, had an edge of hysteria to it now.

Margot couldn't blame her—she'd asked herself these same questions, even as she insisted she would never leave.

All she'd wanted was a home. Somewhere safe, somewhere permanent. Margot wasn't afraid, not the way Sadie was, but she was furious. How dare they take away her peace? Her quiet retreat?

Maybe you don't deserve peace, Ed's voice said, an afterthought, but an ever-present one. *You're the killer in the family, after all.*

She shook it off, trying to push the unpleasant notion down.

Most days Margot didn't think of herself as a killer. Some days, she didn't think about Ed at all. But sometimes, when her guard was down and she thought she might be on the cusp of feeling pretty good about her life, there he was, a little voice she couldn't get away from, reminding her of all the things she wanted to leave in the past.

A part of her, though, a part of her wondered if all of this bullshit being directed at Wes was actually the universe's way of punishing *her*. She was the one who had killed someone. She was the one with a closet full of skeletons.

There was, perhaps, a tiny piece of her that wondered if she deserved this.

But even in the murkiest pits of her own self-doubt, she *knew* Wes didn't deserve it. And right now, Wes was who it was targeted at.

"Tell me what happened," she said, wanting to focus on details instead of her own self-doubt and pity. "Is everyone okay?"

It was obvious that, at least physically, Wes and Sadie were in one piece, and neither of them appeared to be injured.

"The dogs are all accounted for," Wes answered, knowing

what she was really asking. "Five of the cats were in the house. We haven't seen Lucy." His voice cracked at the end of that sentence and Margot's heart sank.

Lucy wouldn't have been in the barn, would she? She stayed close to the house, close to Margot. She only went outside when Margot did her rounds.

But Margot hadn't been home.

What if Lucy had been outside looking for her?

A pit formed in her stomach, but she tried not to let it grow. There were strangers everywhere. The fire truck would have made a lot of noise coming up the driveway, not to mention all the water and shouting.

No. She couldn't believe that her sweet Lucy had been in that barn.

"Okay," she said, her voice thick. "Did you see who did it?"

Wes shook his head. "Sadie and I went to Orland. We wanted to avoid Willows, but we needed a few things to finish sealing the window, and I wanted to fill up the fridge." His attention drifted to the smoking hull of their former barn, and the immediate guilt that clouded his expression almost broke her heart.

"Hey, look at me." She crouched in front of him and took his hand in hers, squeezing it firmly. "This isn't your fault. They would have done something no matter what, because whoever is doing this, they're scared and they're fucked up and they're cruel. But you were safe. Sadie was safe. That's all that matters. This isn't your fault."

"Isn't it, though? They wouldn't have come if..."

"Wes, you didn't hurt that girl. Don't think like that."

His skin was dusty from sitting outside and she brushed back his sandy hair, using one hand to turn his face towards her.

"Would Steve McQueen blame himself for this?"

This little inside joke seemed to be enough to pull him out of his self-induced shame spiral. He let out a little snort of laughter and managed to catch his breath, taking one shaky inhale before he squeezed her hand back.

Sadie gave them a funny look. "Didn't Steve McQueen notoriously abuse his wives?" she asked, her nose wrinkled. "And cheat on all of them?"

Margot nodded. "It's not the *actual* Steve McQueen we invoke. It's the *idea* of Steve McQueen." She smiled at Wes.

"You guys should invoke the idea of Paul Newman instead," Sadie said, resting her chin in her hand. "Fewer car chases, much happier marriage."

Margot smiled at this, happy Sadie was feeling more easy with them.

"Did the security cameras get whoever did this?" Margot asked, hoping that by keeping Sadie involved, it might keep their relationship from veering towards the unfriendliness Margot had felt from her earlier.

She knew why Sadie had been keeping her at arm's length. Sadie and Wes were the closest in age of the Fox siblings, which had formed a tight bond between them that never loosened. Sadie would do anything for Wes, even if that meant protecting him from Margot if Sadie decided that was necessary.

Margot hoped she could mend her friendship with her sister-in-common-law, and the easiest way to start that was to make sure she felt included in what was happening.

"Yes and no," Wes said with a sigh. "We think they might have realized they were being filmed last time, or maybe coming up in daylight they saw the signs. We can see a black truck drive by about twenty minutes after Sadie and I leave, and then nothing until we got back."

Their camera only faced the road and driveway. They'd never anticipated needing coverage elsewhere.

"You think they drove down the road and then came in around the side?" she said.

Wes nodded. "Yeah. When we got back there was no one on the street, but the barn was fully engulfed. We called the fire department but there was no saving it."

Margot sat down on the steps next to Wes and held his hand

while the three of them took in the scope of the damage. There was an aching spot in her chest that she didn't want to give name to, or pay too close attention to, but she knew it wouldn't go away until she saw Lucy.

When Margot was a child, she had talked her parents into letting her get a pet. She'd chosen a hamster and named him Phillip. She had *loved* that tiny ball of fluff, even if his squeaky wheel kept her up at night. She loved sitting in front of his cage, coaxing him into taking treats from her hand, and she drew sketches of his little face, his nose and whiskers.

But one morning she woke up and Phillip was gone.

Her father said he must have gotten out of his cage. Escaped.

But Margot knew. She knew deep in the darkest recesses of her soul that Ed had just gotten sick of the noise. That he didn't want to deal with it anymore. That Phillip had to go.

Margot hadn't owned another pet until she was in her late thirties and Betty came into her life.

Sweet, old Betty. Mostly blind, she'd had the misfortune of being owned by a man who Margot learned was a killer. And that man decided he wasn't going to go to jail.

In the end, Margot had gone home with the dog, because no one else was likely to give an ancient Maltese dog a chance.

Betty, who had already been a super-senior when Margot took her in, somehow lived another three years. It was Betty who had convinced Margot it was okay to open your heart to things. That it was okay to let love into your life that way.

That no one was going to take her pets away in the middle of the night and kill them.

Except now, looking at the barn, and not knowing where Lucy was, Margot felt a terrible misplaced guilt in herself. She had brought those animals into her home promising them a better life. She had believed that they were safer here, that they'd be happier here.

She had thought Phillip would be happy when she'd brought him home, too.

Maybe this was her.

Maybe she was the dangerous one.

A man wearing a soot-covered firefighter's uniform approached them, and the strong smell of burning that radiated off him brought Margot's memory back to a crime scene, a burnt-out car, a woman who should have been dead.

She had to force herself back into the present so as not to get totally bogged down in the past; it was remarkable, really, what scent could do to memory.

"Hey folks, it looks like we've got this under control, but we have to warn you not to go looking through the building after we go. There could still be hidden hot spots, and structurally that thing just needs one strong breeze to take her down. You'll want to get the insurance folks out here to have a look, but our report is going to say this is a clear case of arson. Found a half-melted jerry can about ten feet from the back of the barn. Really sorry this happened to you."

He did seem genuinely sorry, too, which was a surprise to Margot. Given how the last week had gone for them, she'd started to believe everyone in Willows and the surrounding areas hated them unilaterally, but this man wasn't looking at Wes and Margot like they were villains. He was treating them like victims, which was what they were.

The man went on. "Just between us, Coach, I think what they've been saying about you is a load of horse manure. I think it was that Seaver boy that did her in."

Margot perked up, the investigator in her never able to ignore a potential lead. "Seaver?"

The fireman looked at her, then nodded. "Well, sure. My son told me that Whitney and Clayton Seaver had been dating for over a year, mostly kept it quiet, but said things were a little rocky between them at a party a few weeks back. He's the one that told me they were barking up the wrong tree with Coach Fox. Not that anyone thought different."

Margot wanted to point to her burnt-out barn to remind him

that, yes, there were indeed people who believed differently, but he was giving her a lead, and that was more than they'd had in this situation since Wes had gotten home.

"Does the sheriff know about Whitney's relationship with Clayton?" Margot asked.

The fireman shook his head. "I'm sorry, ma'am, I couldn't say. I don't like to gossip."

He left them huddled together on the porch, and though Margot knew this wasn't her case, and she *knew* she shouldn't get involved, every single fiber of her being was telling her she needed to talk to Clayton Seaver.

THIRTY-ONE
WILLOWS

He'd left California.

He'd gone to Oregon, craving cooler weather, greener environments. He couldn't stay in one place too long. It was too dangerous to establish a pattern, to become known.

When he'd left Willows behind him, the feverish discussion in town he'd been able to pick up was that one faction of locals believed it was a local coach. Another believed the girl had a secret boyfriend.

They were all so busy looking for the bad apple in their own bushel, they hadn't bothered to wonder if it had been someone else.

They hadn't been looking for him.

That was good, because he needed to go back and take care of the rest of the evidence he'd left behind. It was tucked away, no one was likely to find it by accident, but he didn't want to take any unnecessary risks.

He spent three days driving around, creating a history for himself in other places. He rented a motel room for two nights in northern Oregon, then left. He didn't spend a single night there, but his credit card said he did. He was sure to buy gas there on his own card as well.

Then he headed into Idaho, this time using a stolen debit card.

The man he'd taken it from must not have anyone looking too hard for him, because the card still worked. Eventually it became useless, they all did, but he had plenty to choose from. Taking out cash would be easier, but ATMs had cameras and large withdrawals were bigger triggers for banks and investigators than small things. A tank of gas, a drive-thru meal, these were normal purchases, even if they were being made in unusual places. Families might think they were just dealing with someone who had decided they didn't want to be found.

Someone alive.

The man couldn't blame people for holding out hope.

Hope kept him paid.

But the previous owner of this debit card was never coming home. And sooner or later someone was going to realize it. He just had to make sure he dumped this card and was on to the next before that happened.

On the road, finding a *next* was never really an issue, it was just being prepared to take on that challenge when he found it. The girl in Willows might have been a mistake. The town was small and she was young; it was too much attention—even if none of it was directed at him—so he needed to go back and make sure his trail was completely covered.

He hadn't wanted to leave her like that, so easy to find. He'd meant to take her body back to her car after, drive it somewhere well outside of town where it could be hidden, where no one would find her for months, and he would be like a ghost who had barely been noticed as he passed through town.

Right now, he was lucky. Their focus was on people who knew the girl.

That gave him an opening, a chance to go back and cover things up, make sure no one found his kit.

The kit would give them too many clues. Too much insight.

He didn't need anyone to find it.

He had others, but that wasn't the point.

Night was falling in Willows by the time he drove back

through. The streets were nearly empty, like people were afraid to be out after dark.

This made him smile, because he knew the truth.

People should be just as afraid of being out in the daylight as they were of the dark.

There was no safe time.

THIRTY-TWO

After they had eaten a tense and simple dinner—thank goodness Wes and Sadie had bought groceries—Margot went to her office and found the file Andrew had given her.

She brought it out to the living room, where Sadie was already starting to nod off on the couch, but also didn't seem to want to go back to her room. Margot could understand that. There was an unresolved tension in the house, a guitar string pulled too tightly, and they were all just waiting for it to snap.

Waiting for the next thing to go wrong.

She hated the feeling of walking on tiptoes in her own home, of not being safe. But she knew this was just the way it was going to feel until there was some real resolution in the case.

Maybe when the BSU finally came through with a profile, things would ease up, but who knew when that would be. The BSU had an endless pile of requests from both within the FBI and outside law enforcement. Anyone who wanted a second set of expert eyes on their crime turned to that division, which meant they had very little time for each case, and never enough time for the cases still coming.

Margot didn't envy them the work they did. A never-ending parade of horrors with no closure.

Well, she wanted closure for this one.

She slapped the thick file down on the coffee table. Wes looked up from the book he'd been pretending to read and eyed the folder warily, as if it were a rattlesnake that might suddenly decide to jump at him.

"What's that?" he asked.

"I think you know what that is." She settled into the armchair across from the couch.

"I probably shouldn't be looking at that." But he was inching closer to the edge of his seat, his apprehension turning to interest before her eyes.

"Well, I've looked at it, so I don't really see the harm in *you* looking at it." She had considered that it might not be such a good idea, especially if it meant that Wes might know things specific to the case that only the killer would know, but she realized that her having the file was its own insurance in that regard. He would know because she knew.

She also believed that, despite everything happening to them, the sheriff had to know Wes wasn't actually guilty. Otherwise, he wouldn't still be a free man.

"How did you even get that?" He looked up at her, brows pinched.

"I didn't steal it from the sheriff, so put that expression away, please."

"My expressions make themselves, I can't help it." He picked up the folder.

"I got it from the FBI. It looks like at least someone in the local sheriff's department has some common sense and they were convinced that help from the BSU might actually be beneficial."

Wes made a small *hmm* sound and started to leaf through the documents. Sadie wrinkled up her nose and looked away, not wanting to see what was inside. Margot hadn't brought the file out to upset her, but she wanted Wes to have all the information she did, and she didn't want to make Sadie feel excluded from the family discussion.

That evening had been exhausting. They'd had to contact their insurance company to file a claim on the barn. They'd reported the situation to Deputy Cassidy, who had come out to have a look, but didn't say much that sounded very helpful. She did, however, take the partially melted jerry can with her to see if they might be able to lift any prints off it.

After all that—and still no sign of Lucy—they had decided they should eat dinner, even if they didn't feel like it.

Margot left a dish of kibble out on the front steps. It would probably just attract wildlife like opossums and skunks, but still, she clung to the hope that Lucy was just hiding somewhere, spooked by the day's happenings.

She didn't have the emotional bandwidth to believe the worst-case scenario.

She also had a meeting invite for first thing in the morning with the team so they could share reports on what everyone had learned. While the headway she and Greg had made that morning was minimal, it was still something. They hadn't previously known that DeGraff had employed not one but multiple assistants. Despite everything else going on in her personal life, she couldn't help but be excited about the prospect of sharing their new knowledge with the rest of the team.

It was becoming clear the further they dug into this case that there was a lot they didn't know about Ricky DeGraff.

Margot headed into the kitchen and made them each a Tom Collins. She drank a lot less these days than she once had, but nevertheless there were still times in your life that gin was a welcome friend, and tonight was one of those times.

She passed around the cold drinks and then sat back in the armchair to watch Wes look over the file. He was perched on the edge of the couch, wearing his reading glasses. He only ever wore them at home, so whenever she saw him put them on it gave her an unexpected feeling of warmth, that she got to see him like that. Sadie was on the opposite end of the couch with a crochet project in her lap, her dark blonde hair piled in a bun on top of her head.

Wes was putting the pages of the file he had finished with beside her, letting her see them if she wanted, but Sadie didn't so much as glance at them. She was evidently not curious at all about how Whitney had died, a very normal reaction for those who hadn't spent time working in homicide.

Wes's expression gave away very little of what he was thinking, but she noticed that he only took a cursory look at the photos before tucking them behind the other reports. Margot wasn't sure if this was to keep Sadie from seeing them, or because he didn't want to look at them himself.

There was a big difference between being an objective observer when the victim was a stranger, and looking at photos of a dead girl he had personally known. Wes had too much empathy to look at those photos and not see Whitney, the person.

It was also impossible not to see his rumpled jacket lying close to her, and that couldn't be easy.

It hadn't been easy for Margot.

"Do you know what the BSU said about this?" Wes asked.

"What's the BSU?" Sadie interjected, focusing intently on their faces so she didn't accidentally look at the folder. Wes seemed to realize what she was doing and closed the file, setting it back on the coffee table. He took a long sip from his drink.

"The BSU is a special investigative unit within the FBI. They help create profiles for unsubs..." Margot paused, trying to gauge Sadie's knowledge of FBI case lingo, before adding, "Unknown subjects, the likely killer or killers in a case. This can help local law enforcement narrow down their suspect pool or help them hone their focus. The profiles are rarely perfect, but they're usually eerily close. And to answer your question, Wes, I don't know if they've even seen it yet. I'm not technically supposed to have any involvement in this."

"But they still let you have a copy?" Sadie asked.

Her incredulous expression was entirely too close to Wes's for Margot's taste. They usually looked quite different, but now, side by side on the couch, both looking to her for an explanation, Margot was feeling the full weight of the Fox family judgement.

"BSU didn't let *me* have a copy. But my boss got a copy..." Her voice drifted.

Wes gave the faintest smirk, and nodded.

Sadie looked unconvinced by this weak explanation, as she sipped her drink. "So, does it prove Wes is innocent?" she asked.

"No," Wes answered plainly. "But it does at least include all the evidence I have in my favor. And most of the interviews they did seem to suggest I still have a few friends in this town." He gave Margot a soft smile.

"Vice Principal Aldean is coming off the Christmas card list, though," Margot said. "Bitch."

That made Wes snicker. "She was never my biggest fan to begin with. But, no, while it doesn't show I'm guilty, there's still the circumstantial evidence. Still, if I were the one investigating the case, there isn't enough here for me to take this to the prosecutor. The case is loaded with reasonable doubt."

"And for good reason," Sadie said, bitterly. "Because you didn't fucking do it."

"Hey, you don't need to convince anyone in this room," he reminded her. "We're all on Team Wes."

"The main problem is, there isn't a lot in that file about anyone else. Unless they get trace fibers off whoever did this to her, which is unlikely because of the rain we got that night, they don't really have anyone else to look at," Margot said.

She had passed on the comments the firefighter made about Clayton Seaver to Deputy Cassidy when she came to look at the fire damage, but even Flo had sort of batted those notions away.

"He's a good kid, just gets into a little trouble sometimes," she'd insisted.

Margot liked Flo, and she appreciated that the younger woman's bottomless pit of optimism was supporting Wes. But she did have to wonder if Flo was simply incapable of seeing anyone in town as being a potential killer.

"I'm going to go out for a bit," Margot said now, setting her untouched drink down on a coaster.

Wes raised an eyebrow. "Out?"

"Yeah, I'll go grab us some ice cream or something, have a look around for Lucy."

"Do you want—" Sadie began, but then caught a look from Wes.

Margot knew the silent sibling communication was telling her not to ask any more questions, but a shift in Sadie's expression told Margot she wasn't impressed by what was happening either.

Margot had already grabbed her keys, though, and despite Elk Creek being tiny, and despite it being a place where most people didn't lock their doors at night, she was still now, and always would be, the daughter of Ed Finch. She locked the door so no one inside would forget to do it. Before she left, she checked the app on her phone that was connected to the security camera, just to make sure everything was still running smoothly.

They had already ordered an extra camera for the back.

It wasn't just wildlife that might sneak up behind them anymore.

Margot climbed into her car and backed out of the driveway, her pulse racing, and a heady flush of adrenaline coursing through her. She wasn't just going for a drive to clear her mind. She had a very specific destination in mind. If she was calmer, less reactive, she might have talked herself out of it.

But despite all her better angels, she was still someone who could make a stupid choice if she felt it was the necessary one.

The stretch of land between her ranch and Willows was a desolate drive, with almost no traffic. The only car she saw was a truck, which once again made her do a double take.

Once again, it was not black.

It might have even been the same one she'd seen parked a few days earlier. A local, just like her, minding their own damned business. She didn't mingle with the people around her, perhaps to her own detriment, so she had no idea who the truck belonged to.

When she looked back, it was gone, disappeared either around a bend or into a driveway she had failed to pay much attention to.

Margot needed to get better at learning her surroundings. Complacency was how people got killed.

She should at least know who was living nearby.

In case.

What that was in case of, she didn't want to think.

When she got to Willows it was after dark, and, aside from the cars parked outside the diner and a few other food joints in town, things were relatively dead. Most of the shops closed at five, so there was very little to bring people out after dark, especially now that the weather was getting colder.

And now that someone had been killed.

Those sorts of things tended to drive people inside.

Margot had never been to the Seaver house before, but it wasn't hard to find out where it was. Everyone knew where everyone lived in a town like Willows, and that meant the area's phone book—something that did indeed still exist—was up to date with addresses.

The Seavers lived about a minute or so from downtown Willows, but still technically out of town. They didn't have an address—a road marker, instead—and Margot hesitated on the dirt road where they lived. The lights were on inside, and the place looked homey. An American flag in pristine condition fluttered beside the door, and there were pots of mums on the front step.

It wasn't any of this that made Margot's mind up for her.

It was the black truck in the driveway.

There might be a lot of black trucks in town, but she recognized this one as if it had just driven out of her memory and into the gravel.

It was the same truck she'd seen in her own driveway.

Margot pulled into the drive. The pulse-pounding adrenaline she had felt when she left the house had faded, and a familiar sense of calm suffused her. The same feeling she'd had in the past when entering a building with a potentially armed suspect. The excitement or shock would settle in later. In that moment she was as Zen as a Buddhist monk. She was armed—FBI agents were required to be armed at almost any time they were outside their own home—but she didn't really care what message that sent. Besides, they'd be hard pressed to see her weapon with her jacket over it, and if Clayton Seaver *had* been the one to kill Whitney, then Margot wasn't going to be confronting him without a weapon.

As stupid as all of this was, she wasn't *that* stupid.

She knocked on the door and a moment later a small woman with round cheeks and a rounder body opened the door. She was wiping her hands on a dishrag, but the moment she saw Margot she went entirely still, her eyes widening.

"Good, you know who I am, then," Margot said coolly.

"Yes, ma'am."

"And I'm going to assume that big black truck out there isn't the vehicle *you* regularly drive around town."

The woman's face turned red, a visible mix of anger and frustration crossing her features, and then she bellowed, "*Rodney!*"

Margot was impressed by the volume that a relatively small woman could manage.

A moment later the sound of footsteps clamored from the stairs behind her, and a man appeared who was very much the woman's opposite. Rodney was at least six foot five, built like a lumberjack, and looked about as dumb and as mean as a box of bricks.

"What?" he asked, directing his question at the woman. Despite her small stature—she looked pint-sized next to the man Margot assumed was her husband—the woman didn't show the slightest sign of fear. Instead, her expression hardened, and she jerked her chin in Margot's direction.

"Don't you *what* me, Rodney. Why is the FBI woman standing at my front door asking me about your truck? What have you been doing?" The fury in her features was more of a threat than just about anything Margot could have come up with, and she had to admit it was a bit of a joy to watch.

Rodney blanched, then gave Margot a cursory once-over. He was trying to pretend he didn't know who she was, but he was doing a piss-poor job of it.

"I'll take care of this," he grumbled to his wife. "You go finish the dishes. Nothing to worry about."

"Nothing to worry about my ass." But she obeyed his request and disappeared into the kitchen.

Rodney didn't invite Margot into the house. He stepped out onto the small front landing so she was forced to take a step down, which made him tower over her. Whether the move was intentional or not, Margot read it as an implicit threat, and it pissed her off.

"What do you want to know about my truck?" he asked, with an exaggerated sniff at the end.

This man was never going to win any awards for his acting chops, and was probably the worst poker player among his friend group. Margot hoped they wiped him clean every time they played.

"I think you know perfectly well why I'm here."

"Didn't know the FBI was handling this case."

This took Margot a moment to process. Only after a long pause did she realize there actually *was* a misunderstanding between them. Was it possible that all the shame and uncertainty she'd been reading on his face wasn't his own guilt, but his fear over his son being guilty of something?

She took a moment to really look at him, trying to get a read on those expressions with a new perspective.

"Where were you this morning around eleven?" she asked, ignoring his comment.

"I was at work."

"On a Saturday?"

"Yeah, you got a problem with a man working on a Saturday? You can fucking check if you need to."

"Where was your son this morning?"

"Fuck if I know, lady. I was at work, wasn't I?"

"Did he have access to your truck?"

Rodney shrugged. "I use the company truck during company time, guess he could have used it. He's not supposed to, but when has that ever stopped a teenager?"

"And what about three days ago? Six in the morning. You working then?"

"No, I was sleeping at six in the goddamn morning like a man with some sense. You need me to get my wife out here so you can ask her? What the fuck is this about, anyway, if it's not about that dead girl?"

Margot pulled out her phone and accessed the recording she had from the morning of the gunfire incident. She held up her phone and pressed play on the recording, letting Rodney have a good look at it.

At first his face was impassive, and then it became steadily more angry. She could see how similar he and his wife had the capacity to be.

"That's your truck," Margot said, once the video had stopped playing.

"That could be any black truck," he replied, the rebuttal coming much too quickly.

"No, I think we both know that's your truck. But if you were sleeping when this happened, then I think we both know who did this to my house. And who came by this morning when no one was home and lit my goddamn barn on fire."

"What the fuck do you want me to do about it, huh? All you have is some dark footage and a guess."

"I'm very good at guessing."

Margot got the sense this was a man who liked to use his size and his bluster to get people to back down, but she wasn't like most people, and he was about to learn it didn't matter how tall, how broad, or how loud a man was. She wasn't going to yield to intimidation.

"Then go to the cops."

"I will. And while I'm there, I'll tell them all about how your son was involved with *that dead girl* as you call her. And that only days before her murder, multiple witnesses saw them arguing. And I think that information, coupled with things like arson and threats, is sure going to make them want to take a good, long look at him."

"My son didn't kill anyone," Rodney snapped.

"And how the fuck would you know that if you didn't even know he'd done this?" She waved her phone at him. "Do yourself a favor. Tell your son to admit he's the one who has been harassing my family."

"Or what?"

Margot was already heading back to her car, her blood boiling, hands itching to throw a punch. She spun around and looked at him, not an ounce of friendliness, fake or otherwise, in her expression.

"This isn't an *or what* situation, Rodney. You tell Clayton to talk to the police. I don't need to make threats. If it doesn't happen, you'll find out pretty fucking quickly why he should have."

She got into her car, slamming the door behind her.

While it hadn't been the visit she'd planned on, she couldn't help but feel the first bit of relief that she'd felt in quite some time.

It felt *good* to have a target for her anger.

Even if that target was a teenaged boy.

Now it just remained to be seen if he would do the right thing.

THIRTY-THREE

Cold cases, by definition, were used to long waits.

But cold cases once opened by Margot's team waited for no one. It was the morning after her barn had burned down, but Margot still had a job to do. Once again, the team were politely aware of what was going on in her personal life, but it ultimately wasn't going to slow down the work they were doing on the DeGraff case.

While Margot waited for Clayton Seaver to face the music, she might as well distract herself by putting her head down and working through the DeGraff case with the others.

This was something she could sink her teeth into, a case where she could actually find some immediate resolution. Knowing that made her eager to delve back into its depths and push her own troubles aside for a few hours. Like getting absorbed in a great jigsaw puzzle.

She locked herself into her office and listened to the team get into details about what they'd learned over the past few days. Margot's head wasn't entirely in it, though. She kept thinking about her confrontation with Rodney Seaver, and wondered if it was possible that he was covering for his son about more than just the vandalism on Margot's property.

Would he also be willing to help cover up a murder?

And then, closer to home, they still hadn't had a single sign of Lucy. The food Margot had left out overnight had remained untouched. While Margot wanted to cling to hope, she couldn't bear to think about the more likely reality. It was more than she could handle just then. She knew how hard it was to lose pets; that was one of the biggest pitfalls of adopting senior dogs.

But Lucy wasn't old.

Margot had had her since she was a kitten. She was one of the first animals they'd adopted when she and Wes had bought the ranch.

Lucy was supposed to be around until she was twenty and couldn't get up from the couch.

She wasn't supposed to be lost at five, and in such a horrific and unnecessary way.

Margot shifted her attention back to the call. Sydney was talking about the work the tech team had done, and it was impressive enough that Margot soon found her sole focus was back on the case.

Using the photo Margot and Alana had gotten from DeGraff Senior, they were able to reverse-search the internet until they found what appeared to be a match. The doll they believed to be Mathilda was from a manufacturer called Bellson's Belles that made a variety of high-end collectible dolls in the twenties and thirties. The company was eventually bought out by Sears and both the quality and cost of the dolls dropped considerably, according to the online doll forums Sydney and the tech team had scoured.

The doll that Ricky's mother had bought from the estate sale was a model called the Rosalind. Adjusting for inflation, the doll would have cost about five hundred dollars new in its time. Even at estate sale pricing, there was no doubt it had been more than DeGraff Senior could afford, but he had still bought it for her.

This also went a long way towards explaining why that particular doll was one that both of Ricky's parents would not have wanted him to play with on his own.

He had perceived it as them not wanting him to play with dolls at all—and that might have been true for his father—but, seeing it from this perspective, there was more to it than Ricky had understood at the time, or even understood now.

"Are they valuable now?" Margot asked. She sometimes worried about being the odd one out on their group calls owing to her special circumstances, and tried her best to remain involved, even if that just meant asking questions to keep the conversation moving forward.

"There's a very niche market for doll collecting now, it's definitely not as big as it used to be, especially with the ubiquity of things like American Girl dolls changing the national market," Sydney explained. "But for certain dolls, there is definitely a market, and our Rosalind is a very sought-after doll. I guess the short-lived manufacturing window and her initial high value have made her a bit of a star on the doll collector market. There have been six sales in the last ten years, and the dolls have all sold from between ten thousand on eBay, to twenty-five thousand in an auction for a Rosalind still in box. So it's safe to say that for the person DeGraff entrusted with his Rosalind, there could be a fair bit of temptation to get rid of her, especially considering he's never going to see the light of day again."

"And she's a fucking creepy thing to keep around," muttered Alana, and Margot couldn't help but agree.

"Have we looked into those sales made over the last ten years?" she asked. "Sellers and buyers."

"We're working with eBay to determine who owns the accounts for the online auctions, and they should be able to get that to us this week. The auction house is proving to be a bit stickier, but we'll get the information soon enough."

Margot was impressed. When they'd been in Montana Sydney had seemed uneasy about her place on the team, as if she was trying hard to both fit in and stand out so Andrew would notice her. Margot suspected she hadn't done much to impress him on the road, but right now she was doing a remarkable job. The efforts she had gone to over the last week had really put them on a new trajectory on the case.

"There's more," Sydney said, having allowed enough time for her pause to be considered dramatic.

"Oh?" Andrew asked.

"We were able to find one doll currently for sale. It's being listed by an antique store in Dallas. We've been in touch with the store owner, and the doll itself isn't in pristine condition and isn't a lead, as it belonged to a local woman who had been known for her doll collection and recently passed away at the age of ninety. But..." She was making sure they were all paying attention and Margot had to stifle a smile. "He said we could borrow the doll if it might help our case."

Everyone on the call was quiet for a beat, looking at her, waiting for some kind of response. Margot, as bogged down as she was in everything currently happening in her life, knew that leads like this didn't come along often.

She nodded once, mostly to herself, then said, "I guess we're going back to Montana."

THIRTY-FOUR

The plan was to return to Montana in two days, which gave Margot forty-eight hours to decide how she was going to use their new prop to get Ricky to give up information on his accomplice, and also to make sure that Wes was beyond suspicion before she left.

As far as she knew, Clayton Seaver hadn't yet been to the sheriff's office to confess about what he'd done to their house. Margot wasn't known for her patience, but she was going to give it another day before she told Cassidy what she knew.

Another day of looking over her shoulder.

She just had to hope that Rodney Seaver had confronted his son, and the fact that Margot knew what he'd done would be enough to make them do the right thing. And that *knowing* he was responsible would keep him from doing anything else stupid.

They had started to sleep with a shotgun next to their bedroom door, something Margot hadn't even done at the peak levels of her paranoia in San Francisco. Of course, there she'd also had a doorman and multiple deadbolts in place. The gun had never felt necessary.

Out here, at least now, it *did* feel necessary.

She prayed that wouldn't always be the case.

As she did her Tuesday morning chores, she kept her FBI-issued handgun with her. Another thing that would have seemed outlandish a few weeks earlier, but now felt like the bare minimum in protecting herself and her family.

She fed the chickens and collected the eggs. With fall setting in, their egg production was slowing. That might be a good thing, though, because they currently didn't have any of the regular ways to get rid of their egg surplus. Wes used to take them to school by the dozen, or share them among his friends in Willows and on the other farms nearby.

Margot felt a pang of regret that Wes was not experiencing those connections now. He was being stoic about missing teaching at school and relentlessly positive about when, not if, he got back to work. Margot herself often felt she could live without outside contact, but Wes was more sociable. Over her adult life she had learned a lot about depending only on herself and avoiding close relationships. Learning to trust Wes had been a big step outside her comfort zone. She had even started to form what could be considered friendships at work, with Alana and Greg specifically, but that was as far as it went for her circle.

Wes was the kind of person who liked to talk to strangers, who wanted to do nice things for his neighbors. He was the kind of man who created and craved connection in a way Margot was only beginning to understand.

The fact that it was something he needed and was currently being denied made her sad and angry in equal measure.

She left a basket of eggs on the front porch to bring in later, and checked the cat food dish she had left out the last several nights.

It hadn't been touched.

Margot took a shaky breath, then returned to the chicken coop to shake out the bits of cat food. Chickens would eat just about anything. She wasn't ready, yet, to give up on Lucy, but she knew at this point she was doing this more for herself than for any real chance the cat was still out there.

If the fire hadn't gotten her, their ranch was home to at least one roving pack of coyotes. Margot could hear their mournful choir singing at night, and it was beautiful, in a haunted kind of way, but they were also constantly trying to take her chickens, and she had to keep an eye out when she left any of the smaller senior dogs outside.

The realities of what was out there on the ranch were dark and unpleasant, but at least for a little while longer Margot had to hold out hope. If she didn't, she was just going to lose it. And she *had* to keep everything together. If she lost it, what would Wes do? He shouldn't have to take care of her, not with everything on his shoulders right now.

She headed to the shed and got the dog food and medication prepared, before returning to the porch, laden with food dishes, setting them out at the precise places she knew each dog liked to be fed.

By the time everyone was fed and medicated, the sun was starting to rise. Margot couldn't help but feel a lump of worry in the back of her throat, as if she was waiting for that truck to come in again, like it had before—

Gravel crunched on the driveway as Margot rounded the side of the house.

Her pulse leapt as she saw that familiar black truck, the very one she had been imagining, roll to a stop in the center of the driveway. The dogs started to whine and bark. Margot whistled, then they all rallied around her, but the uneasy whining sound didn't abate.

Margot hadn't realized it, but her hand had gone to her gun, and she released the clasp of her holster as she waited by the edge of the porch to see what was about to happen next.

The driver's door opened, but it wasn't Clayton Seaver who got out. Margot immediately recognized the hulking form of Rodney jump down from the cab.

She watched as Wes came out of the house.

He was radiating an easygoing energy, but Margot hadn't missed that he'd been holding their shotgun and had placed it just inside the screen door before he came out. He was holding a cup of coffee, the steam unfurling into the air.

The passenger door of the truck opened, and a boy got out.

Margot didn't *know* Clayton Seaver, she had never met the boy, but there was no doubt in her mind who she was looking at when he stepped around the front of the truck. He was the spitting image of his father. He seemed too large to be a teenager, over six feet tall and broad across the chest. The only dead giveaway of his true age was his face, which still had round cheeks and the softness of youth. Where his father was dark-haired, Clayton was blond, right down to the fine smattering of facial hair making a valiant but ill-advised effort to grow over his lip and on his cheeks.

"Coach Fox," Rodney greeted them with a nod in Wes's direction. "Mrs. Fox."

Margot didn't correct his assumptions. She and Wes were married in every way that mattered. If someone wanted to assume it, it didn't bother her. Besides, it didn't seem like an important point to be arguing right now.

"Rodney. Good to see you. Clayton." Nods all around, but Margot knew that not saying *nice to see you* to Clayton was about as close to rude as Wes got these days.

The boy and his father came to stand at the bottom of the porch steps, but Wes didn't invite them up and they didn't ask to come in. Margot let her hand fall away from her gun and pulled her cardigan close around her against the morning chill. She didn't need them to realize what she'd been doing, and it was cold enough out here that the move looked natural.

The dogs were circling her legs still, none of them terribly intimidating, save for Tootsie, but she was also the most cowardly of the lot and was currently hiding behind Margot's legs.

Margot decided to stay where she was, so she could see what was going on up on the porch but the dogs wouldn't be further stressed.

Plus, if this was a setup or a trick, she was in a good position to cover Wes until he could safely get back into the house.

She had no idea if he understood her motivations or not. He was sipping his coffee like this was any normal morning visit, pretending not to have a care in the world. Someone would need to be an expert in Wes's body language to recognize how stiff his posture was, or the way he was rocking on his heels to stay mobile, just in case he needed to clear the gap behind him to get the gun.

This didn't *look* like a situation destined to go south, but Margot wasn't really sure what she believed in anymore when it came to how things should play out.

Better paranoid and safe than lax and dead.

She wasn't sure if that was her own thinking or what she'd gotten from her father. It was almost impossible to pick the thoughts apart sometimes.

"We're really sorry to bother you folks so early, but I'm glad we caught you up and about. Wanted to make sure we did this before Clayton got to school. Clayton, you have some things to say to Mr. Fox?"

Rodney shot a look at his son that spoke volumes. None of this had been the boy's idea. Margot wondered if Rodney had given him a couple of days, hoping he would do the right thing on his own, before forcing the boy into the truck and bringing him down here to face the music.

Margot hadn't thought much of Rodney in their first encounter, but seeing him in this situation, her estimation rose slightly. He was just a working man, tired and spread thin, trying to make his son do the right thing.

He was probably terrified of what could happen to the boy if the worst-case scenario was the reality.

For their sake, Margot hoped Clayton hadn't killed Whitney.

For Wes's sake, she kind of hoped Clayton *had*.

It was a terrible thing to think, but she was human.

"Coach Fox, I'm really sorry."

"Sorry for what, Clay?" Wes was stoic, his body almost completely still except for the movement it took to lift the coffee cup to his lips and back down. To anyone who knew him less, he might look calm. Margot knew this was about as angry as he ever let himself be. Wes's rage worked in a quiet simmer, quite the opposite to her own explosive tendencies. He wasn't going to let the kid off easy for this one, which he might normally have for a lesser infraction. His kindness had its limitations, and Margot was glad he was putting pressure on Clayton.

She hadn't realized that Wes had coached the kid in some capacity, which must have made this situation extra difficult for both of them.

This was someone Wes *knew*.

That had to hurt almost as much as it infuriated.

"I'm sorry for coming around and shooting up your driveway, and for what I did to your window." He paused, like whatever he was about to say next physically hurt him to say aloud. "And your barn. We didn't think the whole thing would go up like that, I swear to God. We started the fire nearby and thought you would see the smoke before anything else happened."

Wes sipped his coffee.

"Who is *we*?"

"Me, and some of the guys. Mark and Fitzy."

Wes just nodded, considering this. "You and Mark and Fitzy must have seen me leave on Saturday. That's how you knew when to come in. So how did you think we were going to be able to see the fire before it spread?"

Clayton looked down at his shoes, scuffing his toes in the gravel. "We thought you would drive in and see the smoke."

"Mmm." That one sound was so loaded. Margot knew he wasn't buying what Clayton was selling.

"I am *really* sorry, sir. I have money for the window. And I can come help rebuild the barn." He held out an envelope, his hand shaking, and Wes just stared at it.

Margot watched him carefully, wondering if that quiet anger of his might bubble over.

"I don't want your money, Clayton. You can go donate that to the animal shelter, because since you pulled that little stunt with the barn, we haven't seen one of our cats. And then I want you to apologize to my wife."

Clayton seemed to realize for the first time that Margot was present, and looked at her as if she was a ghost who had just made herself visible.

"I'm really sorry, Mrs. Fox. About the barn. And your cat."

"Lucy," Margot said coldly as she went to stand beside Wes. "Her name was Lucy."

This was the first time she had referred to Lucy in the past tense, and the word *was* caught in her throat like a barbed fishhook.

"I'm sorry," was all he said.

"I'm assuming your next stop is the sheriff's office?" Margot asked, though it wasn't really a question.

"Yes, ma'am," Clayton said.

"We are hoping, mind you," Rodney interjected, "that you might see it in your hearts to not press charges after Clayton tells them what he's done."

Wes sipped his coffee again, like he really had to think about this.

Margot stared a hole through the side of the boy's skull now that he refused to look right at her. If it was up to her, they'd throw the whole book at him.

"We'll see," she said at last.

In her heart, though she was furious about what he had done, and that fury wanted to manifest in revenge, that wasn't who she was. Not really. And she knew without a doubt it wasn't who Wes was.

He was pissed, and he was probably biting back some choice words right then.

"Whether or not we press charges," Wes said, "you're going to have to do a *lot* of work to earn my trust again."

The boy nodded, looking both relieved and sick at the same time.

"Clayton, where were you the night Whitney Eflin died?" Margot asked bluntly.

"Wh-what?" He looked back at her again, almost like he was newly surprised she was still there. "Can you ask me that?"

"She's an FBI agent," Rodney said. "Just answer the question, Clay. They're going to ask it again when you talk to the sheriff."

Clayton stared at Margot, incredulous. She had to admit that in her ratty thrift store cardigan that came to her knees, her leggings and her Ugg boots, she didn't exactly radiate FBI authority. She looked like a farm wife, doing farm chores.

But she hoped her expression told him she was as dead serious as her question implied.

"Fitzy and me were out driving around."

"You happen to drive by Whitney's?"

He shook his head vehemently. "Hell no. Whit's parents *hate* me. I didn't want to get her in any trouble. Maybe I should have, though. Maybe if I did..."

He looked back down at the ground, burying his toe in the gravel.

Margot didn't need him to finish the sentence. She knew all about the potent danger of those *maybes*.

Maybe he could have saved her.

Maybe he would have seen who did it.

Maybe, maybe, maybe.

But Margot had a few of her own.

Maybe he was lying.

Maybe he *had* been there.

Maybe he killed her.

So he wasn't going to get a lot of sympathy out of her. Not with an alibi like *driving around with someone who would make up an alibi for me if I asked.*

"We appreciate you coming by, Clay," Wes said finally. "I assume we don't have to worry about any more... incidents."

"No, Coach," Rodney answered, squeezing his son's shoulder so hard the boy winced. "Clayton won't be getting himself into any more trouble."

He nudged his son back towards the truck.

Clayton looked at Margot one last time. "I really am sorry about your cat," he said, his tone pleading.

"Yeah, well, your fucking apology won't bring her back, will it?" she said, not trying to keep her tone quiet. Wes put a hand on the back of her neck, squeezing gently, putting his anger aside to comfort her. Or perhaps letting her know that he was in it with her.

The boy blanched, then got into the cab. The truck backed out of the driveway and disappeared onto the main road.

Margot looked at Wes, who was regarding her carefully.

"You think he did it?" Wes asked.

Margot thought about the boy who had just been standing there, afraid to look at them.

She thought about the photos of Whitney's body. How carefully it had been cut open, how bold and assertive the attack had been.

How she hadn't been covered up during or after.

She didn't need a profiler to tell her what she already knew.

"No," she muttered, reaching down to scratch one of the dogs behind his ears. "But our lives would be a hell of a lot easier if I could say yes."

THIRTY-FIVE

Margot, good as she was, could not solve a murder that she was not technically investigating in less than two days.

With Clayton Seaver all but eliminated from her consideration, it was back to square one, and square one had precisely zero good persons of interest. She just had to hope that the BSU would come back with a decent profile, something that would help clear Wes completely.

She knew he was dying to get back to work and was sick of roaming around their house with nothing to do.

Sadie had volunteered to stay on until Margot returned from Montana. This time the trip wasn't slated to take more than two days, which she felt okay with. There was nothing she could do at home right now, and for the time being they didn't need to worry about any additional damage being done to the ranch.

At least with the DeGraff case she might be able to find some closure.

Though even there, she was less and less certain they were actually going to be able to find Ricky's accomplice, if such an accomplice even existed. They still had stones they would need to turn, just to see what cockroaches crawled out from underneath. But she also knew that flying out to see Ricky again was a real Hail

Mary. They were going to have to hope that seeing the Rosalind doll would be enough to get him to admit to having worked with someone.

It was a long shot, because the obsession Ricky DeGraff had with Mathilda made Margot wonder if he would realize that their doll was different. He hadn't seen Mathilda in years, and memory was a tricky, slippery thing. They'd agreed that the best tactic would be to convince him that they'd bought the doll online from a private vendor, and see if he slipped up and said anything that might help point them to the person who had—or might have already offloaded—the doll he had been willing to kill for.

Margot was also itching to ask Ricky about his sister.

She was still astonished that in all their research into his past they had missed him having a sister. But they had been digging into that since their meeting with Senior, and an unsettling possibility was unfolding.

There was a birth certificate for a Mathilda Anne DeGraff that had been filed with the county about five years after Ricky was born. No death certificate was ever issued for the girl. However, Ricky's mother had been a nurse before becoming a stay-at-home mother for her son, and eventually her daughter. If something had happened to the baby, there was a chance the DeGraffs had dealt with it at home.

There were no burial records, and Andrew was working to get cadaver dogs out to the DeGraffs' old property, with the suspicion that young Mathilda DeGraff might have received a home burial. The family were so withdrawn, it was possible that no one knew they had two children, let alone noticed when one of them simply stopped appearing.

It was as if Mathilda had just vanished off the face of the Earth one day. Margot had believed what Senior said about the baby's sudden death. And she believed that *he* believed Ricky was innocent of any involvement in Mathilda's death, but Margot wasn't so sure.

She wanted to find out right from the source.

Once they had cleared security—the doll had been checked thoroughly to ensure it didn't contain or couldn't be used as a weapon—Margot found herself back in a familiar, featureless room, with a large shopping bag next to her on the floor.

For the first time since their very first meeting, she felt like she could actually focus on DeGraff and not on what was happening in her own life. Wes was okay. Sadie was there with him to make sure he didn't start bouncing off any walls. The insurance inspector would be out that afternoon to settle things regarding the barn.

Margot was trying to stay positive. If there was a settlement, they could build something new, and then they could help rescue farm animals. Goats, sheep, maybe a donkey. Those were the thoughts she tried to carry with her while she was so far away and unable to help.

Once this was over, and the DeGraff case was solved, and the sheriff had a real suspect for Whitney's case, and well-meaning but judgemental Sadie had gone home, Margot and Wes could really try to find their way back to normal.

Whatever normal was going to look like going forward.

For right now, though, her normal was sitting in a prison, talking to a serial killer.

Ricky shuffled in, arm and ankle shackles jangling, and Margot nodded that it would be okay to remove them. There was an armed guard inside the small room, and another one just outside, able to see everything going on. Margot wasn't armed, but she felt safe enough.

As safe as one could feel, sitting across from a serial killer.

"Good morning, Ricky," she greeted him, offering him a stiff smile.

"You probably shouldn't do that," he said, his voice soft.

"Do what?"

"Smile at people. Not like that anyway." He gave a little exaggerated shiver. "You got that smile that crocodiles have, you know. Grin at you right up until they eat your face."

"I have a face-eating smile?" Margot asked.

"Something like that."

"Good to know."

"You know, I looked you up after you left last time."

"Oh yeah?" Margot leaned back in her chair, resting her hands in her lap. "You find out anything interesting?"

"You've been doing this sort of thing a while." He gestured between them. "That ever get tiring?"

"Any job can wear you down if you do it long enough. But I'm not sick of it yet."

"Guess it must be easy for you. Well, easier than for most."

Margot had suspected this was where things were going the moment he said he'd looked her up. He was acting like he'd discovered some kind of state secret, but the truth about her past was out there to be found by anyone with a Netflix account or an interest in true crime subreddits. She didn't hide from her past anymore, not the way she once had.

And that meant there were newspaper headlines out there that said things like *Daughter of notorious serial killer helps solve fifty-year-old cold case.*

She bristled at the inference that being Ed Finch's daughter was how she became so gifted at solving crimes. But maybe it was.

She smiled at him again, intentionally this time. "I think there are plenty of reasons I'm good at this job."

"You a daddy's girl?" he asked, leaning against the table, his hands clasped in front of him.

Margot mirrored the gesture. "If you really looked me up, then you'll know just what happened to my *daddy*."

Their eyes locked across the table, but it was Ricky who blinked first, seeming to remember only then how little he liked meeting her gaze. He started to fiddle with his hangnails again.

"Well, I guess we all gotta die someday."

Margot smiled in what she hoped was a pleasant manner. "I think this is a very good topic, Ricky. Fathers. I think I want to talk a little about your father."

"What about him?" The bravado from moments earlier was

gone. But Margot had seen inside Ricky, just for a flash. He played the shy, unassuming role so well, it was sometimes hard to recognize that there was still a monster there. There would always be a monster there.

"I met your old man," she said, keeping an eye on Ricky to see how he would react to this. He stiffened, but didn't immediately say anything. "He didn't have an awful lot to say about you."

"No, I bet that was a wasted trip." His shoulders were up around his ears, making Margot wonder just what he might be imagining.

"I don't think it was. We had a very nice chat with Ricky Senior."

Ricky scoffed. "I don't think anyone has *ever* had a nice chat with Richard DeGraff." He peeled off one long hangnail, leaving in its wake a bloody line. He stuck his thumb in his mouth.

Margot let him stew for a moment and tried not to let her disgust show.

"I have a question for you, Ricky."

"I bet. If you didn't it would be pretty dumb for us both to be here right now."

"Where did you come up with the name Mathilda?"

She was expecting a big reaction to this, some kind of obvious show of distress, or realization of what she knew. Instead, he just wiped his wet thumb on his jumpsuit leg. He didn't seem at all upset, which surprised Margot.

"My mom called her that. I just stuck with it." Margot had no way to know if this was true. But Senior had told them that the doll had been purchased a year after the real Mathilda had died, so it was certainly possible that a grieving mother might have started to use her daughter's name with a beloved new doll.

But Ricky was acting as if there was no connection between the two, which was surprising.

"Ricky, tell me about your sister."

Ricky wrinkled up his nose and looked at Margot in a way that knocked her off her course entirely. His expression clearly said, *what the hell are you talking about?*

"I was an only child," he said, and everything about his tone suggested honesty. Margot would have bet that they could have hooked him up to a polygraph and he would have passed.

She didn't know how to continue. Her planned segue into bringing out the Rosalind doll was to get Ricky to admit that he was using Mathilda as a proxy for his beloved baby sister. She wanted to ask him if he had, possibly, loved baby Mathilda *too* much, and if all the things he had done after were just his way of atoning for his first victim.

But now she didn't know how to get there, and while she was usually quick on her feet in these situations, she wasn't sure how to proceed.

If he was lying, he had become infinitely better at it than he'd ever been in their previous conversations, or in the recorded interviews she and the team had spent hours listening to.

The thing about Ricky was that when he knew he'd been caught out he didn't seem to mind confessing to things. He didn't dance around the truth. The only likely reason he hadn't confessed to any additional crimes while he was behind bars was because no one had asked him the right questions or shown him that they'd done the work to figure out the connection.

Margot didn't know how to back him into that corner when he was acting like her evidence didn't exist.

So she pulled out a copy of Mathilda's birth certificate she had brought with her and slid it across the table to him. She had brought it so she could ask him if he'd remembered what his parents had done with Mathilda's body after she died, but now it seemed to have a different purpose.

Ricky unfolded the paper and stared down at it, his brow furrowed so deeply that Margot briefly wondered if he could read.

"This is fake," he said. "You guys printed this off or something. Photoshopped. I could have photoshopped something like this with my eyes closed." He shoved the paper back at her and it fluttered to the floor.

"Why would we fake something like that, Ricky? What would our motive be?"

"You're just fucking with me. Getting me unsettled or something. Well, good job, I'm feeling pretty fucking *unsettled*. What the fuck?"

"Ricky, your father told us about your sister. He told us how much you loved her, and how devastated you were when she died. You were very young when she was born, only five. She didn't live long, died while she was still a baby."

"You're a liar. I would remember having a sister. You don't just forget something like that."

"You were very young," she repeated. "And it was very traumatic. Did you do something to her? Do you remember if you were holding her? Maybe you wanted to be close to her, and something happened by accident. Your father said—"

"Fuck what my father said. He's a goddamn liar, just like you are. There is only one Mathilda, and she was a doll. There was no *baby*."

Margot wished they'd thought to get any photos Senior had of the baby, rather than just the doll. But given the scant number of photos in his possession, and how his son had been excised from most of them, she wondered if the family had done the same to Mathilda. Eliminated proof of the thing that brought them pain so they could pretend it didn't exist.

She wasn't sure if Ricky was being genuine or if this was an act, but given how angry he was with her right now, she was coming increasingly down on the side of him truly not remembering he had a sister.

The guard in the room had taken a half-step forward, his posture rigid, and she knew he was getting antsy about Ricky's volume and language. These were all precursors to someone lashing out violently.

Margot lifted her hand slightly off the table and the guard

stepped back, but he was still radiating tension and likely would be until this interview was over.

"Okay, let's talk about something different, let's forget this for now."

"Don't pull shit like that," Ricky cautioned. "I'm not here to play games with you."

Margot had been ready to pull out the doll next, but his phrasing and his attitude bothered her.

"Games?" She frowned and leaned forward, staring hard at his forehead, since he was back to staring at his hands. "You think this is my idea of a fun time? That I have nothing better to do with my life than travel across multiple states to sit in a room with you and smell your goddamn stink, and listen to you prattle on about nothing because you love the sound of your own voice? You think I want to be here? Because, buddy, you are sorely fucking mistaken. This isn't a game, there are no jokes."

Ricky's gaze flicked up at her for a moment, then back to his hands.

"There it is," he said mildly.

"There what is?"

"The gator. Going in for the kill."

THIRTY-SIX

Margot paused for a moment to take in some steady breaths. She felt like she was at an impasse.

They needed to move forward, but Ricky didn't seem to remember having a sister, and knowing if he had *killed* his sister was a big factor in understanding why Ricky might have done everything else he'd done after that.

Finally, when the silence between them had stretched to the point of feeling awkward, Margot changed tactic, abandoning the sister angle entirely.

"When I was here last time, you told me that you had left Mathilda with someone you trusted. I want to ask about that. About how much someone like you, in a situation like yours, can actually trust anyone."

He looked up briefly, but didn't make direct eye contact. He seemed to be looking at the door behind her.

"Trust is very important."

"You don't have a lot of people that you trust, do you?"

"I don't trust you, if that's what you're getting at."

That made Margot laugh, a sharp, empty sound. "No, that wasn't what I was getting at."

"Then what?"

"I'm just wondering how well you know the person you left Mathilda with."

He stared at her. "They're my best friend."

Margot gave a dramatic nod of agreement. "I'm sure you believe that. But you're in here, you're never getting out."

"So?"

"Do you know how much Mathilda is worth?" Even as she asked this question she realized, with horror, that once this story became more widely known Mathilda herself would become ever more valuable than a standard Rosalind doll. A doll that had inspired a man to go on a child murder spree? That was the sort of fucked-up serial killer trophy that seemed to get a lot of traction in niche weirdo groups online. The kind of people who would spend ten grand on a napkin Richard Ramirez had once wiped his nose on while in court.

People with that level of obsession with serial killers worried Margot.

But it was impossible to dispute that DeGraff's doll would draw a lot of attention from the people who were into that sort of thing.

Though she had noticed, in her time working in the realm of serial killers, that those who murdered children weren't as popular as the ones who murdered adult women and men. Apparently even the nutjobs who spent their spare time collecting Ed Gein's paintings or writing love letters to men behind bars didn't spend as much time or money idolizing kid-killers.

Margot guessed even freaks had to draw the line somewhere.

Ricky was staring at her, contemplating her question. "She's priceless. She doesn't have a value."

"Are you sure about that?"

She could have shown him evidence of all the auctions where the Rosalind doll had sold for tens of thousands of dollars, but she didn't need to remind him that other dolls like Mathilda existed. For this little ploy to work—and it was already off to a rocky start—

she needed him to think that Mathilda was so rare that there might only be one. His.

"I would never sell her, so she has no price."

"But you don't have her, do you? Someone else does. Someone who might not think she's quite as priceless as you do. Because Mathilda is actually worth a lot of money, Ricky. Money that someone on the outside might need very badly. How can you be confident that the person you've left it with is someone you can trust, even if times get really bad?"

She gave him a meaningful look, holding her gaze long enough for him to yield and look up at her. His typically stoic features were furious even though he wasn't saying anything.

"I left it with someone I trust."

"Trust only goes so far when money gets involved."

She picked up the paper bag from the floor, then removed the doll from inside and set her on the table.

Margot found dolls to be creepy, and this one was especially so. She might not be Ricky's doll, but she was the same model that had inspired a man to kill at least ten little girls. Maybe more.

That made her more macabre than just a regular run-of-the-mill creepy doll could be.

But all that aside, Margot could appreciate the craftsmanship that had gone into making Rosalind. Her hair had to be real, there was no way around that. It was lovely and soft, even after all these years living in the Texas heat. Her skin was porcelain, cheeks painted with just a subtle wash of pink, and the detail work of her glass eyes was remarkable. They looked damn near human. Her eyelashes were applied with care, and her face looked so close to being that of a real little girl and not a doll that Margot would have done a double take if she'd seen her in a store window.

The doll was wearing a pretty blue and white dress that seemed to make her brown hair darker. The dress, Margot noted, bore a striking resemblance to the one that Maddie Moore had been wearing when she'd been found.

Not identical, but enough similarity that it likely hadn't been coincidental.

She had a little bonnet on her head, a ribbon tied around the chin.

The dealer who had loaned them the doll said that the ribbon was the only thing not original. It should have been satin, but had been fixed at some point with a velvet one in a similar color. She had her fingers crossed that it was a small enough detail that Ricky wouldn't notice.

It was all a gamble at this point.

"Where did you get that?" he asked, his voice hushed. Trembling.

"You'd be amazed what you can buy online if the price is right. See, after last time we talked, we started looking around, seeing if we could find Mathilda. Seeing where the path might lead us if we asked the right questions and went to the right people. And there are a *lot* of people online who will spend an obscene amount of money to get their hands on something like this." She held Mathilda's smooth porcelain hand between her fingers, gently stroking the soft finish. Her fingernails were faintly rosy, but not garish.

The attention to detail was incredible, really.

No wonder it had cost so much when it had been released originally. It was a collector's item, without a doubt. This wasn't the kind of doll that you would call a toy, and only the richest of families would have allowed a child to play with it.

Yet Ricky's mother had allowed him to hold her, with supervision.

That had to be connected to his sister and her death. Did his parents recognize that there was something unusual about their son after Mathilda had died? That his grief looked different from their own?

That he had forgotten the girl ever existed?

And why had they covered up the death, instead of bringing the baby to a hospital or a funeral home for a proper burial?

Margot would love to have answers to those questions, but she didn't think either of the living Richard DeGraffs were going to give her the details she so craved.

"Where did you get her?" Ricky asked again.

"Why don't you tell me who had her? Who betrayed your trust for a few thousand dollars? Who did you think you could rely on, because, Ricky, they *fucked* you."

He was staring at the doll with a ferocious intensity, his hands on the table trembling, like the only thing he wanted in the world was to reach out and touch the doll. Margot intentionally kept Rosalind out of arm's reach. She was on loan, after all, and there was no telling what Ricky might do if he got his hands on her.

Besides, the closer he got, the more likely it would be that he'd realize this wasn't his doll at all.

The magic could so easily be broken that Margot wasn't willing to test her luck.

"Tell me the name," she urged.

"She wouldn't," Ricky said, pulling his hands close to his chest, trying desperately to control himself, though it was clear that he was losing it as the seconds ticked by.

She.

She.

That was something.

It eliminated fifty percent of the population. Narrowed their focus. But everything they'd learned about Ricky over those past months meant Margot wasn't surprised by this revelation. Ricky had no close relationships with men. And while he didn't have female friends in adulthood either, he did seem to favor female company over male in most situations.

So him putting his trust in a woman seemed inevitable.

"Who wouldn't do it?" Margot asked. "Because someone did." She smoothed her hand over Rosalind's hair, fluffing it over the doll's shoulders. Her patent leather Mary Jane shoes were polished to a high shine and almost glowed thanks to the fluorescent lights directly above them.

"She wouldn't," Ricky insisted. "Because I gave her *everything*."

He pushed his chair back, and the guard descended in a split second, and cuffed his wrists and ankles. Ricky's hands were still trembling, but he looked at Margot one last time before the guard began leading him from the room.

"I'm not stupid, Agent. I know you might think I am. But I would know Mathilda anywhere, and that is not Mathilda."

And with that, he let the guards lead him down the hall and out of sight.

Margot felt certain, deep in her bones though she couldn't have explained why, that that was the last time she would ever see Ricky DeGraff.

THIRTY-SEVEN

As dive bars went, the Milkmaid was on the nicer end. Which was to say that the floor was only sticky, rather than both sticky and covered in peanut shells.

The glasses were dirty, but the bathroom had been cleaned in the last five years. And the bartender had only made a little *harumph* sound when two women in blazers had walked in and asked for drinks.

At least the gin had ice and the lime seemed likely to have been cut sometime that week. Margot wasn't complaining.

"What a fucking day," Alana said.

They were seated across from each other in a booth that had high backs and striped fabric, like at one point this bar had aspirations of being an English pub, but had just given up all pretense somewhere along the way.

Alana was seated sideways in the booth, her feet up on the padded seat, one high-heeled shoe dangling precariously from one toe. Her hair was pulled back in a tiny ponytail at the base of her neck.

Margot was nestled against the wall on her side, picking at a bowl of peanuts and trying not to think about where she'd been only an hour ago.

The team weren't meeting tonight. They would have a review in the morning before checking out of the hotel, then they would return to California to stew over what they had learned.

She was exhausted from her day, but she couldn't help but feel a slight glow of pride considering what she'd been able to pry out of Ricky. It wasn't a name, but every little bit got them one step closer.

She sipped her gin. Bombay. Not her favorite, but it would do in a pinch. Now that she didn't drink just to numb the pain of being alive, she had given herself permission to like really good gin, since she was only having it every so often. She favored a Japanese gin called Roku, and failing that her preference was Hendricks, but in the middle of nowhere Montana she would take what she could get and she'd say thank you.

Alana was drinking whiskey on the rocks, her glass starting to sweat thanks to the almost too warm air inside the bar.

"They're all starting to feel like that kind of day lately," Margot said, setting her glass on a coaster even though the tabletop was a lattice of old ring marks from decades of drinkers before her.

"You're just in the thick of it now. Once this case is done and things settle at home—"

"But then it'll just be the next case. And everything we have waiting in the wings is just as demoralizing and shitty." Margot poked at an ice cube. She knew she was being whiny, but damn if she didn't feel like she deserved to have her woe-is-me moment.

Unfortunately, her friend was many things, but sympathetic to someone being bitchy wasn't one of them.

"So quit," Alana said bluntly, before sipping her drink. "You're not an indentured servant, Margot. You've been working with this team for five years—that's more than enough time to have proven yourself within the Bureau. Take another posting. Or quit this altogether. Start teaching knitting classes or doing goat yoga on the ranch. You don't have to stay."

Margot settled back in her booth, staring up at the genuinely nice glass light hanging over them. She let out a little laugh.

"I think the idea of leaving is somehow worse than the idea of staying."

That made Alana smile. "Stockholm Syndrome at its finest."

"This is the only thing I know how to do," Margot said. "How ridiculous is that? I change my name, change my life to get away from a killer, and then my entire life from that point on just keeps me coming back to them. I don't really know how to hold a normal conversation anymore. When Wes would force me to go to community events, everyone would be talking about their kids, or sports, and the only thing I could come up with to talk about was watching their kids for the Macdonald triad."

Alana chuckled and raised her empty hand, lifting one finger for each item as she mentioned it. "Bed-wetting. Arson. Animal abuse. Bet that got some tongues wagging in the PTA afterwards."

"They stopped insisting Wes bring me to things after that, so I guess it was a small win in the end."

"The triad has been largely debunked, you know," Alana said, sipping her whiskey.

"I know, but they bring it on themselves. Do you know how often people ask me, *hey, you're a serial killer expert, how can you tell if someone is going to become a serial killer?* Like there's a checklist. Sometimes it's easier to just give them *something*, and that's such a tidy little list of potential red flags."

"Certainly easier than asking Mommy Dearest if she's smothering her son. They don't tend to like that."

Margot took a long drink, her cheeks feeling hot. She should switch to water soon, but she was enjoying this. It felt nice to take some of the pressure of the day off.

"I need the team to make me a PowerPoint of risk-free conversation topics for barbeques and baby showers."

"Margot, no one is inviting you to a baby shower. You are the least *baby shower* person I've ever met in my life aside from myself."

"You never know. Wes's sisters might still unleash more spawn on the world, bless them." Just mentioning his sisters reminded her of the family group chat where Sadie was keeping everyone up to date on what was happening. Margot didn't participate much in the chatter, but she did appreciate all the texts of concern, and even the periodic phone check-ins from Wes's parents and his older sisters.

"Perish the thought," Alana said of the children.

"I think he would have liked to have kids," Margot said, mostly into her drink.

"And you?" Alana was watching her carefully, making sure her tone was non-judgemental. Margot knew Alana was so anti-children she'd had a tubal ligation in her mid-thirties.

"I don't think my life trajectory really gave me a fair shot at answering that question for myself," Margot said, which was honest, but also dodging the question. She met Alana's gaze across the table and smiled almost apologetically. "I think if things had been different, there's an alternative universe where I would have really liked being a mom. But in this one, things were never going to go that way. If I'd had kids, I would have fucked them up. And without getting into a nature-versus-nurture conversation about psychopathy and serial killers, I just don't think we need my family line going further. But I have pets."

Alana took a swig of her drink. "I can't even do pets. Hell, I can't even do plants. So you're more maternal than I'll ever be. Wes never talked to you about kids, did he?"

"We kind of skirted around the issue. By the time we were settled I was getting too old for it. He asked me if it was something I wanted, and I told him basically what I told you. After that we just never talked about it again. I think if I'd said I did want them he would have jumped at it."

"But he wants you just the way you are. All *Bridget Jones* and shit." Alana set her now-empty glass on the table with a soft *thump*. "It's romantic. Gross."

"It's realistic. For some inexplicable reason, he wants to be with me, neurosis, bullshit job, and fucked-up family tree all included. I definitely got the better end of our bargain. He's basically perfect, it's disgusting."

"No one's perfect, but I give him points for having excellent taste." She held Margot's gaze for a beat, then looked out at the dark windows facing the front street. "I want a burger. You think we can find a decent burger in this town?" She set her feet back on the floor, cheeks flushed slightly pink from the heat and the booze.

"I think, of all the things you could be craving, that might be the only option we won't have trouble finding in this town."

"Well then, chin up, buttercup. Quit your bitching, and let's go get a goddamn hamburger and solve this case."

THIRTY-EIGHT

One of the only downsides to not being a borderline alcoholic anymore was that Margot now had to deal with the side effects of being an irregular drinker in her forties.

Which meant hangovers.

She was seated between Sydney and Greg at their conference room table at the hotel—which was really just two folding tables pushed together, since the actual conference room they'd used last time was booked for a wedding—and trying very hard to focus on Andrew. All the while she was cursing the invention of fluorescent lightbulbs and wondering what had happened to the constitution she'd had when she was twenty-five.

Come to think of it, she would also like the body she had at twenty-five back again, if that was an option.

Or just transport back into that body so she didn't have to be where she was right now.

"So, we know more than we did after our last visit," Andrew said, pacing in front of a blank whiteboard they had borrowed from the hotel. "We know that DeGraff's conspirator is a woman, which will help narrow the focus slightly. We'll have to revisit any known acquaintances. Margot, you and Greg got us on a good path by speaking to that former apprentice at the pageant last week."

"Sam Reed," Greg offered.

"I think we need to talk to her again, and also see if we can find the other apprentice she mentioned. Even if they aren't involved, by working with him they might have known who he spent time with or talked to. They're going to be our best bets, so Margot, I'd like you to talk to Ms. Reed again before you head home today."

Margot was going to protest, having already tried that route, but she didn't have the energy in her, so she just sipped her water and gave a thumbs-up in Andrew's general direction.

"Sydney, I want you and your team to dig into DeGraff's finances again. If he was employing these women in some capacity, we should be able to find old tax records. His photography business was an LLC. He didn't have any regular employees, but we know he was pretty meticulous about keeping his professional reputation above reproach. If this woman was paid, even as a contractor, there should be a record of it."

Sydney nodded, making notes on the pad in front of her. The sound of pen scratching paper was so obnoxious Margot had to resist the urge to bat the pad onto the ground.

"I know it might not feel like it, folks, but we're getting close on this one. Greg, I want you to go with Alana to the old DeGraff place in Idaho. The dogs are scheduled to start searching the property this afternoon, so you'll fly straight there after we get back to San Francisco. Any issues with that?"

There were no complaints—everyone knew what they needed to do next.

Andrew was right, it didn't feel like they were close, but that was the way things like this worked sometimes. They weren't running towards the finish line at a mile a minute, they were inching forward on their hands and knees. It was a long, painful process, but they *were* getting somewhere.

It was just difficult to wait for the end result sometimes. Margot was impatient and wanted results quicker than this.

. . .

Margot returned to her room to change and pack her few scattered personal items back into her weekend bag. When she'd bought the pretty leather tote she had envisioned getting away with Wes, maybe an overnight stay in Napa or Solvang. She hadn't expected it to become her serial killer travel bag.

Unfortunately, it was perfectly suited to short trips with minimal luggage required, which was most of the travel she did these days.

She texted Wes before leaving for the airport. She didn't want to bug him about himself, she knew he was starting to feel over-coddled between her and Sadie, so she just said:

> Everything okay at home? Any sign of Lucy?

It took a moment before the reply came through.

> Insurance guys stopped by again, said they talked to the fire department and it all seems pretty clear-cut in terms of our payout. So good news! And we haven't burned the house down in your absence or murdered each other, so we're really killing it here. No Lucy, but I refilled the bowl this morning and put one of your sweaters out on the rocking chair. We both know you're the favorite.

Margot would have protested this in person, but the truth was that Lucy didn't like men very much for some reason. Margot had had her for her whole life, and it was just the way she was. Some people said that calico cats were known to be quite particular and have a bit of an attitude, which was certainly true of Lucy.

> Thanks. I have to stop for an interview on the way home. I won't be too late.

> Stop at Rocco's if you get the chance.

Rocco's was a chicken spot about thirty minutes away from the ranch that happened to be right on Margot's drive home. It was a hole in the wall, but they loved the food, and if she turned on her car's seat warmers the chicken was still hot by the time she got home.

> You got it. Get some Advil out for me, gin is no longer my best friend.

> Oof, you're too old for hangovers, babe.

> I'm exactly the right age for hangovers, as it turns out. XO.

She met the rest of the crew in the lobby, where a van was waiting to take them to the private airport. Everyone's eyes were glued to their phones, fingers tapping a mile a minute, so no one seemed to notice or care when Margot slipped on her sunglasses, held up her own phone, and started scrolling through old case notes.

By the time they landed back in San Francisco, everyone knew where they had to be next. Andrew and Sydney headed back to the office. Margot's car was at the airport waiting for her, and Greg and Alana were just waiting for the plane to refuel before they headed off to Idaho to hopefully unearth some baby bones.

Not a sentence Margot thought she'd ever put the word *hopefully* in.

The team at the office would be working to identify Ricky's previous assistants, and, between them all, they might *just* find what they needed to prove that Ricky had been the one to kill Maddie Moore—he had said as much, but they still had no evidence—and get the leads they needed to discover if there was anyone else out there they could tie him to.

And put an accomplice in jail while they were at it.

It would be nice to see at least one case wrapped up in a tidy little bow. Things with the Whitney Eflin case were so messy that Margot wasn't sure they were ever going to find a resolution, or not an easy one, anyway. She wanted to rip out her hair over how inefficiently they were handling the case. It made her crazy that she couldn't do anything to help personally. Which meant the spectre of that murder was going to be hanging over them all for the foreseeable future.

They were just going to have to learn how to move on. Either the school would reinstate Wes, or they'd need to start looking for other jobs for him. It wasn't so much their income that worried Margot, it was Wes's mental health. He needed to be doing things to feel like he had value, and the past two weeks had been exceedingly difficult for him. He sometimes just sat still for hours at a time, staring out the window, which wasn't like Wes at all. He was usually restless, moving from one task to the next. It might not read like a sign to anyone else, but it did to her.

But one thing at a time, and for right now there was a case in front of her that she felt like she had all the pieces to solve but hadn't quite got there just yet. It was only a matter of time, though, and she had one concrete step she could take to get them a little closer.

Sam Reed's address had been on the business card she'd given Margot, and it turned out that her office was also her home. She lived in a small town called Penngrove, not far outside Petaluma, with a sign on the driveway for Like Magic Photography, and, somewhat more surprising, a larger sign over the gate for Patchwork Kennels.

A kennel was not something she had been expecting to see here.

Sam's house was a rambling ranch-style home right out of the 1950s, and it looked like she had about ten acres of surrounding land. There was a massive outbuilding behind the house with chain link fencing around the outside, creating individual kennel spaces on both sides of the building.

Margot glanced at her phone when she parked and saw that Harper, who had been working back in the main office while they were gone, had sent an update to the team.

Did some scouring, and found that Sister Mary Callahan's birth name was Donna Partridge. No current files on her, have a request submitted to pull any updates on her social security number, see if she made an official name change at some point. Still digging!

Margot had been hoping for something more useful, perhaps a smoking gun on the employee angle. She thought Harper was wasting her time looking into the nun. So a retired nun had visited Ricky? That was strange, certainly, but it wasn't really *helpful*.

The sound of barking dogs was evident as soon as Margot got out of her car. In a paddock beside the house with a large fence built around it, a trio of wiry-haired dogs with intense eyes and bushy eyebrows had clustered together and were all barking to let anyone in a two-mile radius know that company was present.

This evidently set off all the dogs in the outbuilding as well, who began to bark and howl even though they weren't able to see Margot.

The front door of the house opened, and a sharp whistle filled the air. Almost immediately the barking stopped. Sam stood on the front step, wearing a loose denim shirt over a pair of jeans, and somehow didn't look ridiculous in the denim-on-denim ensemble.

"Special Agent... I'm sorry, I've forgotten your name."

"It's fine," Margot said, offering a smile and hoping Sam didn't take it the same way Ricky had. "Special Agent Phalen. Margot."

"Margot." Sam nodded, as if deciding this would be the easiest thing for her to remember.

"What kind of dogs are these?" Margot asked.

"You like dogs?" Sam inquired, without answering the question.

"I adopt senior dogs who have trouble finding homes. We have five right now. Mostly mutts, though—I've never seen a dog like this. They look like that Dr. Seuss character. You know, the one who speaks for the trees."

This made Sam snort and look at the trio of dogs, their slim tails wagging aggressively. "The Lorax. Yes, I've heard that one before. Also Gandalf, Dumbledore, old-timey boat captains, haunted Regency portraits. They get compared to a lot of things. They're Pudelpointers."

"You do this on top of the photography?" Margot asked. She was still standing in front of her car, Sam on the top step. Neither of them had given any indication of asking or offering to sit. Margot's headache had just started to subside, and the cold, fresh air was likely a contributing factor.

"The dogs were my husband's passion," Sam said.

"Were?"

"Yes, he passed away three years ago. Pancreatic cancer."

"I'm sorry."

Sam shrugged off the sentiment, still looking at the dogs. "I didn't intend to keep up with it, but it turns out we're one of the only vetted breeders in the country and our dogs are not only popular but profitable. So I kept the place going, but I do the photography thing whenever I can. I'm not sure if you know this, Agent Phalen, but it's pretty expensive to own land in California, so every little bit counts."

Margot nodded. "Are these three yours?"

"They were Liam's favorite bitches. All retired now, of course. We never overbreed our bitches."

"Mmm," Margot said, like she knew a damned thing about dog breeding.

"Well, I expect you didn't come here to talk about dogs. Would you like to come in?"

"Sure, that would be great, thanks."

Margot climbed up the few steps to the porch and followed Sam through the screen door.

The house was warm inside, for which Margot was grateful. The air had the faint scent of cinnamon and cloves, maybe from some kind of fall-themed candle. Not entirely unpleasant, but a little cloying in its sweetness.

The house itself was cleaned so thoroughly Margot wondered if Sam had been expecting company. She couldn't fathom someone just living in a space that was so damned *tidy*. Throw blankets on the couch in the living room were neatly folded, and all the decorative pillows had that little chop in the top, as if they had been staged by an interior designer.

Considering Sam raised dogs professionally, the place looked incredibly clean as well, with no hair sticking to things. Margot, despite her best efforts, and a sticky lint-roller that she kept in the car, always had hair on her. She didn't know how Sam avoided it.

Maybe these Pudelpointers were a non-shedding variety? They hadn't looked it, considering all that wiry hair, but then again Margot hadn't known the breed existed fifteen minutes ago.

The living room looked like it belonged to a display home, and Margot realized it wasn't for guests, as she followed Sam into what she assumed was the kitchen.

This space looked unnaturally clean as well. Not a dish in the sink or a sign of dinner in the making. Sam went to a Keurig coffee maker on the counter. The machine made a rumbling sound as it prepared their individual cups.

Despite the cleanliness of the kitchen, it was more dated than the living room, looking like it hadn't changed much since the 1970s. There were vintage paintings of hunting dogs on the wall, and old wallpaper that was in remarkably good shape. Margot wasn't surprised, since it seemed like Sam took incredible care of the place.

The house was quiet, though, and Margot had to wonder if the space felt lonely with one person living there, or if Sam found the companionship she craved in her dogs.

Sam gestured towards a small wooden dining room table and Margot obligingly took a seat. The table smelled of Pine-Sol cleaner.

"Do you take milk? Sugar?"

"A little of both if you don't mind."

Sam set a small container of milk and a bowl of sugar on the table in front of Margot.

"I hope you don't mind that the coffee is hazelnut flavored. Liam got me hooked on the stuff and now it's all I order."

"That's fine, thanks." Margot fixed her cup and soon Sam was sitting across from her. Margot noted that both of their cups had vintage dog paintings on them.

"So I'm guessing you have a few more questions about Ricky?" Sam said, sipping her coffee black.

"Yeah, if that's all right—it won't take too long."

"No, it's fine, but can I ask you something first?"

"Of course."

"Why are you guys digging into all of this mess again? I mean, Ricky's in prison, he's not going anywhere. He's going to die in that prison, either of old age or with a needle in his arm. Do you really think it helps anyone to go rifling through his past again? I know I didn't ever expect to hear his name again."

Margot stirred her coffee to give herself time to think about this and how she would answer. Sam seemed like the kind of person who appreciated honesty, even if it was blunt. She was a woman with hard edges and an even temperament, and Margot thought that the best way to get her to open up would be to cut through the bullshit and be honest with her.

"What we're doing has very little to do with Ricky DeGraff himself, which might seem strange given the context, but let me try to explain it. Ricky is in prison, yes. He is facing, some might say, a few life sentences too few. Nothing about my current work is going to net him any additional punishment. He's unlikely to go to trial for anything we uncover in our work, considering he's already behind bars and will be until he's dead, just like you said."

"Okay, so... you can see my point, right?" Sam said, looking confused.

Margot was surprised how young the woman looked under these lights. The lighting at the convention center, coupled with her silver hair, had made her look a bit older. But Margot was realizing now, doing the mental math of when she said she'd started working with DeGraff, and when he'd gone away, that she was probably only in her mid-thirties.

"I don't want to say that you'd need to be a parent to understand, because I think that minimizes the human capacity for empathy. But try to imagine that someone you loved very much, as much as you are capable of loving another person, was taken from you."

Sam's mouth formed a thin line, and Margot knew it was because that had happened to her. Except it was natural causes that had taken Sam's husband away, and no one could put cancer in jail. Still, the younger woman gave a stiff nod.

"Imagine knowing, or suspecting, that something horrible had happened to them, but you never found out what. Maybe you never got to see their body, to have the closure of that final goodbye, because they just vanished one day, and you never got any answers after that. Just a long lifetime of wondering. The reason we're doing what we're doing isn't about getting more punishment for Ricky. He doesn't care at this point what happens to him. The reason we do this is because there are hundreds of thousands of families out there who go to sleep every night wondering where their loved ones are, what happened to them. And if we can help those families find the answers to those questions after all this time, well, we think that's worth waking up a few sleeping dogs."

Sam watched her carefully for a moment, her face showing almost no emotion, beyond a slight tick in her jaw. Finally, she nodded.

"All right, but I'm not really sure how much more I can tell you beyond what I said at the pageant. I didn't know Ricky all that well personally. We weren't friends, we were just co-workers."

"Did he ever show you this?" Margot asked, pulling out a photo of Mathilda.

Sam stared at the photo, then slid it back. "No."

Margot didn't believe her. Because if Sam had never seen the doll before, she would almost certainly have follow-up questions. It was, unquestionably, an unusual thing to ask about, and only moments ago Sam had seemed incredibly curious about the case.

Margot's phone buzzed in her jacket, but she ignored it for the time being. She was pretty sure this conversation was hitting a brick wall because Sam didn't want to be honest with her, which was somewhat suspicious. Margot had thought that opening up to Sam would have made her more willing to talk, not less. She needed a different approach.

"You mentioned that Ricky had another assistant before you."

"Yeah, but not in California."

"Do you know where? Or what her name was?"

Sam shook her head. "I don't, sorry. I know she was older than me, but only because Ricky couldn't stop pointing out how young I was. You know, *you're so talented for someone so young* or *you're so mature for someone your age*. I feel like if the other assistant was young, he wouldn't have been making such a big deal about my age all the time. But I never met her, don't know anything about her. Sorry."

Margot stared at the other woman for a long moment, trying to get a read on her. She couldn't quite decide if Sam was lying or being honest, which usually meant that someone was just lying very well.

Something in the back of her mind told her not to push this any further. At least not tonight. And not here.

She pushed her chair back, signalling her exit. "No, that's fine. I knew it was a bit of a long shot. Appreciate you humoring me with a little more of your time."

"Yeah, no problem. But if you have more questions, maybe just call me next time."

"Sure."

They both stood and Sam walked Margot to the door. When Margot glanced back, she saw that Sam was watching closely. There was something unreadable in her expression, and Margot wondered if she had made the right choice to leave so quickly. She debated turning back and trying again, but instead she waved and set off down the driveway.

It was only when she was back at the main gate and out of sight of the house that she felt like she could pull over and check her messages.

There was a text from Sydney in their group chat.

> Records for the DeGraff LLC showed several independent contractors, but two around the same period. One was Sam Reed, current address...

And the address in Penngrove that Margot was currently staring at on the fence.

> Weird thing though, and maybe it's a mistake in the system. The other employee was a woman named Donna Guenther.

Margot scrolled down to see what was so weird about the woman named Donna.

When she saw Sydney's next message, she froze.

> She was originally from Utah, but according to her last tax return she now lives at 1400 Chatham Lane, Penngrove.

Margot looked back at the sign on Sam's fence.

1402 Chatham Lane.

Then Margot looked at the name again. Donna.

Donna wasn't an uncommon name, to be sure, but the fact that the nun *and* Ricky's former employee were both named Donna was notable.

Now there were coincidences that Margot could overlook, and then there were big old red flags that were waving in front of her face that couldn't be ignored.

She wondered, as she shifted the car into drive, how long it would take for Sam to warn her next-door neighbor that Margot was coming.

THIRTY-NINE

The sun was starting to get lower on the horizon when Margot made it the half-mile to 1400 Chatham Drive. She paused before turning into the driveway to text the group chat.

> I'm at Donna Guenther's address now, I'm going to see if she's willing to chat.

If Donna *was* the same woman who had visited Ricky in prison, it brought up new questions. Why had she taken a brief detour in her life to become a nun? Why had she visited Ricky and then stopped? Why change her name? Sydney hadn't indicated whether or not Donna was married, so perhaps the answer to a lot of these questions was innocent enough. Maybe love had compelled her to leave the fold.

The biggest question of them all was why Sam had lied to her about not knowing Donna. There was simply no way the two of them lived in such close proximity out of pure coincidence. Sam had done her best to keep Margot from discovering anything about Donna.

It might be innocent—perhaps Donna was hiding from an abusive ex, and Sam had learned to become protective of her over the years. Margot could even stretch her imagination to believe

Donna could have a natural reason to be afraid of law enforcement.

But she wanted to ask *Donna* those questions.

Margot suspected Andrew might protest about her impromptu interview, but she was already here.

Margot wasn't going to go in without being careful, though. She called up the local county sheriff's office and reached a competent deputy on her first try.

"I'm with the FBI investigating a cold case, and I just wanted to let you know we might have a potential situation evolving on Chatham Lane." She gave him the address. "I'm not sure if it's going to amount to much, but I'd appreciate it if you could have a car drive by."

"Of course, ma'am. Er, Special Agent. We'll send someone out that way as soon as we have a share car."

Margot sat in her car at the end of the driveway, looking at the little house at the top of the hill.

It looked to be a part of the same property that Sam's place was on, with a more newly developed lot. The house was much smaller, but also newer, than Sam's. That newness meant it was missing a lot of the character of the other house, though. This was just a run-of-the-mill bungalow, painted a deep navy blue with white trim.

There were well-maintained flowerbeds outside, though anything with a lot of color had died off for the season. Still, the house projected a tidy kind of coziness that made it seem entirely non-threatening from the road. All the curtains were drawn and the lights shone through them.

Margot checked that she had her weapon on her and loaded, then pulled into the driveway, gravel crunching under her tires.

There was a little beige Toyota parked there already, and a teal women's bike was leaned up against the garage door. A pair of boots were resting on the steps up to the small porch in front of the door, and though the outside light wasn't on, the glow coming from inside the house illuminated a Halloween-themed wreath hanging on the door, complete with little bats and witch hats.

Margot realized it was time to start thinking about things like pumpkins and candy. They might not be close to town, but a lot of families drove around looking for any places that were decorated, and Wes was a fiend for any holiday.

Though, perhaps, they might not have any kids stopping by this year.

She didn't want to think about that depressing possibility. Instead, she knocked on the door and waited. After a moment the inside door opened, and a pleasant-looking woman appeared behind the screen.

If she'd been expecting Margot, she didn't let it show. "Hello there," she greeted her sweetly. "Can I help you?"

She was shorter than Margot, maybe just a little over five feet, and had dark hair with only a few streaks of gray, but looked to be older than Margot, if the lines by her eyes and mouth were any indication.

Still, there was a warmth about her that put Margot's nerves slightly at ease. Margot knew there was something strange about this situation, yet there was something about Donna that Margot felt naturally soothed by. She realized, with some surprise, that Donna reminded her of her own mother.

Margot pulled out her ID badge and held it up so the woman could see it. "I'm Special Agent Margot Phalen. And I believe you're Donna Guenther?"

The woman smiled. "Well, sure I am. But FBI? That's awfully serious. I hope everything is okay?"

"Would you mind if I come in for a few minutes? It won't take long. I just wanted to ask you a few questions."

"Oh, sure. Forgive me, though, the house is a bit of a mess." She opened the door and ushered Margot inside, directing her to a living room just off the entrance.

Unlike Sam's house, this place felt warm and lived in. The throw blankets and couch cushions looked as if someone had just gotten up from their cozy seat, and the air smelled of something delicious, though Margot couldn't tell if it was dinner that was in the process of cooking, or the lingering scent of what had already been eaten and cleared away.

Margot took a seat in an armchair and Donna sat down on the couch and fiddled with the crocheted blanket. "Sorry, you've got me a little nervous. I've never even spoken to a police officer, let alone an FBI agent. I hope everything is okay."

"Yes, ma'am, nothing to worry about. I actually work as part of a cold case unit with the FBI. We specialize in trying to resolve murders that may be linked to already imprisoned serial killers."

Donna frowned. "I'm sorry, maybe I'm a bit silly, but how can serial killers in prison keep killing people?"

Margot forced a patient smile. "These would be unsolved cold case homicides that we think the killers committed before they were imprisoned."

"Oh, yes. Of course." Donna mimed knocking on her head as if it was empty. "Silly of me. Well, that certainly sounds noble, but I'm not sure how I can help."

"We're currently working on the Ricky DeGraff case," Margot said plainly, then waited to see how Donna would react.

There was a long moment of consideration as Donna took in this information and seemed to debate what she wanted to do with it. She stared at Margot with that same stoic resolve that Sam had only ten minutes earlier. A face that said nothing, but said a hell of a lot in that nothing.

Donna didn't speak.

"I believe you knew Mr. DeGraff," Margot said. She tried to keep her tone light and friendly. This was just a conversation, nothing more. She only wanted to know about Ricky.

Once she had a feel for Donna, she could come back with more agents if it felt necessary. Right now, she wasn't entirely sure she knew how this would play out.

Finally, Donna shook off the shadow that had crossed her features, and her warm smile was back. "Well, sure. Yes. I used to know Ricky, but that was almost twenty years ago. I was newly single, finding my footing, and I started working for him as an assistant."

"How was he to work with?" Margot wanted to ask about Sam, but she thought that was a surefire way to set this going down the wrong path. That question, and the accusation that went along with it, could wait.

"This is going to sound so strange of me to say, given everything that happened, but he was really lovely. Just a wonderful boss. He taught me a lot about photography, helped me prepare myself to own my own business, but honestly, I spent a long time just working for him in Utah while he worked in other states. We were a good team." She was smiling when she finished, then seemed to catch herself. "I know, like I said, that sounds like an awful thing to say, given what's come out about him. But that wasn't the Ricky I knew."

Margot nodded. "Yeah, well. Sometimes people like that are really good at hiding who they are."

"I suppose that's true. You must see a lot of that sort of thing in your line of work."

"More than I'd like," Margot said honestly. "Do you know if Ricky had any close friends?"

Donna let out a little laugh, almost girl-like in its lightness. "Oh, gosh. I don't think so, not really. I think, well, just between us girls, I think Ricky was..." Donna mimed a limp-wrist gesture. "Now, I don't have anything against that personally, of course. I'm not prejudiced. But in Utah that isn't something people really are, you know?"

"Gay people don't exist in Utah?" Margot asked, just to confirm she understood this non-prejudiced statement clearly.

"No, not that, but you just don't see so much of that rainbow flag-waving stuff. Not like what's all over San Francisco." She wrinkled her nose to emphasize she had nothing against it.

"Sure. So, if I understand you correctly, you think Ricky had a hard time making friends in Utah because he was gay."

"Yes, thank you! I knew you knew what I was saying."

Margot wished that wasn't the case.

"Now that I'm thinking about it, though, he might have sent me some pictures of him with some friends. Friends in a different state, mind you, not people I knew. But he'd sometimes send me little greetings from the road when he was working the out-of-state circuit." She smiled warmly. "Give me a minute, I think I know where they might be."

She disappeared down the hall, leaving Margot alone in the living room, unsure of what to do next.

She was being lied to, that much was obvious, but what were Sam and Donna hiding? Was it their involvement with Ricky, or their knowledge of each other? There was always a small chance neither of them was guilty of anything, and they had just bonded after learning someone they both knew had been doing horrific things when they knew him.

The chance was slim, but it was *possible*.

Margot's eyes drifted around the room and landed over the brick fireplace. She got up, wandered closer, and saw that there were a dozen pictures of a beautiful blonde girl. She didn't bear much resemblance to her mother—Margot assumed this was Donna's daughter just based on the volume of the photos—but she was a gorgeous and happy-looking girl. The girl in the photos got younger and younger as Margot moved from right to left, but when she got to the farthest-left photo on the mantel she had to pick it up.

Something about the photo bothered her, a nagging kind of familiarity that she couldn't explain as just seeing the same face over and over in the dozen other photos.

A door opened somewhere in the house, then closed again, and Margot heard footsteps in the kitchen, which was just off the living room, an open doorway between them. "Mom, I'm home. Dinner smells great." She looked towards the kitchen entrance, where the fridge door opened, obscuring whoever was behind it, but showing Margot the clear face of the door itself.

There, too, were more than a dozen photos, each of them of a different little girl. Smiling portraits, all with the same tilted head and soft lighting blurring the features enough to make everything smooth.

Margot recognized each and every one of those faces.

She had been looking at them day after day for the last four months.

Then Margot looked down at the photo in her hand and suddenly understood exactly why it looked so familiar.

The sweet little blonde girl who couldn't have been more than two or three years old in the oldest photo was Rini Fawcett. The little girl who had been snatched from her own front yard while her mother worked inside.

The girl they'd never been able to pin on DeGraff.

The fridge door closed, and Margot watched as a blonde teenager straightened up and turned to come into the living room. The girl had a can of Diet Coke in her hand. She froze when she saw Margot, a bewildered expression on her face, but there was no doubt in Margot's mind who she was.

"Who are you?" the girl asked.

"Margot," was all Margot could think to say.

Another door closed and Donna's cheerful voice called down the hall, "Kelsey, baby, can you go to the garage and get us some more Cokes for the fridge please?"

But before the girl had a chance to respond or move, Margot turned, to see Donna enter the living room.

And she wasn't carrying photos.

She was holding a shotgun and pointing it directly at Margot.

FORTY

Sixteen Years Ago

Ricky DeGraff had never set out to kill anyone. It hadn't been his plan.

But as soon as he felt those delicate throat bones crush under his palms, the moment he'd seen the light go out in that first girl's eyes, he had understood something about himself that he had never known before.

Even though he hadn't planned to kill anyone, he realized he didn't mind the process of it.

Killing someone might not be easy, but that was just because of the physical exertion it demanded. It was a lot of work to choke the life out of someone, especially a teenaged girl.

The lesson he learned was not *don't kill*, it was *choose easier victims*.

Of course, he never thought of them as victims.

They were his beautiful dolls. They were all so lovely, so perfect, until they stopped being lovely and perfect. When they started to cry so hard snot poured from their noses and spit foamed in their mouths. When they sobbed and screamed for their mothers.

When they pissed themselves.

They were all his dolls until they reminded him how horribly human they were. How imperfect they could be. How loud and smelly and disgusting.

Ricky didn't want things he had to take care of. He didn't even have pets because the effort of living up to the demands of another creature was not something he wanted to deal with.

Each time he picked a new girl, he watched her. Watched how she behaved, how she presented herself. Each time, he hoped she would be the right one, the one who could meet his expectations, and be everything he wanted.

And he didn't think he was asking for too much.

Mathilda was lonely, and she wanted a friend. He just wanted his new dolls to be good enough for Mathilda. But half the time, once he had them, he realized they weren't even worthy of getting to meet her, let alone being her friend.

Mathilda was delicate, she was precious. Even now, he was ever so careful when he picked her up, remembering the way his parents had spoken to him. Support her head. Don't hold her too tight. Don't pick her up unless we're with you.

They wanted him to be so gentle, as if she had been a real baby, a real thing that needed to be protected. And he had obeyed.

Mostly.

He remembered when he'd broken the rules once, remembered how he'd badly wanted to play with her one night, and went to the place his parents kept her.

He remembered the way she smelled. Even now he'd never known what perfume or soap his mother had used on the doll's clothes to make her smell that way. Baby powder and a hint of something milky. A beautiful smell.

He'd snuck in to hold her, but found that night that she was hard to position. Her head felt heavier than usual, her body didn't fit easily in his arms, as if it were moving on its own, which was impossible, of course.

It hadn't been Ricky's fault when he dropped her. He remembered the sickening *thunk* she had made when she hit the floor. The way she was still, then, still like she was supposed to be. He'd checked, to make sure she didn't look broken, and there were no obvious cracks.

He put her back where he'd found her, worried the sound might wake his parents, and returned to his own bed.

For a while after that, he felt very guilty. His parents never seemed to realize he had dropped her, but for a long time he wasn't allowed to play with Mathilda or even see her. His mother was very sad, and for months she didn't want to play with Ricky, and she barely got out of bed.

He wondered if maybe he *had* broken Mathilda and his mother was sad because the doll was so fragile, and it was cracked now.

He was sad along with his mother, because he missed playing with her, and he missed playing with Mathilda.

And then one day, when the house felt like a swimming pool that had been filled to the top with sadness, and no one inside seemed to know how to swim out of it, his mother came home smiling.

She had a doll, and it was Mathilda, but different. She had much longer hair now, beautiful brown hair, and she smelled different. She was cooler to the touch. But Ricky saw the way his mother held the doll, and touched the doll. The way she smiled when she ran a comb through that lovely long hair, humming a song under her breath as she did it.

It was Mathilda, and not Mathilda, but he couldn't understand the differences enough to be bothered by them. He just knew things in the house felt lighter again, and his parents were smiling and talking to each other again. The sound of his mother's soft sobs didn't fill the house anymore.

Things were good again, and so he was happy.

And since Mathilda had made them so happy, he promised he would never be careless with her again. He would never let anything happen to her.

He would find her a friend, because he understood clearly that, with each new doll he returned broken, there would come a day when he would be caught. His time would run out, and he wouldn't be able to be with Mathilda anymore.

All that mattered before that happened was making sure she was cared for.

Ricky had to find a friend of his own. He knew he couldn't entrust Mathilda to his father. His father had been the one to throw her in a box and send her to Ricky in the first place. He didn't love the doll the way Ricky and his mother had. For him, it was just a thing.

Ricky had needed to find someone who understood him. Someone who could appreciate what he was trying to do. Someone he could trust.

It meant getting to know someone, letting them learn who he was, what he had come from.

Ricky didn't like to let those little bits of himself show. He didn't like talking about himself, didn't like talking to people at all, most of the time. Usually after a pageant, when he had spent all day wooing mothers and speaking gently to shy little girls, he didn't have the energy left for anything else. He was spent.

Trying to find company outside all of that was asking too much for him.

Instead, he went looking inside that world. Who could understand him better than someone who also spent their time around all those glittering dolls?

He put out an ad for assistants. For people who wanted to learn photography and about how to run a business like his. He immediately dismissed any men who were interested. He didn't trust men.

But there were two women who applied who had potential.

There was Sam, who was young and vibrant and a talented photographer. And there was Donna, recently divorced, in her thirties, with no photography experience, but desperate for a way to take care of herself. Her earnestness made Ricky like her immediately. Sam was more closed off, but if he was going to entrust someone with his secrets, he needed options. It helped that the women lived in different states, Sam in California, Donna in Utah. They could both work with him without ever needing to meet each other.

He could test their reliability, but he could also expand the places he was able to work, if they both started working for him. They could cover more pageants at once.

They could look for more girls at once.

It hadn't taken long for Ricky to realize that Donna was the one. Sam was too independent, too motivated about her own goals. She took to the business well, but she wasn't right for his needs.

Donna, though, Donna was different entirely.

The photography was entirely secondary to her, and she didn't have a natural aptitude for it. Thankfully, most of the work of their photos was done by the lighting and backdrops. All Donna needed to do was point the camera and click, which she was more than capable of.

What Ricky realized within months of meeting her, though, was that Donna was *hungry*. She was so needy for affection that she didn't care where it came from or why. She just wanted someone to pay attention to her, to talk to her, to tell her from time to time that she was beautiful and worthy.

Ricky could do all those things.

It was no different, really, from telling a hovering stage mom that her homely daughter was gorgeous.

Donna was pliable, eager, she wanted to please him, wanted him to see her and talk to her, and it didn't take long for him to realize that yearning for connection was the precise thing he needed.

She didn't even realize how deep she was in until she picked up the first girl and brought her to him.

Because Donna, unlike him, wasn't going to turn any heads if she picked up a little girl walking down the street. And little girls weren't going to think twice about getting in a car with Donna. She had a pleasant appearance, but a largely forgettable face. She also had a great demeanor with children, something she honed during her time with him. She was soft-spoken and warm, and it made kids trust her immediately.

Yes, Donna was the one he had been hoping for.

And once she had brought the first girl to him, she seemed to realize that she was in too deep to back out now, so she yielded with almost shocking ease. Of course, she seemed to see things differently than Ricky. Where he was looking for a perfect friend for Mathilda, Donna thought they were trying to create their own perfect family. She talked often about how, when they found the right little girl, they would all be happy together. Her, Ricky, the child, and Mathilda.

It was her inclusion of Mathilda in these plans that let Ricky know she was the one to trust long term.

He told her she could look after Mathilda for him, because he knew she was the only one who could.

And then Donna had brought a girl home, one who was too young, as far as Ricky was concerned. But she coaxed, she pleaded, she promised. She said this one was so young she wouldn't remember anything else. She wouldn't fight them. She could be the daughter Donna had wanted for so long and hadn't gotten from her ex-husband.

Ricky was unconvinced, but Donna was obstinate. She would prove to him this girl was the right one, not just for her, but for Mathilda.

And Ricky had relented.

After all, Donna never asked questions about why the previous girls hadn't worked. She just helped dispose of them when Ricky was done, whispering her quiet little prayers over their bodies, and saying the Lord would bring her the right baby soon enough.

Ricky wasn't convinced.

He wasn't sure anyone would ever be suitable for Mathilda.

No matter how hard he looked.

But he would keep looking. Because at least now he knew Mathilda was safe, no matter what happened to him.

FORTY-ONE

Donna had entered the room as casually as if she was bringing them cups of coffee. She was even smiling, still, as she raised the shotgun's barrel and pointed it at Margot.

Because of this, for a moment Margot didn't perceive the gun as a threat. She looked at it, and then at the part of Donna's face she could see, and for some reason she thought this might be a confusing joke.

"Donna, what are you doing?" she asked.

"*Mom.*" The high-pitched, terrified voice of the girl—Rini Fawcett—pierced the room, capturing Donna's attention enough that she took her eyes off Margot.

"Kelsey, baby, your mama is just keeping you safe. Now go to the garage like I told you."

Margot saw the teenaged girl look between the two women, her face a portrait of confusion. It was clear she wanted to listen to Donna, because the woman was her mother. At least she believed she was. But Margot knew she understood that something was very wrong with the scene unfolding before her.

Margot's brain had finally decided to register that the gun pointing at her chest was a real threat. Her heart had started to pound, sweat was beading across her brow, and she forced herself to take deep, steadying breaths.

Panic wouldn't do anything to help her. She needed to keep a cool head if she was going to get out of this alive. And right now, that felt like a very big *if*. Kelsey was close enough to her that Donna might not shoot for fear of harming her. Margot said a silent prayer Kelsey wouldn't turn and run.

"Donna, you don't want to do this. If you do this, you'll never see the girl again."

Donna snorted. "Now that you've found us, if I *don't* do this, I'll never see her again. At least if I get rid of you, we've got time to disappear. We've done it before."

"Mom, what is happening? What are you talking about?" The girl sounded terrified.

"Shush, Kelsey. Be a good girl and go to the garage, okay? You don't need to see this."

"Kelsey?" Margot said, looking at the girl. God, it was astounding now, looking at her face, how much she still resembled all the baby pictures of Rini that Margot had seen. They'd never bothered with age-progressed photos, because everyone believed that Rini was dead. But if they'd ever done them, Margot knew they would be a mirror of the girl she was looking at now.

"Kelsey," she repeated, making sure the girl was looking at her. "My name is Margot. I'm an FBI agent."

"She's a liar, baby. She's here to take you away from me."

"You can check my pocket. I have a badge," Margot said, keeping her voice as steady as possible. If the girl did come forward to check her badge, she'd be standing right between them, and Donna wouldn't have a clear shot.

"Don't you listen to a single thing she says," Donna insisted, shaking the gun so fiercely that Margot worried it might go off by accident.

She wished it was any other kind of gun. A rifle, a handgun. Something where she could hope that Donna's aim might be bad enough or unlucky enough that Margot could avoid being hit.

But a shotgun? The buckshot couldn't possibly miss her from this distance.

Margot had to think of a way out of this. She had a whole life waiting for her. A home she loved, Wes, and her stupid chickens. She wanted very, very badly to wake up tomorrow morning to feed those chickens.

As Margot watched Donna, she noticed the way the woman's hands were trembling. This was a woman who was moved by desperation, but not necessarily ready to pull the trigger.

"Kelsey, do you have a cell phone on you?"

"Y-yes."

"I want you to pull out your phone, okay? I want you to look up a name for me. Maddie Moore." She couldn't just jump right to Kelsey's real name. The girl wouldn't accept it. She needed to lay a groundwork of belief. But she wasn't sure how much time she was going to have to do that.

"Don't do it, baby. Don't listen to her."

But Kelsey caught Margot's eye, seeming to understand this situation wasn't right. That she needed an answer to what was happening that her mother was never going to give her. The girl pulled out her phone and tapped at the screen.

Margot locked eyes with Donna, whose whole body seemed to be shaking with anger, her eyes filled with tears. "I won't let you do this to us," she said.

"No one did this except you," Margot replied.

"What... what am I looking at?" Kelsey said.

"Look at the fridge door," Margot commanded. "Her picture is there."

"Those are girls that Mom helped train for pageants," Kelsey said, though something in her voice belied a new doubt.

"No," Margot said flatly. "Those are girls who were killed. Those are girls your mom helped someone kill."

"Don't listen to her. That's a lie."

"Kelsey, look up one more name for me."

"*Go outside*," Donna screamed, understanding she was losing control of the situation.

She edged towards Kelsey like she might swat the phone out of the girl's hand, but she'd need to put the gun down to do it.

"Just one more name," Margot insisted. "Then I think you'll understand. Just look up the name Rini Fawcett. Two I's, a W in the last name."

The girl looked hesitant. Margot could see that she knew that, if she did what she was asked, things would never be the same again. But just looking at the scene in the living room, she had to know that was already true. Maybe some small part of her remembered that name, deep in the recesses of her mind.

She started to type on her phone.

"Please don't do this," Donna screeched, her voice tight with panic and emotion. "Please."

It was unclear which of them this was directed at, or if it was more of a universal plea.

Kelsey was staring at her phone.

"I don't understand."

"That's you," Margot said softly. "That's you right before you vanished from your front yard one summer morning, and no one ever saw you again."

The pain and confusion on the girl's face nearly broke Margot's heart, but she prayed she'd done enough to convince Kelsey of what she was saying.

"Your mom isn't your mom, Kelsey," she said softly, though there was no way to take the edge off a blow like that. "Your mom was helping a very bad man named Ricky DeGraff. You can look him up. He killed little girls, and your mom helped him find those girls. You were supposed to be one of them. I don't know why you're not."

She recalled, then, what Ricky had said in their last meeting.

About why he could trust Donna.

I gave her everything.

Then she looked at the girl, at the house decorated to show that a perfect, happy family lived there. The dozen photos on the mantel behind her.

Of course.

Ricky hadn't killed Rini. He'd let Donna keep her. It was his way to guarantee Donna would never betray him. Because he'd given her what she wanted most.

Margot felt sick to her stomach.

Donna was crying, but she still had the gun pointed at Margot, and her trigger discipline left a lot to be desired.

"Donna, put the gun down," Margot said, her voice impossibly calm even to her own ears. "You don't want Kelsey to get hurt or to see something she shouldn't."

Since the girl—who was also crying now—seemed as if she wasn't planning to go anywhere, Margot felt the slightest bit safer. But there was still a chance Donna would pull the trigger anyway. She'd done a desperate thing to get Kelsey.

What was one more desperate thing, if she thought she might be able to keep her?

Except Margot had ruined that by telling the girl the truth. Donna probably could have kept running, could have constructed new lies, moved to a new town and maybe changed their names. But she couldn't do that now, not as easily.

Maybe she could convince the girl it was necessary, that Margot had been lying, but if she pulled the trigger, there was one thing she could never erase.

"You don't want her to see me die," Margot said. "She can't unsee that, Donna. No matter what else you tell her, no matter how good you might be at lying, you can never do anything to wipe that from her mind. Her mother pulling the trigger, and a woman's torso being obliterated by buckshot. Have you ever seen what a shotgun blast does to the human body at this range? That's not something you can ever unsee."

"Shut *up*," Donna snarled.

"She won't be able to sleep at night. She'll wake up with nightmares. She will always remember watching you kill someone. And you're many things, Donna, but I don't think you've ever killed anyone before. Not yourself. You helped Ricky do it, but he did all the dirty work, didn't he? I doubt you even watched it. He would have wanted to be alone with them."

"I never killed anyone," she said emphatically.

"Then don't start now." Margot's pulse was hammering so loudly she could barely hear the words coming out of her mouth. Everything sounded distant, distorted, like she was underwater and hearing her voice come to her from far away. Suddenly, she could remember with perfect clarity a Bible verse that she'd found in her research on a different killer. It came to her then, despite her not being a religious person.

She might not believe in God, but Donna did.

"There are six things that the Lord hates, seven that are an abomination to him. Haughty eyes, a lying tongue, and hands that shed innocent blood, a heart that devises wicked plans, feet that make haste to run to evil—"

"*Stop it*," Donna shouted, squinting her eyes closed briefly, and jerking her head from side to side like she could unhear Proverbs.

"Mom," Kelsey said, her voice shaky even on the one word. "Please put the gun down."

Margot's heart clenched, both for the pain in the girl's tone and for her fear that Donna might not listen to either of them.

Then Margot heard the distinct crunch of gravel in the driveway, and all three of them looked towards the sound. The blinds were drawn but they were gauzy, and Margot could see the hazy shape of a black and white Sheriff's Department cruiser.

The momentary distraction was all Margot needed.

She dove behind the couch, even as Donna's kneejerk reaction to the movement caused the gun to go off, buckshot embedding itself into the brick fireplace, glass falling to the carpet from the shattered picture frames.

"Oh, fuck," she heard Donna say.

"*Mom*," Kelsey was screaming.

Margot had to think fast, and get ready for what was going to come next. If Donna came around the back of the couch, Margot was a sitting duck, but she also didn't dare move, in case it drew Donna's attention to her and she decided to aim true this time.

Voices outside were shouting, but Margot couldn't make out the words.

Then she heard the sound of the front door being smashed in and the shouting got much louder but no more distinct. Margot got out her weapon, now that she was protected and her brain wised up enough to remind her she had it.

There was so much shouting, but Margot knew she had to add to the din. "I'm FBI, I'm behind the couch," she yelled, waving a hand over the couch, then jerking it back before someone could shoot it off. "I'm armed, is it safe to stand?"

"You're clear," came a sharp female voice. "But raise both your hands when you come out."

Margot holstered her weapon, then slowly got to her feet, both hands in the air.

One uniformed deputy had Donna on the floor, his knee in her back as he cuffed her. The deputy who had been speaking to Margot had her weapon drawn but it was aiming down as she waited for Margot to stand.

"I'm going to reach for my badge now," Margot said, waving one hand and moving it slowly to her jacket pocket. The deputy looked uneasy, her stare intense, but once Margot removed her ID badge and opened it, the deputy's posture changed immediately. Not relaxed, exactly, but less taut.

"She fired at you?" the deputy asked.

"She fired where I used to be," Margot said, turning around to see the new holes in the fireplace, all the destroyed photos, before looking at Kelsey, who was thankfully unharmed and still standing in the kitchen doorway, her eyes wide and horrified at the scene unfolding before her, her mother on the living room floor in cuffs, the shotgun now in the hands of the male deputy.

"The girl is a missing person," Margot said, trying to keep her breath calm and even. "If you look up Rini Fawcett, you'll find she went missing about fifteen years ago."

The two deputies exchanged baffled glances, clearly wondering what the hell they'd gotten themselves into.

Margot, for her part, was just relieved they'd come as a pair.

"Someone is going to need to find her parents," she said. "Her real parents."

Kelsey didn't seem to hear a single word she was saying. She just kept staring at her mother. The woman she thought was her mother.

On the floor, Donna was crying now, ugly, deep sobs. She couldn't take her eyes off her daughter.

"I'm so sorry, baby," she said, between gasps. "I'm so sorry. Your mama loves you, Kelsey, baby. I love you so much."

The deputy who had cuffed her helped Donna to her feet, while the other spoke animatedly into her radio.

Margot crossed the room in Kelsey's direction, knowing the girl was going to need comfort and guidance through what came next, even if Margot might not be the right person to offer it. She got the feeling there was still a very long night ahead of her.

FORTY-TWO

When the police cruiser pulled away an hour and a half later with Donna in the back, Margot spotted Andrew sitting on the hood of his car, arms crossed over his chest as he observed the scene unfolding around them. There were more cruisers, their blue and red lights swirling over the front of the house. In the distance, she could see more of them in front of Sam's house and could hear the dogs howling discontentedly.

She vaguely wondered what would become of all those dogs.

There was a chance, with a good enough lawyer, that Sam might still walk away from this. She could lie, pretend she had no idea what Donna had been doing with Ricky DeGraff. She could say she didn't know who Kelsey was.

She could pretend that she had just been helping a mutual friend, someone who she had shared a boss with, who was doing her a favor by renting a vacant property on her land, and that whatever went on in someone's house was none of her damned business.

She might be back in her house in a few days.

Then again, she and Donna might end up with side-by-side cells. It was hard to call.

There were a crew of FBI agents who Margot didn't know moving in and out of the small house, removing boxes of items.

Margot headed over to Andrew and sat next to him on the car hood. From this distance she could almost feel removed from it all. Except there was still a girl sitting in one of those cruisers, crying her eyes out because she had just learned that her mother wasn't her mother at all.

That was going to take her some time to process.

Margot knew the local PD were trying to locate Rini Fawcett's biological parents, but it wasn't going to happen instantly. The girl was going to need to be taken in somewhere overnight, probably an emergency foster. Things were going to be very hard for her.

That hadn't been the outcome Margot had been expecting when she had pulled into the driveway of the little house a few hours earlier.

Andrew nudged Margot with his shoulder, and then jerked his chin towards the scene. "I owe you an apology," he said, which was a sentence Margot was unaccustomed to hearing from him.

"Why?" she asked, frowning.

"I'm the one who told you to come here on your own. I never should have let you come into a situation like this without backup."

Margot let out a little laugh. "We had no idea what this situation was going to be when you sent me here. We both thought this was just going to be a run-of-the-mill follow-up interview. I wasn't even supposed to be here." She waved her hand in the direction of Donna's house. "What a fucking mess."

An FBI agent exited the house. In her hands was a doll, clearly visible through a massive plastic evidence bag.

"Guess that's her," Andrew said, watching the doll get loaded into the back of a van. "All of this, because of that one doll? What a fucking mess," he added, echoing her earlier statement.

"She had pictures on her fridge, Andrew. Of Maddie Moore. Of so many of the girls. Ones we'd been sure he couldn't be involved with. They were portraits, and she had them up there the same way I've got my nephew's school pictures on my fridge." She grimaced at the thought of it. "Pictures we've been looking at for months. How could she look at those, day after day, knowing what had happened to them? *Because of her*."

"I think, Margot, that we sometimes fall into a trap in this line of work of wanting to understand things better. Of trying to uncover the *why* of some things to make them knowable. But we're talking about a man who killed children so his doll could have company. And a woman so desperate for a child of her own, she was willing to steal one. I think it's okay to not understand that. We can know the *why* and not have to be able to know how they justify it to themselves. This is a woman who was and is clearly mentally unwell. Things aren't going to make sense in these scenarios, no matter how much we would like them to."

"I feel bad for that girl," Margot said.

"Worse than if you'd learned she was just another photo on the fridge?"

She stared at the house, the people moving in and out and dismantling the only life that girl could remember. And she thought about sitting next to Andrew in a very different car, a very long time ago, as her mother collapsed onto the lawn sobbing, and her father was tackled to the ground by multiple federal agents, and she wondered if these scenes were really all that different.

Margot thought. It wasn't an easy question to answer. "I don't know, honestly. Her life is going to be so hard. She's going to get so much attention from the media. How do you get anything like a normal life after all this?"

Andrew must have been thinking the same thing she had, remembering their first meeting almost thirty years earlier.

"Maybe she doesn't get to have normal. But she's alive. And that's something," he said.

They both continued to watch what was unfolding at the house. Andrew was likely in charge of this whole show in some capacity. He was certainly the most senior person on site. But no one bothered them with questions or seemed to be paying any attention to them in the least.

"We got a call from Alana and Greg right before all this kicked off," Andrew said, as if it was only now occurring to him to share this information.

"Oh?" Margot was so tired now that the adrenaline had worn off that she wasn't sure she even cared what they had discovered at Ricky's childhood home. But maybe she was wrong. Maybe this final little piece would make everything make sense. "Did they find anything?"

Andrew nodded, stuffing his hands in the pockets of his jacket, both to fend off the cold and likely because he wasn't sure what to do with them. "We had the dogs there, a dig team ready, and a forensic anthropologist on site."

"You were pretty confident we were going to find something, then?" she said.

Andrew shrugged. "It seemed like a strong possibility, and I was starting to feel a little pressure on this one. The money guys don't love when we visit a prison more than once."

Margot snorted softly. "No doubt."

"They found a place in the yard that the new owners said had previously been a garden shed. They'd torn it down years ago. The dogs hit on the area right away. It didn't take them long at all to find the grave. Guess no one thought they needed to bury such a small body very deep."

He pulled out his phone and handed it to Margot. She swiped through the pictures from the scene, which showed a delicately unearthed grave site, where the tattered remains of a baby blanket were wrapped under a thick plastic sheet. In the next photos the sheet and blanket were peeled back, showing the skeletal remains of a baby, bits of a sleeping onesie still stuck to her frame.

Margot knew she was supposed to be desensitized to death by now, that nothing was supposed to shock her. But sometimes things crept up and made it hard to be dispassionate. There was an ache in her chest that was hard to ignore.

The DeGraffs had buried their own daughter in their backyard.

Another photo showed the skull from a different angle, which seemed to give their strongest indication yet of what had killed baby Mathilda. There was a long crack in the skull.

Margot handed the phone back, not looking at anything else. "What did the anthropologist say?" she asked, her mouth suddenly dry.

"We'll want an opinion from a medical examiner, I think, but the anthropologist was confident it was not an accident that caused the baby's death. He believes that someone very intentionally hit her head against something hard—the floor or another object that dense—and possibly did so repeatedly."

Margot grimaced, wishing she hadn't asked.

"So it was Ricky, then," she said, mostly to herself.

"That seems like the most logical conclusion. I don't think he was faking during your interview with him, though."

Margot nodded. "So DeGraff did intentionally kill his baby sister, but he doesn't remember doing it, or even remember that he had a sister. He took all of the feelings and guilt he'd been carrying over that murder and transferred them to Mathilda the doll. Everything he's done since, then, is his own twisted penance for that first kill."

The cruiser with Kelsey in it turned off its lights and pulled out of the driveway. Margot had no way to know what was next for that poor girl, but she felt a surge of empathy for her.

"I know we should know not to expect things," she said. "There's never a guarantee we'll get answers, never a sure thing that we're even right about there being more victims, but damn, I did *not* see things going this way in this case."

"None of us could have seen this coming, Margot, not even you. It's all..." He gestured towards the house, the people, the whole twisted mess of it. "It's beyond prediction, even when we do our best to predict the answers, you know?"

"Can I go home?" she asked.

"Yeah, take a couple days. You deserve it. We're back at it Monday, though."

"New horrible things to look at?"

"Always."

"Can't wait," she said, without bothering to fake a smile.

At least, if she wanted to look for a silver lining, Rocco's was still open when she pulled up forty minutes later.

The chicken was hot when she got home, but Margot barely noticed.

As soon as she pulled the car into her driveway and saw the familiar glow of lights on in her home, her hands began to shake. She was able to put the car into park and kill the engine before the trembling became too violent, and that was about the same moment she realized she was crying.

She'd been here before, the place where shock took over after something traumatic. But knowing what was happening didn't make it any easier.

Her body had taken over, stealing complete control.

It didn't matter that she knew she was safe and no longer in danger. This was the price that had to be paid for being able to stay calm. She'd kept her shit together even when it seemed like Donna might be the last person she ever saw.

She held on to her cool with Andrew and for the long drive home.

But her body needed its moment, and now it was going to take that, whether she liked it or not.

She sat in her car for a good ten minutes, trembling and crying —good, body-rocking sobs—until the shock turned into relief and she was able to take one trembling breath after another to calm herself.

She wiped her face on her jacket, took a breath to steady her nerves, then grabbed the chicken and got out, as ready to enter the house as she was going to be.

She'd only taken a few steps when she saw something moving between the burnt-out barn and the house. At first, she stiffened, wondering if this was some new threat, but it was too small. An animal—probably just a raccoon or opossum.

But she caught the silvery glint of an eye reflection from the light off the porch, and her pulse quickened.

It couldn't be.

She had been certain. She hadn't wanted to believe the worst, but the worst was all that had been left for her.

Then Lucy crossed the beam of light coming from the dining room window and made a beeline for her, meowing loudly, and Margot was almost convinced she was imagining it. Her brain had decided to invent some pleasant thing to reward her for her horrific night.

Lucy brushed against her in her shin and let out a familiar commanding yowl. The one that demanded food and attention *now*.

Margot stooped down, somehow still clinging to the chicken, though she had forgotten she was holding it, and scooped the calico cat into her arms.

Lucy headbutted her chin, purring loudly. Her whiskers were singed and her fur felt slightly oily under Margot's palms, but she was alive, and she was home.

Margot started to cry again, her face buried in the cat's smoke-scented fur until Lucy became annoyed and gently bit Margot's arm, still purring the whole time.

Margot didn't let her go until she was back in the house with the door tightly closed, and then she called out for Wes, longing to share the euphoria of this miracle with him.

Lucy and Margot were both alive, somehow.

They were home.

FORTY-THREE
COLORADO SPRINGS, CO

Present

He liked Colorado. He'd visited several times, and he'd always known it was somewhere he would like to do some work. It was a beautiful state, and it was positively brimming with backroads and isolated places. He'd laid the groundwork during his last stay, though he hadn't bothered to look for anyone. He would have been too rushed.

Now it was October, and the weather was positively chilly in contrast to Northern California, where winter never really learned to stick around the same way it did in other places.

This was a good time of year. Snow would come, but for now it hadn't fallen yet, which gave him a short window to do what he wanted to do.

Colorado Springs wasn't a small town, it was a proper city, a place he could get lost in and slip by completely unnoticed. In other words, it was a perfect change of pace from where he'd just been.

He had to admit, there were aspects of his work in Willows he'd really enjoyed. He'd liked being able to really sit in the aftermath of what he'd done and see how it had unfolded. That wasn't a gift he was normally afforded. It was risky for him to stick around in a small town, he knew that, but he was confident he'd timed things well enough, been strategic enough, careful enough, that there was no risk of any of it blowing back at him.

Of course, he should have wrapped it all up the first time, not gone back for a second trip. If there was anything he'd done wrong, it was going back. But he hadn't stuck around long the second time, hadn't gone anywhere that he might be recognized as a repeat guest. He'd slept in his truck again, though he had considered going into the old house to have a poke around. It was obvious no one had been there for a long time, and no one was likely to notice his disruption, but there was something about the place that had made him wary. All that dust, that untouched space. No, he would likely have left something of himself inside there. Sleeping on an old mattress that was probably filled with mouse nests wasn't worth the added risk. His truck was fine. He had blankets he could roll out in the backseat to make it more comfortable. Though the drop in temperature did mean he got a chill overnight.

That was how he knew it was time to move on, to put Willows in his rearview and not risk leaving any more traces behind.

Of course, he always left the door open to return to the area. Willows wasn't the only town on that stretch of road. There were other places he could work, other venues to explore. There was no need to leave himself unprepared.

For now, though, he had a working bank card, a motel room that didn't care to ask him for ID as long as he paid his stay ahead of time, and a family somewhere who would be confused as to why their missing loved one was spending a few nights in Colorado Springs.

He felt confident they wouldn't come looking just yet. But this would be the last place he would use the card. The trail could end there. Anything else would just be pushing his luck.

The motel was otherwise perfect. No cameras outside, a clerk who seemed more interested in her paperback novel than in anything happening around her. The kind of disconnected place that didn't really exist anymore. He loved finding little shithole gems like this as he moved around. It was good to keep track of them. You never knew when you might need one.

He had just finished taking a shower when his phone rang. He only turned it on for an hour a day, if that. Sometimes he'd leave it off for entire states. It was always off when he worked. Too easy to track that kind of data.

He walked through the hotel room naked, confident, and picked up the phone.

"Hey, little peach, how's my girl?" he asked, his tone husky, charming.

"I've been trying to call you all day," a woman's voice answered. "Where are you?"

"Tonight, Nevada. And you know I don't leave my phone on when I'm working. Is everything okay?"

The woman sighed, a heavy, tired sound that was like the promise of a fight without the execution. She'd stopped asking him hard questions a long time ago, stopped picking fights she knew she would never win.

"Brooklyn wants to say goodnight."

"All right, put her on."

There were some jostling noises, two voices in the background, then the sound of the phone being picked up off a counter. "Daddy?" came a small voice.

"Well, hi there, little lady. You're up pretty late, aren't you?"

"No," she protested. "It's just bedtime now. Not late."

"I get my time zones mixed up sometimes. Did you have a good day today? How was school?"

"Good." She had that way about her, where she was bursting at the seams to share everything with them, but when they asked her anything it was just one-word answers and no elaborations. Things were just *good*. If he asked what she learned it would either be *nothing* or *I dunno*.

She was only four, of course, so *nothing* seemed like a natural thing for her to be learning at preschool. Still, it tickled his nerves in an unpleasant way. She should be smarter than that, better. She should be able to speak for herself, to make herself understood.

He didn't have the energy to try to get more out of her tonight, though.

"That's good, baby, I'm glad to hear it. You're being really good for your mommy, right?"

"Uh-huh. When are you coming home?"

"Monday," he said. "What do you want me to bring you?"

"M&Ms," she said, as he knew she would.

There might come a day she would demand specific things. A Las Vegas snow globe, a mascot of a teddy bear. Things where he'd have to be more careful when he lied about where he was. But right now, the only things she ever asked for could be picked up at a gas station fifteen minutes from his front door. He wife never asked for anything.

Not anymore.

He suspected, at least to some extent, that part of the reason was because she knew he wasn't always where he said he was, and she didn't want to go to the effort of uncovering the lies.

That was one of the reasons he liked her so much.

She had learned not to be a problem for him.

He said goodnight to his daughter, and a more tepid goodnight to his wife, and once the conversation was over, he turned the phone off and got dressed.

It was late, traffic was light. He'd done a little research on his last visit and knew that Pikes Peak College had both a massive student population and the best nursing program in the state.

He also knew what time of night the buses started to thin out, leaving students who had stayed late at the library doing extra work to sit for long periods, or walk home in the cold.

He pulled onto the campus and cruised around, avoiding any areas that seemed too heavily populated. He needed somewhere dark, somewhere more isolated, where it was unlikely people would be hanging out in groups, and even less likely that someone might see him working.

On the edge of a quad, the overhead light blinking on and off, he saw a girl moving slowly, her bag seemingly so heavy she was hunched forward in an attempt to shift the weight of it.

He pulled up alongside her, rolling down his window.

"Hey, you need a lift?" he asked.

She stared at him, squinting across the dark sidewalk. From where she was, she could probably see the Pikes Peak staff badge, and the familiar uniform of the janitorial staff.

"Look, I'm just heading over to the Rampart Center to start my shift, at least let me get you to a better bus stop. It's so dark over here, I don't feel right leaving you by yourself."

The girl looked around, suddenly reminded that it was indeed both dark and isolated here, and then let out a little sigh. "Sure, okay. Thank you so much."

Because after all, she could trust a school employee, couldn't she?

What was the worst thing that could happen?

FORTY-FOUR

Margot's alarm buzzed before dawn, though she had already been awake for a while, staring at the ceiling and thinking. Lucy was curled up between Margot and Wes and had spent most of the night purring so aggressively that Margot could feel the vibration in her ribs.

Margot didn't want the sweet cat to leave her sight. The miracle of her return was the one glowing positive in this entire fucked-up week. Sure, she could be happy about finally wrapping up the DeGraff investigation, but the victory felt hollow.

A family had been destroyed, and a girl now had to live with the agonizing truth of her upbringing. That was a pain that Margot understood all too well. And while the ending had been inevitable, something put into motion almost fifteen years earlier, that didn't make it any less painful for those involved.

While Margot could never sympathize with what Donna had done, because of the hideous, life-altering consequences of it, there was a part of her that almost *did* understand it. She had wanted a baby so badly, and in a sense, she had saved Rini Fawcett's life, even if it meant that Rini grew up never knowing her real parents.

They had considered Rini an outlier for DeGraff, but it all made sense now. She hadn't been picked by Ricky. She'd been picked by Donna. And Donna had made such a case for Rini being a perfect friend for Mathilda, that she was the only survivor among Ricky's victims.

Margot hadn't been able to sleep for most of the night thinking of that girl, almost seventeen, and how her entire life had been obliterated overnight. She certainly wasn't thanking Margot right now. She wasn't feeling rescued. She had just lost her mother, and it was going to take a very long time for her to understand what Donna had done to her. Margot knew how that bitterness felt, because she'd once felt it herself towards Andrew and the rest of his team.

All she knew was being Kelsey Guenther. Margot had heard late last night that her parents—her real parents—now divorced, had been told about her miraculous reappearance. Her father, it seemed, had a whole new family, new wife, new kids. He'd indicated that he would come when he could, but it almost seemed like he had closed that door of his life and wasn't too keen to reopen it.

Rini's mother, on the other hand, had never closed the door. She had lived in the same trailer that Rini had been taken from, keeping the porch light on every night. Never changing the home phone number. She'd left the girl's bedroom largely untouched.

The most important part of her life had been snatched off her lawn one morning, and she had never gotten over it. She planned to drive over to collect her daughter that same day.

Who knew what would happen next?

Kelsey/Rini would be eighteen in a year. She'd be able to make her own decisions about her future. For now, though, she was a minor and needed a guardian, and that guardian would be her biological mother. A woman she barely knew, who would love her so fiercely it would feel foreign.

The horror story should have ended when they put Donna in cuffs and found evidence of Maddie Moore, sealing her fate and nailing Ricky DeGraff for one more murder.

What they'd found was evidence of six more murders that

they'd had on their periphery, but hadn't thought Ricky could be responsible for because he had untouchable alibis for the time.

The real horror story was going to be Kelsey's life moving forward, accepting that her mother was her kidnapper, and a woman responsible for being an accomplice in a half-dozen murders.

At some point, Kelsey would need to come to terms with the fact that she hadn't been kidnapped to be someone's daughter.

She had been kidnapped to be someone's victim.

Margot didn't envy the young woman the psychologically damaging journey she was about to embark upon. Nothing was going to feel easy or carefree for her after this.

Lucy laid a paw on Margot's face.

It was like the cat was reminding her of the golden rule in the Fox/Phalen household. No thinking of serial killers before coffee.

Margot pressed a kiss to the cat's forehead, then one to Wes's cheek, though he was still dozing. She would let him sleep in, because soon enough his early mornings would return.

The principal had called him the previous night. After discussions with the sheriff and multiple appeals from staff and students, he was being reinstated on Monday. Margot knew this return would be bittersweet for him. He would be happy to be back doing something he loved, but she knew it was always going to be a little tainted, now.

And there would be people who still believed he was guilty.

The case seemed to be getting steadily colder, as the leads on both Wes and Clayton had dried up. They didn't know where else to look, and the FBI profile told them not to bother, in a sense. The person who had done this likely wasn't local.

They were probably long gone.

It was going to take them a lot of time, effort, and work to put this in the past, but that was exactly what they had to do. It wasn't Margot's case to solve, and, at least for now, no one was looking at Wes anymore.

"You up?" Wes asked, his voice thick with sleep, his eyes still closed.

"Yes, but you shouldn't be. Go back to sleep." She kissed him even as she grudgingly withdrew from his arms, leaving a purring Lucy in her place, snuggled in the crook of his neck.

"Am I her favorite now?" he asked groggily, pressing a kiss against the cat's singed fur.

"You're everybody's favorite, baby." She smiled to herself, unable to resist leaning back over the bed to brush a lock of hair off his forehead.

"You're obsessed with me," he said warmly, still not opening his eyes.

"Always have been."

"I knew it. Did you hear that, Lucy?"

The cat just purred in response. A moment later, both cat and man were gently snoring.

Margot slipped on her Uggs and headed downstairs to start a pot of coffee. Sadie would be heading home today, and Margot was relieved they would be able to return to life as usual, but it had been nice to have someone else in the house with them. Things hadn't been without tension between them, but at the end of the day they both wanted what was best for their family.

The way Sadie had hugged her when she'd gotten home last night and told them what had happened was all Margot needed to know that she was included in that family, as far as Sadie was concerned.

Margot knew she was going to have to start making more effort to invite their friends and family to come. She had never really been a host before, and it used to take a lot out of her to have people upsetting her routine. But she wanted to keep this feeling alive. For her and Wes.

While she had frequently felt like Sadie was judging her decisions, she also couldn't blame her sister-in-law for worrying. She was protecting Wes, and that was a motivation Margot could understand deep into her soul.

She was so busy thinking about Sadie, it was somehow a shock to see the woman herself come padding down the stairs.

"You're up early," Margot said, automatically pulling down a second coffee cup.

"Had trouble sleeping," Sadie admitted. "It's been a weird couple of days."

Margot let out a small laugh. "You can say that again."

Sadie came up beside her at the kitchen counter and added milk and sugar to her cup before topping it with the freshly brewed coffee. She waited until she'd had her first sip before speaking. "I know you can make light of it, and maybe that's a good thing. Wes does it, too, just lets the heavy stuff roll off him. Maybe that's what makes you both so right for each other. But Margot, can I give you a little advice?"

Margot poured her coffee into an insulated travel mug so she could take it outside with her. "Sure." She wasn't actually sure she wanted to hear what Sadie was going to say, but she felt like she owed her the courtesy of listening after all she'd done for them.

"I know you spent a long time being alone. And you know I'm very pro being alone. I've been doing it my whole life. But don't let that comfort turn into isolation. I know what happened over the last couple of weeks might sour you on your community, and no one would blame you, but I guess what I'm saying is don't build a wall to keep just you and Wes in. Or if you do, at least make sure there's a door in it." She smiled softly. "Does that make any sense? I'm still half asleep."

Margot couldn't help but smile, considering she'd been thinking only minutes earlier about wanting to make more of an effort.

"It does make sense. And I promise I'll build a door." She put the lid on her cup. "I might even give people keys."

"Hey now," Sadie said, shaking her head and grinning. "Baby steps."

Sadie headed back to her room. Margot slipped on a heavy coat before stepping outside. The night had been so cool there was a patina of frost on the grass, making everything look like it had been candied in sugar. The cool morning air bit at her ears and cheeks, but she was happy for it today. She was happy to feel alive and grounded in a place that was just hers.

Even through everything that had happened over the past few weeks—the skeleton of her barn was still a stark reminder of how bad it had gotten—she didn't feel unsafe here. This was a place she had chosen, and she and Wes had made it their own.

Nothing is ever as perfect as it seems.

She sighed.

No matter what that nagging voice in her head tried to tell her, she *was* allowed to be settled. She *was* allowed to make herself a real home, both with places and with people.

She was allowed to be happy.

No matter how hard she needed to fight to hang on to it, she would.

Fighting for happy endings was something she had gotten surprisingly good at.

Lucy was only one step behind her as Margot went through her morning chores. Margot promised she wouldn't tell Wes that he was not, in fact, the calico's favorite. The chickens were spoiled today with a pail of compost scraps from the kitchen. They clucked merrily as they tore through potato peels and bits of discarded carrot and lettuce. The scraps would be gone in minutes.

The dogs had been sleeping in the house when she headed out for the chickens, but she returned to the door and whispered inside, "Breakfast."

This siren call got all five of their rescues' attention, though it did take a minute or two for them all to get their stiff limbs moving enough to get through the door. They followed Margot to the shed and waited patiently as she assembled their food and medicine. When any of them got too demanding or whiny, Lucy would turn around and give them a soft *bap* with her paw. A queen keeping her people in line.

Margot fed the dogs, then returned to the house to feed the cats.

A thought occurred to her as the sun peeked over the horizon. Last week she had told herself she would put in an effort to get to know her neighbors better. Now that Wes wasn't persona non grata in the area and she wasn't bogged down in a case for the next day or so, perhaps it was time to make that effort. Like Sadie had said, she couldn't just wall out the community forever. There were so many eggs on her counter, she could use that as an excuse to build a door.

She showered and dressed, which took her to an almost reasonable time to be visiting someone on a weekday morning, then loaded up a few cardboard cartons with eggs.

She left a note for Sadie and Wes on the counter that she had ducked out to drop eggs at the neighbors, smiling to herself as she realized both of them were likely to think she was making that up.

She made a quick stop to the neighbors she had already met, an older couple named Gus and Wendy to the east of them. Then, recalling the truck she had seen on the road the other day that had turned into some hidden driveway, she headed back in that direction.

She thought, with no small level of smugness, that it might be fun for her to be the first to meet a neighbor, rather than Wes.

The little turnoff where the truck had vanished was so worn down that it almost blended into the hills. She nearly missed it, and was grateful the roads were nearly empty this time of the morning so she was able to do a U-turn and coast up the rather steep drive.

All the plant life along the driveway looked dry, which wasn't unusual for this time of year, perhaps, but she was used to things still being green. Her place, Gus and Wendy's place, they were still lush with life, even though it was almost Halloween.

As Margot crested the hill, her stomach sank and the hairs on her arms stood on end. She couldn't help feeling that something was wrong.

There was no sign of the brown truck, or of any vehicles at all.

The driveway was just a wide expanse of hard-packed dirt. These things, in and of themselves, were not red flags. But as signs started to group together, things began to take on a more sinister appearance.

The house wasn't just currently empty. The porch was covered in dust and leaves. The windows were boarded up. In the pens closest to the house there were no signs of animals, nor that there had been animals in them in quite some time. No fresh dung, no remnants of feed.

And there was no noise. On any farm or ranch in this area, you could hear their animals. Her chickens were audible the second she stepped out of the car. The dogs would kick up a fuss at the mere hint of a guest. When she'd visited Gus and Wendy, she could hear cows lowing in the background even though she hadn't been able to see them.

The air here was so quiet she could hear each crunch of her boot heels on the driveway.

This wasn't right at all.

Maybe she'd picked the wrong driveway.

There was a chance she had been mistaken.

No, you know where you turned. You're in the right place, Ed's voice tickled the back of her brain.

Normally she ignored that voice, but right now it sounded sensible.

It was right.

This was the place she'd seen the truck turn, there was no doubt in her mind. But there was no way anyone had lived here in years, let alone the last two weeks.

Margot left her carton of eggs on the hood of the car and unlocked her glovebox to retrieve her firearm.

Five years with the FBI, she never left home without it, she just didn't always wear it.

She didn't think there was anyone lurking inside the house or in the woods waiting to jump out at her, but she also had no interest in leaving herself exposed and unarmed in case she was wrong.

The memory of what had happened at Sam's place with Donna was too fresh. Margot wasn't sure anyone could ever get used to having a gun pointed at them. And she wasn't about to make herself an easy target.

As she walked away from the car, she knew that, if she was being smart, really smart, she would just get back into the car, turn around, and go home. Pretend she was never here, that her alarm bells had never been tripped.

But now that she was here, she knew that was impossible.

She did a loop around the driveway until she spotted fresh-looking tracks near the treeline at the end of the drive. While they had hardened over, it was clear they were new, because there were no other signs of tracks to be seen in the whole yard.

They could only have been made when the ground was soft. The last time it had rained hard enough to soften the dirt this much was the night that Whitney had died.

Beside the tracks there were boot prints. Big ones, that headed in the direction of a path among the trees.

This wasn't a forest by any means. The trees were skinny and spread out, the earth between them thick with dry grass. Margot followed the trail, keeping sight of the main house. She had once worked a homicide in Muir Woods, among the majestic redwoods, where the trees were so huge and thick the sun barely penetrated to the forest floor. These trees were the kind that could survive months of no rain, spindly but just alive.

The boot prints were gone—the grasses were too thick and high for anything to make it down to the mud—but the path kept going so Margot followed it, the hairs at the back of her neck standing on end. Her fight or flight chose the latter option, but she wasn't listening.

There was something here.

She didn't know what, but she knew if she turned away now she might never know.

About a half-mile from the house, with only the peak of the roof visible and only if she was standing on her tiptoes, Margot saw a patch of disturbed earth. She froze, staring at it, not entirely sure what to do next. She couldn't call the sheriff up to report some partially dug-up dirt. They would laugh her out of town.

She knew she had to see what it was, but her feet were planted firmly in place.

Look.

She didn't want to.

But she knew she had to.

She approached the pile, which had been partially covered in a few branches and some dry grass. Margot imagined that most people wouldn't have noticed it at all. But she had been trained to look for graves, hadn't she? She had spent her life unearthing buried skeletons both literal and figurative.

Margot knew how to spot what shouldn't be there.

She knelt beside the pile and started to push it off. The dirt was loose, so it had been placed after the rainfall—otherwise it would be thick, clumpy. It took her a few minutes to clear a space, but then her hand hit something hard and plastic.

She went still for a moment, then rapped her knuckle against the plastic. A hollow sound came back.

Margot took a pair of gloves out of her pocket. They weren't crime scene gloves, just flimsy mittens to keep her hands warm during her morning chores, but she knew she didn't want to touch whatever she found with her fingers.

The plastic thing she had found, she soon realized, was a lid, which twisted off.

She lifted it clear and peered inside, surprised by the depth. Someone had buried a large plastic bucket, a good two feet deep. But then Margot realized what was *in* the bucket, and she scrambled to her feet and took several steps back, her mind reeling.

The bucket's contents on their own might have been innocuous, but together they told a story. There was a bundle of nylon rope. A roll of duct tape. A flashlight. A pair of rubber gloves. A packet of wet wipes.

A knife.

Margot's pulse hammered as she stared in disbelief.

This was a kill kit.

Most murderers would keep something like this in a duffle bag in their car, so they could access it easily if the situation arose. Many a foolish killer had been arrested because they'd been speeding or missed a signal, and an officer had seen their kill kit in the process of booking them.

But this one was buried.

It looked brand new, though. Like it had never been used.

Margot looked back at the packed-down grass. Thought of the brown truck. Of the treads in the driveway.

Hadn't used it yet... or had used it and re-hidden it?

To use again later.

Margot pulled out her phone, and realized her hands were shaking. She looked around at the spindly trees surrounding her, the dirt track back to the driveway. She was alone out here, but she couldn't help feeling she was being watched.

She dialled the sheriff's office and as it rang she refused to look away from the hole in the ground, as if it might vanish if she did.

"Willows Sheriff's office, this is Deputy Cassidy," a warm voice greeted her.

"Flo," Margot said, her voice husky. "It's Margot. I just found something you guys are going to want to see."

She gave Flo her location, then sat down in the grass beside the open bucket. That morning, she had believed that things were on the cusp of returning to normal. But even in the horror of what she'd found there was a strange feeling of relief. She'd wanted something concrete to prove that Wes was innocent, and she felt absolutely certain she was looking at it.

That sense of gratitude was short-lived, though.

Looking at the glint of a knife in the bright morning light, she thought of the eggs sitting in her car, and wondered how she could have ever believed that a normal life was something she could aspire to.

Death was always going to be waiting for her, whether she liked it or not.

But instead of feeling bitter or frightened of the knowledge that death had made its way to her own backyard, she just felt angry.

There had been a monster here, something evil that had been so close it could have reached out and touched her.

She had missed him once.

She wasn't going to let him go a second time.

Margot stared into the bucket at her feet.

He'd made a mistake coming here and leaving this behind. All killers made mistakes eventually, ones that caught up to them. He might not know it yet, but she was going to find him.

A LETTER FROM THE AUTHOR

Thank you so much for reading *Tell Me Her Name*. I'm so thrilled to be back with Margot again, and I hope you all loved this new chapter for her. If you want to join other readers in hearing all about my new releases, you can sign up for my newsletter!

www.stormpublishing.co/kate-wiley

Or for other news and bonus content sign up here:

http://eepurl.com/ASoIz

Reviews are so important to authors, as they can help new readers decide what to spend their time and money on. If you've enjoyed this new book and want to read more, I would be eternally grateful if you would consider leaving a review. Even a short review can make all the difference in encouraging a reader to discover my books for the first time. Thank you so much!

I feel so blessed that I was able to continue writing Margot books after everyone fell in love with her (flaws and all) in her Detective series. Finding a way to continue her journey was an interesting puzzle to solve, but I knew I wasn't quite done with her yet, she's just too interesting a character to let her go without a few more adventures. Perhaps I should apologize to her for that. I hope you agree that bringing Margot out of retirement after her original five-book series was worth the effort, and I hope you'll continue to read her FBI adventures with much gusto.

If this is your FIRST Margot book, welcome! It was written to be a new entry point, but if you loved Margot and want more, then I'm thrilled to tell you that there are five books already released where you get to know her backstory, and more books ahead that will delve into her in the present.

Thanks again for being part of this amazing journey with me and I hope you'll stay in touch – I have a lot more planned, and if you keep reading, I'll keep writing!

Kate Wiley

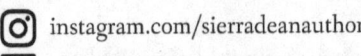

www.katewiley.com

instagram.com/sierradeanauthor
facebook.com/sierradeanauthor

ACKNOWLEDGMENTS

It's hard to believe that only a few years ago, my very first Margot Phalen book was sitting in a drawer collecting dust. Now we're on her second series of books! I knew from the very beginning that Margot had a story worth telling, but by the time her main arc was done, I knew she wasn't ready to be put away permanently. She's too interesting, and far too loud in my head for that. I couldn't wait to find new ways to explore her dark and twisty world, and I am so grateful to Vicky Blunden and the entire team at Storm for agreeing that Margot had more story to tell.

I often see in reviews how impressed people are with my research, but I have a confession to make. My research is just three decades of obsession with true crime. That said, there were several additional resources I found invaluable in writing this book, one of which was the book *Hearts of Darkness* by Jana Monroe. This memoir about life in the FBI for a female agent was unbelievably helpful in learning more about how women are treated by the Bureau, as well as the hard realities of working in the BSU. The insights and nuggets of information here were so helpful to give my fictional FBI team a sheen of truth.

Additionally, other true crime junkies are going to find traces of the serial killer Israel Keyes in our mysterious background serial killer. Like all good crime fiction, the scariest stuff is that which is informed by reality. While our nameless hunter is different from Keyes in many ways, the inspiration remains. If you want a book that will truly keep you up at night, *American Predator* by Maureen Callahan should be added to your list. This book also mentions John Douglas and Robert Ressler, two very real FBI profilers who helped create the modern BSU. Douglas, along with his collaborator, Mark Olshaker, has written *many* compelling books, but *Mindhunter* is a great place to start. Douglas quite literally wrote the book in sexually motivated homicide, while Robert Ressler is credited for having coined the phrase "serial killer" back in the 1970s. These are the guys who shaped our understanding of modern true crime.

On a lighter note, I owe a debt of thanks to Nicky Hardy, a wonderful friend who also happens to be the former Miss Nebraska 2010. Nicky was gracious enough to answer some of my burning questions about the atmosphere of pageant life, and any mistakes I've made are entirely due to my own whimsy and a shoddy memory of watching too much *Toddlers and Tiaras*.

This book was quite a change from writing a fixed location in San Francisco, and having Margot beholden to her role as a detective. It was nice to get to go a bit broader in scope, leaving me with the opportunity to tell so many more stories.

A huge thank you to everyone who read the first Margot series, making it possible to do a second one. Thank you to my friends, who are supportive during my grouchy writing sprints and my complaining about various stages of editing. Writing might be a solitary pursuit, but those on the periphery who listen to writers complain about things are truly unsung heroes.

To my whole Storm editing and marketing team, you guys are amazing, and I will never cease to be amazed at the hard work you do for your authors. Thank you!

And always, to my mom, the first person to ever encourage my writing, I wouldn't have come this far without you.

www.ingramcontent.com/pod-product-compliance
Lightning Source LLC
LaVergne TN
LVHW031537060526
838200LV00056B/4533